"Do You Hear What I Hear?"
By Stephen W. Scott

A huge thanks to the following for their help: Derek Stewart for his wonderful cover design and his creativity, Anthony Libonati for his narration of the audio version, and a huge appreciation for my Writing Coach and Editor, Heather Nuttall-Westover.

This one is dedicated to my cousins:
Eric, Jayme, Ryan, Rhett, and Jason.

This is a work of fiction. All of the characters, organizations, and events portrayed in this novel are either works of fiction or are used fictitiously.

ISBN – 9798308452751

Copyright © 2025

by Stephen W. Scott

All rights reserved.
No portion of this book may be reproduced in any form without written permission from the publisher or author, except as permitted by U.S. copyright law.

Book cover design by Derek Stewart

Contents

PART ONE: BRAZIL 1
  In the Dark 1
  The Survivor 5
  Blind 11
  The Bungalow 14
  Vacation 20
  Jimmy? 31
  Headache 40
  The Secret 46
  Narcissus 51
  The Last Surf 58
  Leaving 70

PART TWO: FLIGHT TO THE PAST 78
  Remembering 78
  In Hell 85
  The Pact 93
  The Escape 102

PART 3 – HOMECOMING 107
  Unseen Home 107
  Dinner 111
  A New Family 117
  Justin and Jason 128
  Seeing School 140
  Mirror, Mirror on the Wall 149
  Dan and Janie 158
  911 Call 167

Faith and Doubt	172
Mission	177
Immunity	195
Waking Up	202
I See You	214
Old Man	228
The Conflict	239
The Last Twin	245
Great News	255
In the Water	260
Scotland	262
About the Author	265

Stephen W. Scott

PART ONE: BRAZIL

In the Dark

(Sao Paulo, Brazil)

Jason shuddered and tried to move, but pain flared in his neck, shoulders, arms, torso, and legs. Needles, connected to tubes and wires, burrowed in and out of his skin. The cold air made him shiver. He bellowed and then coughed, triggering waves of pain in his torso. Pain exploded in his shoulders, elbows, and hips. Strange voices and a foreign language confused him.

His memory tried to recall everything, but it eluded him. What country did the family visit? Ecuador? Argentina? Brazil? Brazil! That's where he was. What happened to him? The car wreck memory returned. The images of twisted metal along with the sounds of smashing glass, screaming, and the smell of spilled auto fluids shot through his mind. They ran so fast; he could not weed them out and focus on just one.

"Jason," said the lone English-speaking voice, "My name is Jonas Gutierrez. I am from the US Consulate in Sao Paulo. Can you hear me?"

He coughed as a pain flared in his chest. Jason grunted as it shot across his sternum and ribs, vibrating like a thunderous bass speaker. A dull, achy pain spread through his left shoulder and arm. It pulsed and spread like wildfire to his back. "Shit, shit, shit, shit – oh that hurts. Please help me, sir, please." Each word was stifled by heavy grunts and breaths. It was like a dance: grunt, pain, speak a word. Grunt, pain, speak a word. The pain ebbed for a minute, fading, but not by much. His breathing softened. Jason stammered. "Where ... am I?"

"In the Sao Paulo Central Hospital. You were in a car wreck. Do you remember?"

"Yes sir." He coughed again, only to be interrupted by the loud sirens of pain. Again, the measure returned: grunt, pain, speak a word. "Where's ... my brother? And ... Mom and Dad?" His heart stilled, anticipating the answer – especially when the man hesitated.

"Your ... parents ... and your brother ... were all killed," the man's voice quieted, but Jason heard the rest.

A warm numbness draped over him. Not knowing what or how to feel, all sensations retreated into nothing. An invisible pain tried to break through the numbing. Cracking it, tears lurched through his eyes. "Mom ... Dad? Jimmy? They can't be ... gone." Sobs punched through tears, snot, and a vile shaking.

"I have called your grandparents and your aunt and uncle in the States. Your aunt and uncle are on their way and should be here tomorrow."

Jason cried – and then it hit him. Something else scared him far worse. He felt his face. Scarred, disfigured – but he was trying to find some sort of mask or bandages over his eyes. Nothing was there. His eyes clenched so hard, they almost hurt. The painful reality triggered more terror than sadness. The blunt truth smacked him hard. Only a dark blackness existed – surrounding him as if a thick blanket covered his head. No matter how much he wiped his tears away, or how much he blinked his eyes, no images formed. No light emerged. The darkness refused to budge or give way. This couldn't be happening!

His heart froze. Jason cringed. "Mr. ... uh ... uh ... what's your name again?"

"Gutierrez."

He stammered. His jaw quivered. The question teetered on the tip of his tongue. He blurted. "Why can't I see anything?"

Mr. Gutierrez hesitated – but only a second. "You had a traumatic brain injury." Another pause. "You're blind."

He was in the dark. Alone. He knew nobody in the room with him. He could only hear them, sense them through touch, and smell the chemicals that provided sanitation in the unseen room. His quivering jaw shook more – and it spread a cold prickly feeling in his body. Just underneath his skin, it felt not like fire ants, but ice ants marching down his neck, shoulders, upper arms, and chest. There, they circled his heart like sharks around their prey. The others continued their descent to his stomach, hoping to steal what little food remained. Wherever they traveled, they left behind an uncontrollable shaking. This continued through his genitals, his thighs, knees, and shins, finally reaching his feet and into his toes. Every part of his skin shook like a subtle earthquake, causing the hair on his body to sway like trees. "I can't see! I can't see!" He repeated the words several times. Each time sent a heavy wave of terror through his mind.

His ears heard the doctors talking with Mr. Gutierrez. They spoke Spanish. No, it had to be Portuguese. That's what Dad told him the people of Brazil spoke. Jason wished he could understand them. The words flew fast, making him feel even more incompetent with learning new languages. Already trapped in blackness, the strange voices and language bounced around, reverberating as in a blackened cave.

The doctors and nurses erupted into conversation. "Sir, what is it? Is this going to be permanent or temporary? What are they saying? Is there a chance of me seeing again?" A few tears lurched through, jumping out the corners of his eyes. The ice ants circling his heart and stomach mounted another attack.

"I have talked to them, and they informed me it is likely the blindness is permanent."

A captivating feeling froze his skin, sank to his muscles, and dug deep into his bones. It shot up through his chest and tried to squeeze his throat. It let go. Finally taking a breath, a saddening wave washed over him. It was not violent like a crashing surf, but gentle, quiet, and calm – like the warm waters of a bathtub slowly rising. He cried.

Stephen W. Scott

The Survivor

"Wolfgang Gerhardt."

Nathan's head turned, responding to the name. Planting his cane on the floor, he used both hands to stand from the hard, wooden chair. The cane added an extra footstep on the hard, oak floors of the Brazilian bank. Leaning on the counter, he removed his hat, immediately losing warmth as the cold from the ceiling ventilation fell onto his naked, bald head. "I am Wolfgang Gerhardt. Do you have the box?"

Nathan handed her the phony identification. He flexed all his muscles, hoping she would fall for it. Fortunately, she handed Nathan a long, metal security box. Nathan held it under his left arm, so he could keep the walking cane on his right. He moved faster, as the anticipation grew in his chest. Reaching a lonely office, he closed the blinds then set the box on the aged, dinged wooden table. Nathan bowed his head. He said a short Jewish prayer in Hebrew. Opening his eyes, he examined the old, scuffed key and kissed it. It fit perfectly, stoking the anticipation that swelled with his prayer. The panel unlocked and it opened. A breath from the past leapt at his nostrils.

He found it. The evidence that eluded the U.S. Military, the CIA, MI-6, and the Mossad for decades rested before his eyes. He found the diary. Glancing at the old text, he took in bits and pieces of the scribbled German text. He had the first insight into the monster's mind. It was dark ramblings, confused diatribes, and evil musings. A few lines confirmed his theory, and the other victims he knew. It ended abruptly.

Do You Hear What I Hear?

Scribbled in different handwriting, Nathan read it with heavy interest, hoping it might give a clue as to the rest. He read the old papers that faded to a yellowish parchment: "To protect myself, the other half is in the second box. It's not in my home, but another small property I own."

Nathan sighed, shook his head and dropped it. So close. Resigned, he examined the old black-and-white photos. They triggered a lone, painful tear. He shuffled them. Although some resolution had faded, he could make out the faces perfectly. The first photo was of all the children – each one with their twin and lined up by age. The following pictures were of the individual twins, and a few triplets. For every set, there were two pictures. One from the front, the other from the back. While some were outside, near the high wired barbed fences, others were inside near the "medical" facility. They could give any fancy name they wanted, but the old man knew it was a torture chamber, cold with sharp metal objects that conducted terror. He felt those objects himself and the trauma that lingered.

The children had their clothes nearly falling from their emaciated bodies. Those children had the glaring yellow star pinned on their shirts. The ones who did not have the star, though, were naked. The pictures from the rear revealed many bruises, scars, and surgical incisions. They all had the same tired, sullen eyes – void of any emotion, save despair.

He found the one picture he sought. Shuddering, his hands shook at the sight. His other hand used his fingers to trace the faces of both boys. He looked at the back of the picture to be sure: "Nathan and Noah Oberst." The perfect memory did not dance, but rather moped through his mind, dragging down his soul. It made the picture before his eyes come to life like a movie. Nathan's lip quivered, remembering those long, insufferable days and nights. He clung to memories he wanted to rid himself of, but he couldn't. Visions, sounds, smells, physical feelings, and horridly frightening emotions gave full life to the miserable recollections. The onus memories still lashed out, inflicting misery to this very day.

Nathan heard the screams echo through his mind far more than the cavernous walls of the torture chamber. Some of those were his own, although his memory perfectly heard the screams of Noah and the other boys as well. Somewhere between the pleas for mercy and the painful shouts of despair, he somehow heard hateful stabs, taunts, and jeers from the tormentors. One scream almost pierced his ears, then suddenly ceased. Nathan, confined with leather straps face down on a cold metal table, shouted for Noah. His twin brother did not say anything. Unable to turn his head, he somehow knew Noah had died.

The scalpel dug into his lower back's skin. The sharp stabbing pain, unbearable, forced him to scream louder than before. Except this time, he did not plea for the monster to stop, but for Noah to return. Spilled tears fell on the metal table as the monster continued his surgery. What was he doing? What purpose did this serve? The leather straps kept his shaking from turning into convulsions. They got worse when the monster started sewing him back. Every suture sent a siren of pain that crawled through his back and upper legs. His nerves screamed almost as much as his mouth. Ironically, his own ears cringed at his desperate cries that echoed off the concrete walls of the facility.

His huffing and sobbing somehow caused the pain to weaken and retreat... Did the monster leave? Or did it just sit detached, writing notes in its book? He imagined its curious eyes, almost like a tiny child that was amused by the torture. The horrible monster had no heart. It spoke the foreign Germanic language to a few other Nazi onlookers. They seemed aloof from the pain and agony as well. The conversation could have been about something as innocuous as the weather, or about the latest play they viewed.

Footsteps distanced themselves from his table. Finding a pool of sweat under his forehead, and a tiny bit of slack in the leather strap, Nathan twisted his head towards his brother. He tried calling out to him, but Noah did not respond. Had the monster taken his life? Or merely drugged him for more torture? His neck strained as pressure mounted on his forehead. Twisting it harder, he managed to pivot his head.

The face of the monster stared at him. Blank eyes stared amidst a tall, thin head covered with dark hair. Nathan wondered if the blood on the fluffy mustache was his or Noah's. Underneath his chin was a doctor's mask, stained in crimson and caking in blood. The monster stared at Nathan as he screamed. Nathan wondered what it had in store for him. The monster stood and took a few steps away, lost in a blinding glare of sun that crashed through the high windows. Nathan saw his brother. Blood caked his head, his back, his ear, and his side. Noah's lifeless eyes still possessed a glaze of unending terror. Hollowed out, his voice faded like fires doused by water or dirt. For the first time, he was separated from the only person who had ever been with him every second of his life.

Blocking his view, the monster returned – except this time it was different. Its long, pointed ears framed a grotesque caricature of an old, skinny man with glaring eyes that emitted a sinister light. Its mouth, agape, revealed many spiked, blood-stained teeth underneath two slits where the nose should be. Its skin, pale in some spots and burnt in others, had bugs and maggots squirming all over. Its arms, long and disjointed, had a deformed, three-fingered claw. Large, bat-like wings spread from its back, draping Nathan in a cold shadow.

Nathan shook himself from the afternoon terror. A few tears leaked from his eyes. After all the decades that had passed, he still wept from the pain – and still shook from the terror. He had seen the monster a few other times in the barracks. For some reason, the real monster only appeared at certain times. He wondered if other children, like his brother, saw it, too. However, it loved the disguise more: the fine, gentlemanly doctor who offered the children treats like chocolates.

Back in the present, Nathan bowed his head – praying to Yahweh. He wondered why the God who parted the Red Sea for his people thousands of years ago sat silent to the desperate, painful prayers of a boy in the German camp. The answer did not sit well with him. In fact, no answer came. He wondered why he still clung to the ancient religion. Tenacity or strength? Or was it stubborn stupidity?

Nathan, thrust back to the present reality, set the picture down, and opened the ancient letters. The first paper had a list of at least 500 names: boys, girls, identical twins, and some fraternal. He guessed the ones with checkmarks next to them died – either from starvation or by the hand of the monster himself. Nathan was one of 200 who survived. His thumb passed by all the checked names, trying to make them live once more, or perhaps out of simple respect for their collective suffering.

Nathan looked at the yellowish, fragile journals. They

were dated. He focused on the one marked 1943-44. Part of him wanted to tear it open and rip out the pages – and maybe toss them into a fire. Another part wanted to read it. Not knowing what to do, and tired from reliving the past, he put them all into his flexible attaché and closed them up.

Using both hands again, Nathan stood, then used his cane as a guide out of the old bank. Just like 70 years ago, he left behind the place of the sadistic tormentor. Just like 70 years ago, he took with him memories of the monster. Sure, the disguise had died, but it surely found a way to continue.

Stephen W. Scott

Blind

Jason felt the warm, soothing flesh of a finger. A long, finely manicured fingernail gently stroked his cheek. "Jason?" His eyelids opened, although he remained in the dark. His head tilted to the right. He wondered if he faced the window. Yes – he did. His hand felt the plastic window that shielded him from the cold, thin air.

"Jason, honey, are you doing okay?" He could tell she sat next to him, and now Aunt Janie stroked his hair. He nodded lightly. "Do you need anything? Something to eat or something to drink? Do you need help going to the bathroom?"

Barely shaking his head, the thought of his aunt watching him pee did not sit well with him. Of course, he doubted she could fit in with him in the tiny bathroom of the commercial jet.

His eyes squeezed, trying to hold back the endless supplies of tears. His hand tried to cover his face, but she gently clasped his hand and whispered. "Honey, your Uncle Dan and I are here for you." She hugged him, then kissed his cheek. "We'll take care of you. Once we get back to Albany, we will get the best medical care for you. I know you're scared but we will get through this."

"Hey, buddy," said a masculine voice. "You doing okay?"

Sick and tired of the question, he almost snapped back but held his tongue with his Uncle Dan. Despite his closest relatives being nearby, Jason felt a wave of loneliness. He had lost everything: his twin brother and both his parents. "I can't see. I can't see." He wept. "Uncle Dan," he said, "I can't believe he's gone. They're all gone. Mom and Dad – and Jimmy. I miss him so much. It hurts so bad." The pain was not his left shoulder, his head wound, or his broken forearm. Instead, it was an invisible weight that wrapped around his heart, his stomach, and soul, and slowly crushed all of them.

"I know exactly how you feel."

The masculine embrace had the same strength and comfort as Dad. Strangely, he could never remember ever hearing Uncle Dan or Dad on the verge of tears. They were both tough men. Both survived a stint in the Iraq War and Afghanistan. Both Dad and Uncle Dan were twins, too. At this point, Uncle Dan was his only link to Dad. Confused, scared, and alone, he clutched his uncle tightly. "What happened? I don't remember much."

"You don't remember the wreck? The Sao Paulo police were confused as well. They don't understand the wreck. It's that ... your father." Uncle Dan gulped, almost sounding as if he blocked himself from crying. "My brother," he took a heavy breath, "ran the rental car off a road leading to a church. And they can't find a reason. No tire blowout, no slick spots or skid marks. Do you remember why he did that? What happened?"

"No. I don't remember much except the noise, crying and yelling. I can," he stammered, "remember the car crunching, the glass breaking, the medics yelling." Every noise he mentioned reverberated, one at a time, like a series of door slams. Each one made Jason shudder. He cringed as the sounds triggered a huge twitch through his entire body. He inhaled deeply and held it. Slowly, carefully, he let it out, hoping it did not rush out like an angry lion.

"Well, can you remember the last thing you saw?"

"Dan," interrupted Aunt Janie, "not now."

"Honey, please." Uncle Dan gulped again. Jason felt his eyes pleading for help, comfort, and solace. "Jason, do you remember the last thing you saw?"

The last image, etched in his mind just like a stoned carving, haunted him. It, too, caused his soul to wretch and convulse. His eyelids acted like spillways in a dam, releasing the pressure again. "I saw Jimmy. He was terrified. He was yelling my name for Mom and Dad to help. He was crying."

Shaking his head, somehow drying his tears on his uncle's sleeve, he tried desperately to eject the memory from his mind. It was the last thing he saw. It jumped at him, somehow crashing through the confused memories. It could not be seen clearly. It faded, then jumped back. It brought back the recollection of a rank, putrid stench he could almost taste – almost triggering his gag reflex. It happened again. It was like freezing a DVR image, except every time, it got bigger, more menacing. Jason recalled the first time he saw it.

Do You Hear What I Hear?

The Bungalow

Nathan hated and liked the walkway at the same time. It provided solid footing for walking, although its slope tired him quickly. He preferred it to the beach sand – which was not the solid footing he needed more and more with age. In his late 80's, he was grateful for a sharp mind, and a body that still displayed adequate strength. Still, the tendons and ligaments in his left knee had depleted strength, thus the need for a cane. On the other hand, he remained lean. Some doctors expressed concern over his frame, but he thought it better than one that was obese and limited movement. He credited this to a two-mile walk before bed – although a decade ago, it was a four-mile constitutional. Back then, he also shared the walk with his wife. He smiled, as her gentle, melodious singing voice resounded in his memories.

Nathan took notice of the sunbathers. They all had thin bodies, thick hair, unwrinkled and tanned skin, toned muscles – and not very modest swimsuits. He cursed and savored the sights of the women in their thong bikinis. In fact, many of the women did not wear a top. Yes, they were immodest, and they stirred his not-forgotten lust. However, they were all young – young enough to be his grandchildren. The boys wore their bikini-style swimsuits, apparently trying to show off their manhood. He shook his head and almost laughed, realizing he might do the same if he still had his youthful virility.

His hat came off for a second as he tried to use it as a fan. He started to wipe the sweat off his bald head until he realized the light breeze cooled the area. Should he leave the cap off? No. Sure, there was plenty of shade, but the glaring sun would easily burn his aged skin.

At this point, he was traveling uphill on a cracked sidewalk, moving further away from the beaches. He smiled at the children running or skateboarding down the slope. The joviality remained even though he had to dodge a few of them. His pace slowed a little bit as the incline steepened. However, something stopped him.

He coughed. A slight pain swelled in his chest. His heart was out of sync. It didn't have the correct rhythm. Nathan knew it was called atrial fibrillation, or A-fib. Sitting on a low-rise wall, he rested. Feeling the medicine in his pocket, he tapped the bottle. Nathan felt grateful for being able to be mobile at his age. Despite his lean frame and his daily constitutional, his heart was not immune to aging. How much longer did he have on this Earth? At 88 years old, he knew that death would come for him one day. Nathan wished he had not outlived his wife. He missed the companionship.

His heart clicked with his breathing. The pacemaker reset it. Both his pump and his breathing started dancing in time once again. The coordination was perfect. Still, Nathan remained sitting for a few more minutes.

Once moving, it only took another twenty steps or so. He saw it. His heart locked, almost beating out of sync again. However, this time the old, forgotten fear triggered it. Fortunately, it got back in time with his body as he prayed to Yahweh. Nathan looked at the small rent house nobody else could find. This was the secret property the former Nazi owned.

The villa looked like any other: rustic, with some decaying patterns, but still very livable. Rich, dark wood had decayed from years of wind, rain, and other elements. In fact, a slight gust of wind triggered a few things. First was relief. He had found it. Glancing at the paper in his top shirt pocket, he noticed the matching numbers. Flipping the card, the picture was unmistakably the right house. It was a rental home used by the monster.

The second reaction triggered within him was a sudden anticipation. This was the one thing he looked for ever since Rebecca died. She never understood his quest, but he never expected her to. A child of the United Kingdom, she was not herded into a death camp, tortured, and starved. She did not bear the shame of being treated like an animal. No, the Nazis treated animals better than their victims.

The third reaction of seeing the villa was an apprehensive fear that kept the anticipation in check. What if the demonic spirit of the monster still resided there? What if it waited to pounce on him and take his life like it did on Noah all those years ago?

Inhaling, he moved up the steps. He took the key he found yesterday in the safety deposit box. It still fitted the lock. One turn was all he needed to open the door. The hinges slightly squeaked. A quiet ticking sound emanated from the main room. An antique clock rested atop an adobe fireplace. The wooden floor had a few rugs to protect it from the legs of a couch, a few chairs, and a table. The same was true for the kitchen. His cane caused a slight echo as he stepped towards the kitchen. Someone had stayed recently. Some grocery bags were left, along with chips, cookies, and sodas.

He moved to the back, realizing the hallway led to the bedrooms. The apprehensive fear had vanished, as he could not detect any supernatural eyes gazing at him. He peered into each room. The master bedroom had an unmade bed, scattered with luggage bags as well as some bags used for shopping.

One bedroom aroused his curiosity. Twin beds, unmade, with lots of shorts, boxers, T-shirts, and souvenirs all over the floor. A deck of cards was on the rug between the beds, as well as a laptop, an iPad, and a few smartphone accessories. A wallet lay near one of the beds. He picked it up and opened it.

A student identification card stared at him. The image was in transition from boy to man. He had sandy-brown hair parted to the side, draping his forehead. His dark pupils were centered in his round young eyes. The name seemed to be a voice in itself: Jimmy Collins. Noticing another wallet, he inspected it, too. The face matched, except the hair had no part to the left: Jason Collins. Twins.

Nathan shuddered, thinking evil might have latched onto them like it did so many decades ago to the twins he knew in the camp. He noticed a coin near the edge of an area rug situated underneath one of the beds. His wrinkled, tired fingers scooped it up and examined it. The symbol, a winged image disgusted him. His anger boiled more at the winged cross, angled about 45 degrees. Of all the symbols he had seen in history, it was the ugliest.

Gasping, he saw himself in the mirror. It chilled him, just like all those years ago – in the monster's room. Nathan recalled being forced to stare at mirrors. He had to gaze at his own reflection … until he saw something else. Unlike all those years ago, he did not see anything else. He stared at the mirror for a moment, wondering if it might happen again. No. Nothing. He caught the image of something behind him. Turning, he saw it: an old cigar box. It had a faded beige

Do You Hear What I Hear?

color, dinged and worn on the corners, and decorated with more Nazi imagery. Hastily opening it, he anticipated finding what he desperately needed. He took a breath, seeing the other half of the diary he had found earlier. He noticed the old pictures sorted on the desk. Puzzled, he quickly took the pictures and put them into his attaché.

"Who are you?"

Startled by the abrupt voice, Nathan's entire body stiffened. He used a sigh and a slight laugh to relax. Carefully, he slipped the coin along with the student ids into his jacket pocket, and he pressed the cigar box between his left arm and his torso. He gazed at the Brazilian who stood at the doorway. Despite the fact his identification would reveal his identity, Nathan lied, using the common alias. "My name is Wolfgang Gerhardt. I am a relative of the original owner."

"I am the owner now." The man had a round face, with a little extra fat under the chin. Still, the arms and hands looked strong and muscular. His black hair was receding, but he also sported a mustache spotted with gray that also needed trimming. The Brazilian continued. "My father bought it a long time ago and willed it to me on his death. I must ask you to leave so I can prepare it for new guests." The man seemed very on edge. His eyes darted back and forth continuously.

"New guests? The old ones left their personals here. Do you rent this for tourists?"

"I don't have to answer to you Mr. … what did you say your name was?"

"Gerhardt. Wolfgang Gerhardt. If you rent this place, I would be interested in staying a few nights. My old relatives …"

"Senor, you must leave." He moved quickly, nervously, as his words shot faster and faster. "I already have a waiting list, and the new guests are anxious to move in now. And I must get these items shipped to the former guests as soon as possible."

"What happened to them?"

"Sir, you must leave, or I will call the police. And I would like that key you have."

Nathan balked at the suggestion and noticed how antsy the renter was. His breath shot fast, he kept looking around, and his lower lip quivered. After a few seconds, Nathan obliged the man and handed him the key. Feeling the sweat of the man's palm and seeing the terror in his eyes, Nathan whispered. "You have seen the monster, haven't you? It lives here. Feeds off the guests – and you, as well? I've seen it, too. A long time ago. I might know how to stop it."

His quivering fingers quickly clasped the key, and he stepped back. "Mr. Gerhardt, you must leave. If I find you here again, I will have you arrested. Leave!"

Nathan sighed, turned, and walked away.

Do You Hear What I Hear?

Vacation
(One month ago)

Jason and Jimmy stormed through the small house and found their room. It had a strange, but not offensive odor. Almost like vinegar, mixed with apple cider, it left a slight sting in their nostrils but was not strong enough to drive them back. The air barely moved amid an anemic, struggling fan that failed to blow the humid heat away. They stripped off their shirts to wipe the sweat already streaming down their heads and torsos. "Dad," said Jimmy, "please tell us this place has air conditioning."

"It better," said Jason, "or it's going to be murder trying to get to sleep." He glanced at his twin, Jimmy. Sometimes, they played "mirror" with each other. Both would mimic every move of their hands, arms, and head - as if they also shared the same thoughts. Occasionally, one of them would try to fool the other on the next move. Their father often said he was envious of their slender, tanned bodies, developing muscles, and abs. Jimmy yanked his head to the side to get the long, sandy-brown hair out of his right eye. Mom kept telling them both to cut it, but they liked long hair to torture their dad. Jimmy and Jason's noses had thinned over the last year, along with their jawlines, making them rigid and tight. Jason took notice of the one tattoo Mom and Dad allowed: a small cross on the left shoulder. She said it had to be on the side closer to the heart. Jason had one, too, because he could never let his twin be any different.

Jimmy blurted. "Hey, did you notice some of those girls at the beach weren't wearing any tops?"

Jason smiled widely. "Are you kidding? I'm sure I saw some totally naked! We gotta get down there. I think some of those girls are our age."

"I LOVE Brazil."

"Me, too. Hey Dad, Mom......... we love Brazil."

"More specifically, we love the naked women of Brazil," Jimmy whispered so Mom and Dad could not hear him.

Dad emerged in the doorway. His tall, lean frame could be intimidating – especially since he didn't smile often. A crown of dark hair outlined the top of his head, and a goatee framed his chin. As usual, his head lowered, almost like an angry ram ready to lock horns with any other alpha male. "You guys need to calm your hormones down."

Jason and Jimmy immediately stood at attention, giving Dad a little respect. Both saluted, "Yes, sir, sir! Awaiting your orders, sir!" Both suppressed a giggle after delivering the same words at the same time. This grated on Dad's nerves more than anything – especially since he was a pilot and Air Force Officer in Iraq and Afghanistan.

They wrapped their arms around each other's shoulders, dropped their heads, and made their usual plea while widening their eyes. "But Dad..." Both boys' voices were still changing, but leaned a little more to the pre-adolescent side, making them sound childlike – or probably childish. It was their usual ploy to get Dad's soft side, which he seemed to show less and less as they grew up.

After a few more "But Dad's," he snapped at them. "I mean it," he said while lowering his head even more. "I don't need twin smart-asses."

"Sorry, Dad," said Jimmy. "I guess we just have an asshole shortage."

"Not so far," quipped Jason.

Dad shook his head. "I should've never introduced you guys to that movie." He referred to Point Break, a 1990s movie that was about surfing and skydiving. He introduced it to them when they got into surfing a few years ago. "Boys – I know you're young, dumb, and full of come – so you can go to the beach for a few hours. I'll call the landlord about the air conditioning."

Glancing at each other, their eyes widened, and their mouths spread: they knew they got under his skin. It was not that they hated him, but it was fun to irritate him and Mom with their antics. They raced putting on their swimsuits.

Something raced past the corner of Jason's eye. He finally noticed the set-up of the room. One twin bed was on the left side of the room, another on the right side. Next to both beds were a dresser and a mirror. Jason nudged Jimmy to look at the amazing image of mirrors within mirrors, reaching inwardly into infinite proportions. They faced their respective mirrors.

"This is so awesome," said Jimmy.

"That is so cool," said Jason. Both raised their arms and made faces. They could not figure out if they stared at a reflection of themselves, or of their twin brother. Strangely, more of them resided in continuing reflections. Jason waved his arms, "Help me, I'm falling into another dimension of time, space, and who knows what?"

Jimmy noticed Mom and pointed at the mirror. "Look, Mom, there's more of us now. We're going to take over the family."

Mom, usually the pleasant one, laughed at the image,

then stepped into view of the mirrors. "Look," she said, "now I've multiplied which means all the moms are still in charge."

"Good one, Mom," said Jason. "Now if you don't mind, please step out of the room so all the young people can change into their swimsuits for the beach."

Mom shook her head. Her eyes had a darker tint than her sons'. They were also flatter, sleeker, and feminine. Her nose was straight, which gave her a fierce look when she was pissed at her boys. Mom's hair was the same color, but shorter than most women's. The hair parted just above her left eye and almost draped it – then flowed back to an almost perfect arc that ended just above her collar. She stared at her sons and tilted her head to the right. She was either about to chastise or tease them. "I've seen your asses when I changed your diapers, and more so when I had to whip them." Fortunately, she still respected their privacy and shut the door behind her.

Both boys quickly unpacked and found their swimsuits and put them on. Both made sure they had everything they needed: sunscreen, wetsuit, sandals, towels, sunglasses, T-shirts, and money to rent some surfboards.

Jason's right elbow caught Jimmy by the neck. "Not yet! The good-looking one always goes first."

Jimmy, laughing, pivoted to the right. Jason fell forward, allowing Jimmy to wrap his elbow around his twin's shoulders. "This has already been settled! You're the ugly one and I'm the good-looking one. Must I..." he grunted as Jason resisted, "teach you this lesson once again?"

Jason countered with his foot sweeping Jimmy's ankle. Both tumbled and bounced hard on the bed. They both laughed but never gave up on getting the upper hand. Their hands and arms tried grips, slaps, and leg moves. Jimmy got control as they rolled onto the floor laughing. "Yes! The King James has won once again!"

The pounding on the door alerted them to Mom's yells. "Boys! No wrestling. We do not OWN this place."

Both continued to laugh and huff, but they stopped wrestling. After a minute, they recovered, stood, and grabbed their surfing gear.

Jason's confidence left his chest. Replacing it was a cold dread, and a feeling of being watched. He glanced at the window and lifted the shade to check the back alley. Nobody was there. The feeling returned, almost like a moth dancing around his head and just barely staying out of view. Looking around the room, a shadow eluded him. It must be one of the numerous reflections in the mirrors.

Although looking for someone or something, he noticed the small twin beds, the light, tan-colored paneling of the walls, and the generic pictures of sailboats. Lamps were attached to the headboard of each bed. On the other side of the dresser and mirror was a small desk for each of them. Like the dresser, they were a light brown color with plenty of scratches and dings. The beds had a couple of pillows in blue pillowcases. The sheets were also blue, but a light brownish blanket wrapped tightly around each bed.

He thought he heard something whisper. Was it Jimmy? Perhaps Mom? A chill wrapped around his skin and penetrated his chest. Feeling as if unfamiliar, hostile eyes glared at him, he took a few deep breaths. His shaky heart quieted. The feeling of being watched disappeared.

With his surfing gear, Jason bolted out the door after his brother.

***

Jason put on his boxer shorts and sat on his bed. The padding had thinned and weakened over time. Some parts felt lumpy. However, after a couple hours on the beach, and Mom's great Teriyaki Chicken, his exhaustion would certainly overpower the lack of comfort. Moreover, Sao Paulo was almost four hours ahead of Albany, NY, so the time change drained him too.

Jason's lamp buzzed and flickered. Turning it off, he got under the covers and turned to his side as Jimmy turned out his own light. Sleep rushed at him, dragging his eyelids closed. Almost asleep, a blast of frigid air hit him pulling him back to consciousness. Did the landlord come and fix the air conditioner already? The chill, too much, forced him to pull the blanket up to his neck and over his shoulders. A rank stench reached his nostrils. The rotten smell almost made him gag. God! What was that? It was something like rotting eggs mixed with some sort of animal shit and some sulfur. His nose and eyes cringed from the rank stench. Mom always told him to breathe through your mouth whenever a foul stench carried, but that always seemed idiotic to him. It was plain gross. He pulled the sheet over his nose, hoping to hide from it. As too many distractions yanked him further from slumber, Jason sat up and opened his eyes.

Stunned, he stared at his brother. Jimmy stood in the middle of the room. A glint of moonlight peered through the curtains, outlining part of his body. The light crept from the floor, up his left leg, and revealed a small section of his naked torso and face. The one eye that could be seen was open. A breath calmly exited his mouth, the cold vapors intertwining with the crack of light.

"Jimmy?"

Do You Hear What I Hear?

His twin, oblivious to the call, continued to stand. The eye stared straight ahead. Keeping a blanket over his shoulder, Jason stood an inch away from Jimmy. He whispered his name a few times. Jimmy did not acknowledge him. Was he hypnotized? Or sleepwalking? Snapping his fingers did not provoke a response. Even slapping his brother lightly did not awaken him. Jimmy did not even blink.

"Mom! Dad! Something's wrong with Jimmy!" Repeating the call a few times, Jason turned on the lamp. Squinting, he tried to keep the light from hurting his eyes. Stepping closer to the door, he opened it and called out again into the dark hallway. He could hear them coming. They, too, mirrored his confusion and discomfort. "What is it?"

"It's Jimmy, he's ..." His voice trailed. Jimmy was no longer standing, but back in his bed. His eyes closed, he had the sheets and blankets pulled tight.

"What is it, honey?"

Flustered, he didn't know what to say. Fighting his own skepticism, and incredulity, he searched for the right thing to make sure he did not seem crazy. "Jimmy was ... out of bed. He was ... standing right here. I thought he was sleepwalking or something. I called his name, but he didn't move. And now ..."

"Are you sure you weren't dreaming yourself?" Mom hugged him gently.

Only looking at his brother, confused, he hunched his shoulders. "Maybe I was – but I coulda sworn ..." His voice trailed to silence.

Dad leaned over him. "Jimmy?" Dad repeated his call, getting louder every time. "No, he's sound asleep." Jimmy, though, twitched. He breathed heavily. His eyes darted underneath the lids. "Looks like he's having a bad dream."

"Dad. Is the air conditioner fixed? It got really cold in here a moment ago. It was almost freezing."

Dad's eyes, quizzical, nodded. "I feel it, too. However, this is ridiculous. I'll check it." His footsteps resonated but faded quickly.

Mom pulled her arms tighter, rubbing them. Her brown eyes glazed with confusion. Her lower lip quivered. Her eyes darted. Her head pivoted as she scanned from corner to corner of the room. Did she see something? Her nostrils flinched as her eyelids clamped shut. She stepped back. Suddenly, her breath became visible. She turned and followed Dad's path. "Derek, do you …" her question faded quickly.

Jason jumped as a shadow moved. Was it Mom merely stretching her shadow while leaving? No. It felt strange, unfamiliar, and dreadful. The reeking odor invaded his privacy again. Using his palm, he covered his nose hoping that it would keep the stink out of his nostrils. His skin chilled. Something passed over his head. Could it be a bug? Perhaps a moth or a wasp? A hot breath pulsed on his neck, partially blowing his hair. Jumping, he turned around, feeling as if something watched him. He kept turning – trying to see whatever barely eluded him.

Jimmy's face appeared. Deformed, bloodied, and bruised, with ashen, cracked skin. The eyes were nothing but a blank, terrorized stare. His jaw agape, with bugs crawling from the inside. Blood trickled from the lower, mangled lip.

Jason's yelp faded in his lost breath. Falling backward, he missed half the seat of the chair and plopped to the floor.

What? Jimmy was back in bed? How? His eyes were closed but still darted back and forth underneath his eyelids.

Do You Hear What I Hear?

He moaned a little. Confused, unsure of himself, Jason clamped his eyes shut for a second, shook his head, and opened his eyes again. Maybe he had to reboot his brain like restarting a laptop. Standing, he stood over his twin.

Jimmy snapped his eyes open. He wanted to scream, but it was rendered silent by his heavy gasps. Clutching his sweaty, naked chest, his jaw quivered. Covering his eyes, he shook his head. His elbows and knees quivered underneath the sheets. His raging breaths, out of sync and in an erratic rhythm, did slow. Jimmy tried inhaling deeply, holding it, then letting it out slowly. Like little steps, his breaths fell back into perfect timing.

"What was it bro?" asked Jason. "What were you dreaming about?"

Jimmy dropped his head and shook it. His voice quivered. Sweat beaded and rolled down his neck, back, and chest. Jason felt his brother's trembling – and even his fear. "I don't know," Jimmy said, inserting a breath between each word. "I can't remember. It was just horrifying."

"Yes, the air conditioner is back ..." Dad stopped abruptly. "Son?" He quickly lowered himself to face Jimmy. "You're soaking in sweat even though it's cold in here. What were you dream-"

"He said he doesn't remember," said Jason.

Jimmy shook his head as Mom returned. She sat next to him, hugging him tightly across the shoulders and head. Almost rocking him like a baby, the adolescent did not recoil from her touch, nor complained of being embarrassed.

Dad found some clean sheets and a fresh blanket. Jimmy wrapped the sweaty sheets around his waist as he let his parents make a quick change of the bedding.

"Kinda reminds you of a few years ago, hiding it when

you started ..."

"Mom," Jimmy added agitation to his voice – making it a wall to stop the embarrassment. He kept himself hidden with the old sheets and carefully got under the fresh bedding.

"And if you would wear something while sleeping you wouldn't ..."

"Mom," he said, "I understand. Just let me be me."

"Calm down," Dad said while rubbing his shoulder. "Jimmy, are you sure you don't want to talk about it?"

"I don't know what to talk about," he said while hunching his shoulders. "I can't remember the dream. It was something that ... happened ... a long time ago. But I don't know what." He finally faced Mom. "I can see bits and pieces of it. But not enough to get a ... clear picture.

Mom kissed him on the forehead, referring to him as "My poor baby."

Jimmy sighed and gently pulled away from Mom. "I'm alright now. I want to try and go back to sleep."

Mom and Dad said good night again, but not before asking Jimmy if he wanted or needed anything. After they left, Jason knew he could get him to talk. "What was it, bro?"

"I said I don't remember. Leave me alone, shithead."

Jason laughed at the profanity. It was their pet name for each other, and they used it all the time. Even a stranger could realize Jason and Jimmy could call each other that, but really did not mean it.

Jason's smile remained as he closed his eyes. The smile faded and his eyes snapped open. Narrowing his eyelids, he focused on something. At first, he thought it was a shadow. No. It had mass and dimension. The distinction was definite: a head, wing-like ears, and eyes. They barely glowed a faint reddish color. The head turned towards Jason. It stood

Do You Hear What I Hear?

motionless in Jimmy's dresser mirror.

Stephen W. Scott

Jimmy?

Jason squinted as the morning sun hurt his eyes. Palming his face, he tried to ease the acclimation of his eyes from sleep to awake, from dark to light, from dream to reality. Feeling ready, he popped his lids open. He stared at the ceiling for a minute, savoring the morning laziness – grateful to wake up with no alarm.

It hit him hard. Instantly he felt the urge to pee – but he had to contend with the morning wood. He hurried to the bathroom. The shower was running, but his twin never cared. Somehow, Jason's boner faded so he could pee.

As the toilet flushed, he grinned, expecting a profane scream from Jimmy. Surely it would sap the warm water. No. Nothing. The shower water stopped. Jason looked up in the mirror to see the ugly greenish-clear shower curtain pulled to the side.

Grinning, he looked over his shoulder to wish his brother good morning – until his eyes locked with ... something, but it wasn't Jimmy. The image glared back. Empty, sunken eyes had a cold blackness. Ashen and burnt skin rotted. The mouth had protruding teeth and fangs growing in strange fashions, showing no organization. The long neck stretched as the head lifted and expanded. A loud, vicious, high-pitched hiss forced Jason to cover his ears.

His heart thumped so fast it hurt. Tiny creatures seemed to crawl up the skin of his legs, waist, and torso. His chest contracted as a wretched cold spread into his chest and up to his neck. The terror vanished, retreating into various parts of his body, like rats scurrying for cover. He turned and backed up at the same time, slamming his back into the mirror. Finally, the cold let go of his neck and a scream surfaced.

"What's your problem, bro?" Jimmy grabbed a towel and started drying himself. "Looks like you've seen a ghost."

Jason shook his head and tried to calm his heart by putting his hand on his chest. Realizing the ghastly images were nothing but a remnant of a nightmare, he relaxed. The creatures that crawled on his skin disappeared. He cursed. "I thought I saw something weird. Really weird."

"Of course – you were looking at your butt-face in the mirror, shithead."

"You have the same butt-face I do." Turning back to the mirror, he noticed Jimmy drying off. However, his facial expression changed from a smile to a spiteful gaze. His eyes blackened and grew, making him look like some sort of deranged mannequin. A heavy, uneasy feeling circled him. An explosion of fear shot through his chest – forcing his eyes shut. Frenzied and confused, Jason tried some deep breaths to push out the fright. It only worsened. In fact, he felt the dread increase, as if pulling him deeper into an ocean or a pool. After several breaths, the gales inside softened into light winds.

Still a little spooked, Jason sighed and left the bathroom. Ravenous hunger helped him forget the raging terror. He rifled through the pantry, finding Frosted Flakes, a few bananas, and a bowl. Mom shopped well for their month-long vacation. He sliced the bananas, letting them fall into the dry cereal. The milk cascaded down the crevices of the cereal slices, eventually lifting the contents within a pool.

"There's the world-famous American surfer, Jason

Collins, eating his breakfast, preparing for the day."

Seeing Jimmy shove his phone at his face like a camera, Jason somehow spoke through his partially full mouth, using the preferred nickname they had for each other. "Put that thing away, shithead."

"Jason, what's it like competing for the surfing title against your brother?"

"My brother's a shithead," he said between bites. Unkempt, still dirty, only in his boxers, he pushed the smartphone camera away. Jimmy put it down.

Jason wanted to check it and make sure his twin didn't snap a picture of him. Turning the tide, he aimed the camera at Jimmy. He pulled on the towel. Jimmy cringed, caught the towel, and wrapped it around his waist again. Normally, he was the more daring and less inhibited of the two, usually sleeping naked. However, he never liked Mom catching him nude. He turned around.

Jason cringed, gagged, and coughed as his brother's face changed in the phone's camera. It resembled an old woman with deep wrinkles, sores, and black, bulbous eyes. Her matted hair was thin, gray, and scraggly. Streams of darkness seeped from the ears, and her nose had been cut off, leaving two empty black caverns. Long jagged teeth protruded down from a hideous overbite.

Milk nearly invaded Jason's lungs, but a panicked reflex contracted into a cough. Milk painfully gushed from his mouth and nose spurting with some coughs. It spilled down his jaw and chest and onto the floor. The phone had already bounced off the floor, catching a few drops of milk on the screen. His lungs, in pain, did all they could to spew a little bit more milk and flakes to get his breath back.

"What are you doing, shithead?" Jimmy picked up the

phone. "You break my phone, and I'll feed you to the sharks out in the bay."

Jason, finally, able to breathe, found his respiration returning to normal. Looking at his twin, he relaxed.

Jimmy moved closer. "You okay, bro?"

Jason nodded.

"Good," said Jimmy while examining his phone, "because if this screen is cracked, you're dead."

Jason wiped the milk off his skin, then scooped up the remains on the table and floor. A few wipes with paper towels and dish towels did the trick. Jason then went to shower. He kept looking over his shoulder at Jimmy.

**

The sun's rays beat relentlessly, forcing Jason to smear more sunscreen for protection. Looking around at the people on the beach, he started to feel a little more relaxed. These tight-fitting Brazilian male swimsuits were a little embarrassing, but as he viewed the other people on the beach, he felt less self-conscious. It also discouraged him from wanting to gaze at the barely clad, (and often topless) women sunbathers.

Glancing around, he noticed Jimmy running towards him. Jason activated his video app on his phone and aimed it at his twin. Holding his hand over the camera portion, he did his best to block the sun from obscuring the picture. Nothing. Jimmy looked the same as he always did. Jason squinted his eyes, wondering why he kept hallucinating.

"Mom, watch my phone. I'm going out with Jimmy now."

She barely acknowledged him, focusing on her book. Dad had something to do at the U.S. Embassy. This was a huge perk of working for the State Department: fancy vacations during the summer. They had traveled to many places like Buenos Aires, Costa Rica, London, Hawaii, the Philippines, Myanmar – and that was just the last five years! Jason loved the warm locales, mostly because the family lived in Albany, New York. Lots of snow, lots of cold, and very little surfing. Jason and Jimmy both fell in love with surfing when visiting Hawaii for a month in 2018. They learned to surf and fell in love with it. Ever since, Dad made sure they had a good month or so to get surfing in a warm climate (except the summer of Covid). Sure, they could do some in upstate New York, but not enough. They hoped to go to Australia someday.

Moving under the umbrella's shade, he started to put on his surfboard leash. Smiling, he cast aside his fear and tucked the board under his arm. Jumping prone on the board, he kicked and used his hands to move out towards the waves. He glanced at Jimmy, who was about twenty to thirty yards to his left. They both paddled towards the larger waves about 100 to 150 yards from shore.

The tide appeared to encroach on them slowly. He felt nervous but remembered the line from the movie, "Point Break." *Just paddling out is a total commitment. You can't just call 'time-out' and paddle back if you don't like it.*

The wave rolled faster as the bottom shallowed. Still, those swells were high, probably 15 to 20 feet. Both boys went over a wave and saw the perfect one coming right at them. Almost as if they had a psychic connection, they both turned 180 degrees and paddled. Glancing back, Jason noticed the wave rising again, cresting high. A few more kicks and paddles and he jumped up and planted both feet on the board.

The rush surged through him as he rode the wave. The

water foamed, dripping over his head as the waters formed a canopy over him, and a wall behind him. Jason reached back, cutting the cresting waters with his hand. The adrenaline spread from his heart, coursing through his veins, and surging through his arms, legs, bones, and muscles. Still, he felt relaxed and peaceful as he continued to ride the wave.

The water fell apart as the wave rolled further to shore. The wave collapsed and he was knocked underwater a few feet. Rolling on his back, he saw the foaming seawater form racing white clouds above him. They continued forward until they faded into oblivion. Surfacing, he climbed atop his board and started paddling out for another ride. Glancing over, he saw Jimmy. Jason laughed seeing the suit pulled down near his knees, showing his brother's white ass to the world. The surfing leash prevented it from being pulled off his body.

Jason bellowed another line from the movie, "Lose something, brah?"

If Jimmy lost it, he'd just surf naked! He was the daring one. Jimmy pulled it back on, then started paddling again.

They got closer to another mountain of water. At least two other surfers wanted to ride this gargantuan wave as it had a width of at least 100 yards, and a height of twenty feet or more. This wave lifted, appearing fierce, angry, and intimidating. Although scared, he held to the one line of the movie he always remembered: *Fear causes hesitation, and hesitation causes your worst fears to come true.* Again, Jason and Jimmy pivoted their boards back towards the beach and paddled. As the wave lifted behind them, they jumped to a standing position.

Jason again felt the adrenaline shoot from his torso to his limbs, giving him another high as he stood. This time, he triumphed over the surf and his own fear – emerging on top of the wave. A quick move of his hips and knees, he kept his balance and somehow moved to the underside. Although the water cut across his ankles and knees, he maintained his equilibrium. The wave fell on top of his body, knocking him into the waters once again.

Jason rolled on his back to watch the racing foam once again. Something caught the corner of his eye. It was a large torpedo … gray, with sinister eyes, long gills, and a large mouth. Everything inside Jason shuddered to a vicious halt. An invisible force seized him, freezing his body for a split second. He almost swallowed the seawater seeing the large shark open its jaws as it neared Jimmy's leg. As Jimmy looked back, the shark looked as if it hit some sort of wall, then rolled on its side – seeming unconscious. Jason somehow found control of his arms and legs and swam frantically to the surface. He got on his board just in time for a smaller wave to drag him ten to twenty yards from the shark. *What kind was it? Who the fuck cares? It sure was big!*

His jaw quivered and he gulped in some seawater that made him gag. He finally got his legs and arms out of the water and onto the board. His head darted, panicked, trying to see any sign of the predator. He finally remembered what to do in the situation and yelled, "Shark! Shark!" Finally, he caught sight of his brother again. He lay motionless on his board as his legs and arms draped in the water. Of course, sharks often bite boards, injuring the surfer, but a limb in the water just tempted the beast even more.

"Jimmy," yelled Jason, "get your legs and arms on the board!" He hoped his brother heard. Suddenly, a large fin emerged to the right of Jimmy. It swam closer. "Jimmy! To your right! To your right! Watch out."

The shark poked its head out of the water. It turned quickly, swimming away. It seemed scared, using its tail to splash Jimmy. Jason pivoted his board towards his twin. "Jimmy! Jimmy! Come on. We gotta get to shore before it comes back. Come on!"

A scarab motorboat idled alongside Jason. Two lifeguards lifted him and his board out of the water. Although safe in the boat, his breath raced so fast, his chest hurt. His arms and legs shook, and his jaw quivered. Almost crying, he clenched his eyelids shut. That was the closest he had ever been to a shark – and it was the largest he had seen.

The boat purred over to Jimmy and the lifeguards did the same for him. Once Jimmy was inside the boat, Jason hugged him tightly. "I thought it was going to get you." It seemed as if all the heat left Jimmy's body, and his eyes had a blank, emotionless stare. They lacked personality and will. Instead of irregular, fast huffs, Jimmy's were quiet. "Jimmy! What's wrong?"

Finally, Jimmy took a breath and his eyes blinked. "What happened?"

"The shark. Didn't you see that big shark? It came after you twice! I thought I lost you, bro."

"What shark?"

"That huge shark! You didn't see it? It was coming right after you. You were just a few feet from being bitten!"

He grunted, then coughed. He struggled for equilibrium. "I don't remember the shark. All I remember was … the screaming."

"Sharks don't scream. What are you talkin' about?"

"Screaming in my head. Loud." He grunted a few times. "Very high pitch – making my ears ring."

Jason had not noticed the boat picking up the other two surfers and reaching the shore. Mom was right there, ready to hold both boys tightly with all her strength. Her tears mixed with their seawater; she insisted on going back to the bungalow.

Noticing the waters void of swimmers, Jason couldn't agree more. He glanced back at the churning waves in the water, wondering what had happened to Jimmy.

Do You Hear What I Hear?

Headache

Jimmy felt numb, void of any physical sensation, or emotion. He heard a ringing in his ears. It was subtle, tickling the hairs near his ear drums. Or were those voices? A headache slowly worked on its way from the top of his head. It didn't throb but was rather a dull, achy pain that felt like a heavy object on his head. It reached his eyes, somewhat blurring his vision.

Mom's light brown eyes swirled with a bevy of emotions: fear, anger, desperation, and worry. Her tight face still looked young, without any plastic surgery. She did have some wrinkles near the outside of her eyes, the outside of her mouth, and forehead. Still, they were distinguished, giving her a regality of respect and strength. Her hair, somewhere between blonde and light brown, did have a few grays. She pointed her fork at both boys, thrusting it lightly, almost poking it with every syllable. "You boys are not going out tomorrow. I don't want you in that bay for the rest of our vacation!"

"Honey," interjected Dad, "you're overreacting."

Their voices overlapped, not wanting to listen to each other. Dad kept assuring her the patrol would be out early in the morning and make another run every three hours. Fear superseded all logic and reasoning as Mom's voice got louder.

"They are more likely to get stung by a jellyfish or die in a car wreck back in the States," said Dad.

"Mom," interjected Jason, "don't worry. I don't want to

go out tomorrow, or maybe even the day after."

Jimmy thought his twin sounded as if he were talking from within a well, or maybe a cave. The voice echoed, except the reverberations got louder instead of softer. The ringing in his ears got high, sounding like the feedback from a microphone too close to the amplifier. He clamped his eyes shut, wanting to blot out the irritating, grating sounds. He got cold, hunching his shoulders.

"Son! Son!" Jimmy opened his eyes. The sound had faded, but his headache persisted. The cold vanished as Dad touched his shoulder. "Are you okay?"

"I don't know. I gotta bad headache." He got up abruptly.

"Don't you leave yet young man!" Her voice was sharp, but not loud.

"Mom, I hear you and I understand. I just need to lie down for a while."

"Well, take something for it."

"No shit, Mom! Like it's going away through wishful thinking?"

"James Daniel Collins!" Mom interjected.

"Son!" followed Dad.

"I'm sorry, but this headache is bad. Just let me lay … lie down," he quickly added before she corrected his grammar.

He grabbed an ibuprofen and swallowed it without water. Retreating to his room, he reclined, and even though it was dark, he put a pillow over his eyes. He tried to relax, hoping the high-pitched noise would relinquish its power and fade into oblivion. What happened to him? He tried to remember the shark. Did he see it? Was it really that close? Did it really open its mouth at him then swim away

Do You Hear What I Hear?

frightened like Jason said?

His breath slowed. His thoughts faded into quiet. There was no music, no past conversations, no images of movies or TV shows. As his mind felt peaceful, he suddenly felt freezing cold. He pulled the pillow off his head and sat up. A faint light reflected off the bedroom mirror. He turned, seeing his crystalized breath outlined in the faint streak of light. His blank mind suddenly teemed with fear.

He heard it. A subtle voice, dissonant and faint, reached his ears. He looked in the mirror to see his own silhouette. However, a larger shadow enveloped him. It looked as if it had large, folded wings, surrounding a large body and a large head between tall, pointed ears. Red eyes subtly glowed in the head. A long talon extended, pointing to the right.

Spasmodic, irregular breaths burst through both his nose and mouth, leaving a trail of carbon dioxide that collapsed as it fell. A cold, gripping terror seized his chest. He wanted to yell but could not. He wanted to scream, but something cold inside him reached up, and pulled his tongue back. Jaw quivering, Jimmy looked to where the talon pointed.

A door rested at the end of a hallway. Was it there before? No. He did not remember it. It seemed almost as if a wall disappeared and turned into a short hallway. A flickering, low light outlined the ajar door. A few times, it looked as if hands and fingers pushed through the cracks as if trying desperately to escape. Something held them back. Low moans and whispers echoed, except they grew, bouncing from wall to wall.

Trepidation seized Jimmy's muscles. For a second, it felt like he would collapse like a marionette held up by strings. No. Someone, or something, pulled at them. Feeling no will of his own, his legs started walking. The strings pulled on one knee, lifting it up, pulled it forward and set his foot on the cold, wooden and splintery floor. The opposite string pulled up, pulled his other leg forward and let it come down. He would have fallen, but the strings on his shoulders remained taut. Jimmy wanted to turn around and run from the ominous presence that lay ahead. It was something sinister, hiding in shadow that waited for him to walk into a trap. However, whatever had his strings would not let him. A hot breath poured down his neck, followed by a blast of frigid air.

The hallway stretched. The lights flickered more. The hands and fingers disappeared and reappeared. Closer, they looked dead. The skin was sickly, somewhere between blue and gray. Black bruises and cuts marred the skin. Splotches of hand and fingerprints in blood stained the door and walls.

At the door, Jimmy waited. The strings from the puppet would not let him lift his own arms or move his legs. The moans and whispers became silent, as if not wanting anyone to hear their secrets. The lights blinked off and on several times. It remained dark for a while, letting a bitter cold approach him. After an uncertain amount of time, the lights popped on again. turned off and on, off and on, off and on. Off. After several seconds of darkness, the light ignited once again - staying on. A long, painful creak moaned, following the door's arc inside the room. Jimmy wanted to shut his eyes – yet the puppet strings did not let him.

His bare feet, freezing, stepped into some sort of hospital room. No longer wood, it was now tiled, stained with both blood and dirt. The vile smell of rotting and spoiled flesh mixed with body chemicals was so bad, he could almost taste it. The stench triggered heavy nausea, making his eyes water.

Do You Hear What I Hear?

To his right was a metal table, stained in blood. Stainless steel surgical tools not only had blood, but pieces of skin, hair, and teeth. Some blades were long and sharp. Others were dull and round. Some of the round blades had tiny, serrated teeth – and some resembled saws.

A flashing light flickered, revealing the corner full of legs, arms, fingers, hands, and feet. They were small, marred, bloodied, and had the same grayish-blue shade as the hands. The ends of the severed limbs had maggots chewing on the flesh. A wave of the smell crashed on him as a slight breeze pushed the stench across the room.

Another light flickered on his left. Looking down, he saw a child, no more than nine or ten. The child, with no discernable gender, was bald, and in a straitjacket. Scars ran along the side of the head. Turning to face him, Jimmy recoiled at the sight of the child's eyelids sewn shut. Under his eyes, stains of blood resembled tears. He whispered something. It got louder until it finally became audible: "I want my eyes back. He took them. Please get them back."

A whimpering cry further in the room alerted Jimmy. He saw them: girls. Both looked alike, and they were joined at their freshly sutured shoulder stumps where one girl had her right arm amputated – and the other had her left arm removed. Both of them stared ahead at nothing, as if locked in a trance, but somehow had a couple of tears streaming down their cheeks. Jimmy, although terrified, cried with them.

Another cry pulled his attention to the opposite corner. Two boys, malnourished and emaciated, were strapped to chairs, with their legs in small tubs of ice water. Their arms, their hands, even their legs shook as they endured the freezing cold.

Jimmy heard a voice that spoke a strange language. A figure, turned away, dressed in medical garb worked furiously while mumbling to himself. Two assistants, also in medical clothing, observed casually. A horrific, icy yell insinuated a chill of terror through Jimmy's body. If the puppet strings were not taut, he would have jumped at the boyish screams and tried to cover his ears.

Although Jimmy wanted to run, the marionette strings pulled, coercing him to circle them. Rounding the front, he saw their medical garb covered in blood, with pieces of innards attached to their torsos, arms, and hands. Seeing disfigured monsters with scars and bulbous flesh covered in tiny black tumors, he froze. Their dead eyes pierced his soul that shuddered in terror.

They spoke a language he could not understand.

"What?" whispered Jimmy.

They spoke it again.

Sinuous shadows lengthened and reached for Jimmy. Their eyes became empty sockets as their mouths emitted a low-pitched howl. The teeth grew fangs. The ears lifted into pointed spears. The deformed wings expanded, then closed on him, robbing him of any light or warmth.

Jimmy yelled as he sat up. A vicious sweat completely covered his skin and soaked his bed sheets. His screams continued as the lights came on.

Do You Hear What I Hear?

The Secret

An explosive stream of lightning spread across the sky. It stretched out like arteries and veins that carried light until it disappeared into the towering storm clouds. Thunder clapped with an ominous roar. It reverberated, fading into oblivion. Another set of lightning trails burst from nothing, streaking from cloud to cloud. The thunder resounded again. The lightning exploded a third time, but it was further away, not giving the light it emitted earlier. The thunder followed trying desperately to keep up with the display, but it faded faster – along with the drubbing of large raindrops that tapered, turning into a steady drizzle.

Jason stared outside. He hated this. They were trapped inside, unable to go surfing, get a suntan, and meet girls. Even worse, the storm knocked out the Internet, and their cell reception was minimal. Cable was not working well either and they only had access to some local channels that were in Portuguese.

Something peeked out from underneath the rug. The round edge of a dirty silver coin enticed Jason's curiosity. He dropped to his knee to pull it out. A huge bird's wings spread from one side of the coin to the other. Underneath the majestic bird was a familiar symbol that frightened him. It was a tilted cross, with wings. Etched in the coin, Jason rubbed his thumb over it. Turning it over, he saw the profile, also carved into the coin. Although it did not fully look like him, Jason recognized the Hitler portrait. "Hey Dad, Jimmy! Mom! Look at this."

Dad's tall shadow draped over him, drowning the already weak light. He seized it from Jason. "Wow," he said while examining it closer. "That's dated 1939!"

"What's that say?" Jason asked, pointing to the words underneath the Hitler profile. Dad knew the Romantic languages, Italian, French, Portuguese, and Spanish very well, but he was not as keen on the Northern European Languages.

"I don't know."

Jason dropped to the floor and pulled the carpet back some to see if any more coins were there. Disappointed, he found nothing, but instinctively knocked on the floorboards, hearing a hollow sound "Hey, I think there's a secret compartment down here."

Dad, along with Jimmy, knelt and pulled the small cover away. Anticipation swelled more as they peered into the crevice. Their cell phones all turned to flashlights to lighten the small opening. At the bottom was a cigar box. Jason grabbed it and pulled it closer. The corners were dinged, and the color had faded. Brushing away the dirt and dust, Jason cringed at the Nazi décor on the top and sides. Somehow, it possessed an allure, leading to a mystery. It called all of them, almost whispering. Dad and Jason hesitated, but Jimmy's curiosity goaded him to open it.

Opening it, the air from decades ago leapt free, traveling through a time warp and lunged the past forward in an instant. Old, aged, and yellowed papers lay folded in the box, along with part of a diary. It had been torn in half. Some pictures, and currency both paper and coin, laden with Nazi emblems, also littered the box.

"Wow, this is cool! This stuff must be worth lots of money!" said Jason.

Do You Hear What I Hear?

"Maybe some museum will pay us for it," added Jimmy.

"Wait, guys," said Dad, "don't get carried away." He, too, had dropped to his knees. An envelope seemed to beg them to open it. Dad turned it upside down and old photos fell out. Black and white, they were stiff, but fragile.

Jason picked them up, but one glance shocked him so much, his hand froze, and his grip dropped them. He backed away.

Jimmy picked them up and examined them with heavy interest. The children were mangled, malnourished, and emaciated. Some were naked, and if not, their clothes were about to fall off. Some limbs or digits were missing. Definite suturing was aligned on their backs. Their eyes were devoid of emotion, will, or even personality. Many of them appeared similar, and in some cases, the same.

"Let me see them," whispered Dad. After looking at the children, he flipped the pictures and noticed the dates scribbled on them. Barely readable, all of the dates were between 1941 and 1944. Dad inspected the German money, the medals, and realized what they had found. "I think we stumbled across one of the Nazis who fled to South America after World War II."

Jason carefully opened the torn diary. "Look at this." He opened it up and looked at the mysterious words. He showed it to Dad. "It must be German."

"Shouldn't we take it to some university that specializes in Holocaust studies, or some Jewish Museum?" asked Jimmy.

"Well, the house is on Brazilian soil, so we must turn the things into their government. Even if the Nazi escaped here, Brazil has first dibs on the material." Dad glanced at the fragile parchment within the diary. "But I don't see a problem in taking this to the U.S. Embassy first. I know a couple of people there who know German. I cannot wait to find out what this says." He looked at the pictures again and sighed. "Yeah – these are children at concentration camps"

Jason's stomach knotted. He took a step back, feeling uneasy. "A former Nazi lived here? He tortured children?"

"Looks like it," said Dad. "Many Nazis fled to South American countries after World War II to escape prosecution." He hesitated, "And the OSS helped some of them escape in exchange for the scientific material the Nazis discovered."

"What's the OSS?" asked Jimmy.

"They were the CIA before they were renamed the CIA." At this point, Dad shook his head. "The United States should be embarrassed by this part of World War 2." He looked at Jason and Jimmy. "Boys, don't ever make a deal with the devil or you'll become one."

Jason worked up the nerve and examined the pictures more closely. Almost crying, he could hear their desperate pleas for help leap across time. Their eyes, although in a picture, pierced his spirit with angst, begging him to do something and rescue them. Jason gasped at the sight of the dirty skin, scars, sutures, and hideousness.

"Oh, my ... God," Mom could not look anymore, turning her head and crying.

Jason let Mom hug him after he passed the pictures back to Dad. What kind of people would do that to children? It was frightening – more so than any horror movie he had seen. He sighed, almost grieving for them. What were they like? Did they play sports? Go to Church ... or rather Synagogue? What did they talk about? Did they play games like hide-and-go-seek, tic-tac-toe, or something else? Jason almost cried, realizing his worst complaint was the wi-fi being out at the house right now. Those children were starving! They were hacked and tortured! How many were killed?

"Okay," said Dad as he pulled the remaining pictures from Jimmy, "I think that's enough." He, like Mom, shook his head, sighed, and pulled Jason closer to kiss him on the forehead as he tried to protect his son from the past.

Dad looked out the window, obviously noticing the rain had stopped and the clouds spread apart. "Great. I can get these to the Embassy so they can contact the Brazilians."

"Derek," said Mom, "I need to go to the store, so I'll go with you." She turned to Jimmy and Jason. "Are you boys okay to be left on your own?"

"Jesus … I mean … jeez, Mom, we're 14 and we'll be okay," quipped Jason.

Jimmy watched Mom and Dad leave. He glared at the one old photo he snuck from Dad. Two boys, lying on a table as a man in surgical garb stood over them. Blood stained the table, as well as the surgical clothes and instruments. A sneer spread across his face.

Narcissus

Nervous, Jason stepped back from Jimmy. His twin stared at the mirror for minutes, perhaps hours on end. "Bro," Jason whispered, "you okay?"

Unfazed, unmoved, Jimmy's eyes never blinked. His head turned slightly, casting a brief glance at Jason. It swiveled back to face the mirror again.

"Hey," he said louder while pulling on Jimmy's shoulder, "what's going on? You're creeping me out."

Jimmy turned his head, again, casting another, longer glance.

"Jimmy! The wi-fi is back on, and there are literally dozens of games waiting for us. Come on, shithead." After waiting what seemed like several minutes, Jimmy faced the mirror once again.

"At least you can call me shithead, you shithead." Jason sighed. "I give up. I'll play by myself." He waited a minute, wondering if Jimmy would take the bait for a masturbation joke. Usually, he would jump at the opportunity - but all he did was stare at the mirror.

He wasn't the same anymore. Jimmy and Jason had a link very few siblings had: being twins who knew each other so well they could speak the same things at the same time or could respond quickly as if being able to read each other's mind. At first, Jason almost cried, but then an icy sensation carried heavy trepidation.

Jimmy

Jimmy struggled, trying to find personality, identity,

Do You Hear What I Hear?

and agency as if they faded heavily. He tried to speak, but nothing came out of his mouth. Although his eyes had been captured by his own reflection, he desperately wanted Jason's help. What was happening to him? Why couldn't he break free from the hypnotic spell. The air became still as a weighted overwhelming dread enveloped him. It trapped him like heavy chains, keeping him from moving. He tried to flex his muscles. Why couldn't he move?

A mass confusion descended on him. One second, he was in the bungalow by himself, and instantly he was back at home in Albany. For a second, his family surrounded him, then they vanished. He felt the sunshine on him, giving him warmth and life - but then he was cast into darkness as if heavy drapes were pulled over the windows. Growls, metal scraping against metal, wood, bangs, crashes, and inhuman moans disturbed the tranquil silence - as well his spirit. One second, a searing heat baked his skin, triggering a profuse sweat, but then a chilling cold caused him to shiver.

Something whisked him back to his room at home. Metal shutters had replaced the doors. He kept trying to get out, but the doors would not budge. He pounded on them, hoping Mom and Dad would get him out. Looking out the windows, it seemed as if the stars either retreated from the dark or burned out. The moon, although full, was very dim - like a light bulb about to go out. Separating him more were the bars outside the window. When were they installed? He pounded the glass, hoping it might break and then he could yell for someone to help. What? How'd he get naked? Ironically, he liked being naked – often sleeping that way, but not when it was freezing cold.

His eyes opened. Where was he? Oh, yes. The bungalow in Sao Paulo. How did he get back from Albany so fast? He was staring at the ... mirror, yet no reflection existed. Turning around, he noticed the room descended into a pitch-black tunnel.

Looking back at the mirror, his body froze solid at the sight of the creature. Shocked by the monster's snake-like eyes and stitched mouth, he shivered at the sight of horrid, jagged teeth. All his fear knotted his stomach then exploded through his lungs, out his mouth, and into a horrid scream. His skin tightened, froze, then his limbs shook uncontrollably. Wait a minute. The monster stood inside the mirror, mimicking every one of his moves. He moved closer, staring at the mirror - just as the creature did the same.

The creature changed forms, reverting to Jimmy's reflection. His cold breath left a fog on the glass as his own eyes slanted and stared, sending a glare of hatred. It made him colder, forcing Jimmy to shake his lips, fingertips, and toes. His breath got caught in his throat as the image had separated itself. The lips widened and the eyes narrowed. "What ... what ... the fuck" he stammered a few more times in his whispers, "are you?"

Jimmy's reflection changed into something else that grew, thinned, and darkened. Ominous wings spread, absorbing what little light remained. It opened its mouth, bellowing a hideous, low-pitched roar.

Jimmy's fear erupted from his lungs, exploding into a scream. He retreated, backing into the wall while holding his chest to contain the painful, intense pumping. Panicked, not knowing what to do, he stared at the mirror. He could not reconcile this moment of reality.

The glass fogged up from the inside of the mirror and part of it iced over. The creature pressed its three-fingered claw from inside the reflection. The glass cracked. The deformed arm pushed through the mirror without breaking it. The head lurched forward, passing from the reflection, through the mirror and into reality. More cold spread to the walls, the floor, and the furniture as the claws grabbed the top of the dresser and pulled the rest of the way through. Once the wings broke through, they fluttered giving it an extra boost and the entity freed itself. Jimmy felt the wind push his hair and chill his skin even more. As in a victory, it howled a low-pitch scream, splattering drool across the room, onto Jimmy's face.

Jimmy suddenly found himself inside the mirror. His image sneered at him, then turned to look over his brother. "No!" His voice reverberated strangely. He pounded on the glass. "Jason! It's coming after you! Get out!"

Jimmy's doppelganger changed into the hideous beast he saw a few seconds ago. It's howl erupted, feeling like a force that would rupture his ears.

Jason

A thunderous noise jolted Jason awake. He tried to clutch his chest, hoping to force his respiration to a normal, rhythmic pattern. A slick sweat seeped through and drenched his skin. His heartbeat, frantically out of sync, felt like a bunch of deaf percussionists incapable of finding the proper beat. His shaking spread under his skin, leaving behind jolts of electricity. Closing his eyes, he concentrated on finding normal breath. Using the meditation techniques some surfing instructors taught him, his body found the normal, proper harmony.

A heavy stillness dropped on him. Even though the terror existed outside his body, the palpability grabbed him by the shoulders. Something watched him. They were not friendly, warming eyes like Mom or Dad, but rather spiteful ones. Jason saw it in the mirror: a dark, hideous, winged creature in the shadow. Its red eyes glared at him.

Jason wept, somehow knowing what this creature had been doing slowly over the last several days. "Please, please," he whispered, "give me my brother back."

***

Lying on the living room couch, Jason tried to sleep - but it eluded him as fear raced through his mind. For the first time in his life, he was afraid of Jimmy and did not want to sleep in the same room with him. He and his twin had known each other every second of their lives – even in Mom's womb. Jason knew it was something else turning his brother against him - but what? An indescribable hurt pressed on his spirit. He cried.

Jason's head turned and his arms, legs, shoulders, feet, and hands all twitched – even keeping in time with his heart, lungs, and bladder. Jimmy, hidden in the shadow, stood above him, staring down. "What are you doing, shithead?" he whispered angrily.

"Nothing." Jimmy's voice sounded empty of personality. It almost stammered.

"Bro, you're sleepwalking. Go back to bed," Jason whispered.

"What?"

"Go back to bed. God, you've become so annoying."

Jimmy stood still – staring at Jason.

Jason stood and escorted his brother to the bedroom.

"Are we home?" asked Jimmy.

"No," Jason whispered impatiently, "-we're in Sao Paulo. Stop acting so weird."

"Okay," he said.

After getting Jimmy to bed, Jason glanced around,

sensing strange eyes piercing through his skin and into his soul. They seemed to be all over, in the corners, hiding in deep shadows. Glancing around frantically, he could not stand this awful feeling. Tense, it felt like bubbles spreading underneath his skin and out his pores. He rushed back to the living room, sprawled on the couch, and put a blanket over his shoulders. He pulled his blanket tight over his head to keep it dark enough to sleep.

Suzanne

Suzanne heard footsteps. Light, slow, they sounded like bare feet softly slapping the floor. Was she dreaming? No. She was somewhere between asleep and awake. Knowing Derek was next to her, she felt safe and secure. She relished the warmth and strength of his lean body, still with good muscle density.

A vicious chill made her skin shrivel and shake. Pulling the blanket tighter, even covering her ears and mouth, she moved closer to Derek. Suzanne sensed his dreams were troubling. Perhaps he dreamt of the helicopter crash back in the Iraq War? He lost two friends when Iraqi insurgents shot down the chopper. Derek was the pilot and carried a lot of guilt, even though he didn't need to. It plagued his memory and often changed his dreams into nightmares.

The door hinge let out a long moaning creak. A faint light stretched across her cheek and eyelids. Afraid, she returned to a childhood ritual: reciting the Lord's Prayer. Not only did the familiar prayer leave a warm peace, but she giggled because she heard the voice of James Earl Jones. After listening to the Bible on audio so many times, the actor and voice artist had now permeated all Scripture. Maybe God *did* sound like James Earl Jones. She almost laughed out loud but then used the peace to relax and find slumber.

A terrible dread closed in. Dark, and cold, she sensed something angry, malevolent, and sinister. Her spirit jumped across the void, back into the realm of awake. Opening her eyes, she saw it! A huge, hideous beast, outlined in silhouette. Large ears rested on the head. Red, flattened eyes glowed, changing their hue to a subtle yellow. Its head turned, revealing some sort of snout. It breathed heavily, bobbing its head between the tall, thin shoulders. Afraid, she gasped and tried to clutch her heart - hoping to slow its racing rhythm.

She sighed, recognizing the familiar shadowy figure. Even though the boys had an identical stature and build, Suzanne somehow always knew which one was which. "Jimmy," she whispered, trying not to disturb Derek's sleep. "Jimmy," she whispered louder.

Jimmy awakened. His hands covered his body, although Suzanne did not see anything as it drowned in shadow. Rolling her eyes at his insistence of sleeping naked, shaking her head, she whispered, "Jimmy, you're sleepwalking. Go back to bed." He backed up, obviously not wanting to show his naked butt to her, either. "And since you've been sleepwalking, you need to wear something."

Sheepishly embarrassed, Jimmy backed out of Mom and Dad's room. She barely heard Jimmy call himself "stupid shithead" as he returned to his bedroom. Shaking her head, Suzanne whispered a laugh.

An eerie feeling pressed against her. Turning back towards the bed, the shivering returned, coupled with an ominous doubt. Suzanne's head turned back and forth, trying to find the strange eyes that left cold pinpricks on her skin.

Do You Hear What I Hear?

The Last Surf

Jason let out a huge yawn, trying to find the energy he lacked for the day. The nights prevented sleep, robbing him of the rest he truly needed. Maybe going outside and standing under the sun's bright rays would help replenish his vigor and enthusiasm.

He opened the front door and stepped outside, taking in the brightness and the life of people on the sidewalks and streets. Glancing left, the road stretched uphill, with many more small homes. Some were of brick and stood with confidence, while many were hovels, made up of decaying, water-damaged wood, crumbling stone, and old, weakened foundations. To the right was an even terrain with better homes.

Jason cracked a smile for the first time in a few days as he took in the beach. Seeing girls in the skimpy, thong bikinis he got excited. Torn, part of him wanted to hit the waves and the other half wanted to keep an eye on Jimmy. Moreover, they worked as a team to spark conversation with girls. A common one they liked to use to meet girls was, "My twin and I were wondering: which one of us is the best-looking?" Almost laughing, Jason remembered the girls who would laugh at the comment and then make goofy eyes at them. The humor was nothing more than a lost memory.

Jason ran back to the bungalow. As soon as the door closed, darkness circled. He glanced out the window at the bright sun, occasionally hidden by clouds. Despite the large windows, little sunlight penetrated the inside.

A knock alerted Jason to someone's presence. He partially opened the main door, leaving the screen door locked in place. An unfamiliar man stood outside, wearing khaki shorts, a polo shirt, and sunglasses. The Caucasian man smiled. "Excuse me, young man, is Derek Collins your father?"

Jason hesitated, ready to slam the door. Dad always told him to be less trusting in foreign countries, even if they were Americans and appeared friendly.

"I'm Brian Sammons with the U.S. Embassy and I work with him, is he here right now?"

With his foot on the screen door, Jason shook his head. "No, sir." He started to tell the stranger Dad and Mom went out to do some shopping and sightseeing but remembered never to give details to people they don't know. "Is there something I can help you with?"

"I called his cell phone and left a message but thought I would try to stop by as well. Your Dad found a box that had a diary and some pictures, and … well … it's missing from the safe."

Remembering the box that had the German manuscript, the photos of starving, tortured children triggered an uneasiness in Jason. He never wanted to see the pictures again – and wished he could remove them from his memory as well. Suddenly, what Mr. Sammons said registered in Jason's mind. "Missing?"

"We put it in the safe a few days ago, and when our experts arrived, we opened it, and the diary was missing. Did your dad bring it back here?"

"Not that I know of," he said, hunching his shoulders.

"Weird," mumbled the man. "If you would, please, tell your dad I stopped by, and ask him to give me a call. I'd really appreciate it. Again, I'm Brian Sammons."

Jason considered going to the beach by himself. He was

Do You Hear What I Hear?

tired of being cooped up with his brother. All Jimmy wanted to do was sit in the dark. And he kept staring at the mirror! What was it with that mirror?

This was ridiculous. The shock of the shark attack a few days ago had worn off and Jason was ready to get back in the water for some surfing. If Jimmy wanted to sit in the dark room by himself, so what? Jason's steps were heavy and hard, making sure Jimmy felt the anger. He shook his head and changed into his swimsuit, grabbed a towel, put on some shoes, and grabbed a wetsuit.

"Jimmy," he said, "I'm tired of being stuck in here with you. I'm not wasting any more time. I'm going surfing." Maybe he could get him to respond with a movie line they often used on each other before. "In the last few days," he yelled, "you've done squat! Squat! Now do you have anything remotely interesting to tell me?"

Jimmy continued staring. Usually, he'd counter the Point Break line, "I caught my first tube today … sir." Instead, his twin said nothing, not even looking at Jason.

"I give up." Jason made his words hard and sharp as if to hit or stab his brother. "You wanna stay in here and be spooky, that's fine by me, but I refuse to sit in the dark when there are waves, and a lot of hot, topless chicks out on the beach."

Jason grabbed a house key, his phone, and some sunglasses and went to the beach.

***

Exhausted, Jason fell to the sand on his knees. Surfing felt like a religious experience that satisfied his hungry soul. He pulled a fresh breath through his nostrils and inhaled deeply. Afterward, he exhaled slowly, taking his time to fully purge the carbon dioxide from his lungs. The sun beat on his wet shoulders, chest, and back, evaporating the droplets of seawater. Many other water beads fell onto the sand.

Sitting on the beach, Jason stared at the orange sun. Part of it dipped behind a tree line on the western side of the bay, leaving enough of it to cast a shade of purple on the underside of some cumulus clouds. The surf rolled continually until the shoreline broke the waves into a bubbling foam. The fresh smell of ocean water, the air blowing across his face and drying his hair felt peaceful. He missed Jimmy. This was their time to talk about their day on the waves, how they felt, what their accomplishments were, and how surfing put them at ease with each other, the world, and Mom and Dad. Unsure if it was a drop of seawater or a tear on his cheek, he rubbed it dry. "What's wrong with you, Jimmy?" he whispered. "We'd always do this together."

After five more meditative breaths, he stood, found the beach shower to get the sand off, then returned the surfboard and leash to the rental facility. Afterward, Jason retrieved his belongings out of a rental locker and went back to the bungalow.

"Hi, Mom."

Looking up from her book, she smiled widely at him. Her short, reddish-brown hair framed her face perfectly. Her head was not overly thin, nor was it round or fat – but somewhere perfectly in between. She wore white shorts and a black tank top shirt that showed her thin arms. "There's my other handsome young man."

"Mom, please," Jason protested, "you're embarrassing me."

"Well, then, I'll come to you for my hug and kiss from my favorite twin son," she said, giving him a kiss and a hug.

Do You Hear What I Hear?

"Let me guess ... you want me to help you with dinner."

They both smiled. "I tried to get Mr. Grumpy to do it, but all he does is sit in the dark, looking into the mirror."

Jason nodded slightly. "He's acting so weird lately," he whispered. "Let me change into some dry clothes, okay?"

Mom nodded. Jason went into the room. Dark, he wondered if Jimmy slept. Turning on the desk light, he saw Jimmy sitting in a chair, glaring at the mirror. "Shit – Jimmy! You scared me."

Jimmy said nothing. His head turned to face Jason, then after 10 or 20 seconds, it pivoted back to the mirror.

"Are you ever going to help Mom with dinner? I've done it two nights in a row, shithead."

Jason noticed something in Jimmy's hand: it was the old box they had found a couple of days ago. Jimmy was reading from the old journal they found a few days ago. It was the same one Mr. Sammons was looking for. How did Jimmy get it? Even stranger, Jimmy's lips barely moved as if he could read the old language. He then stopped to inspect a picture. After examining it for a few seconds, the left corner of his mouth sneered. He put the photo on one of the piles he had on his bed.

"Jimmy," said Jason, "where did you get that? Someone from the Embassy is looking for it. Do you hear me, shithead?"

Although Jimmy did not fully face Jason, the sneer slightly grew. Glancing at the mirror, Jimmy's reflection broke free from its source. The head moved. The light around Jimmy faded. His eyes narrowed. They glowed yellow.

As Jason dressed himself, he heard a subtle ring become louder, stretching into a high pitch and broad volume.

Shocked, numb, Jason finished dressing and went to the kitchen.

Mom nudged him playfully, then whispered. "What's going on with your brother?"

"I dunno," he said, hunching his shoulders.

She hugged him again and delivered a kiss on his forehead. "I'm so proud of you."

His head turned sharp. "What for?"

"You were surfing again, right?"

He nodded.

"Because you got over your fear of the shark. It took a few days, but you went right back out there to face your fears.

"I thought you didn't want me back out there."

Somehow, she started a conversation between her orders on what ingredients to get out and how to prepare them for dinner. "I'm sorry for overreacting. I was wrong. And ... what's more important is that facing fears is how you become stronger, mature, and gain confidence. And that's what girls like in a guy: confidence. You are handsome, but confidence is so much sexier – and it'll get more girls than your handsome looks."

Jason tried not to smile, but somehow one broke across his face.

"Hey!" said Dad as he walked into the bungalow. "How's everyone?"

"We're fine," said Mom, "but Mr. Depressed is still in his room."

"He's not depressed," said Jason, "just weird." After a slight hesitation, he turned to Dad. "Uh, do you know a Mr. Sammons from the embassy?"

Dad nodded.

"He stopped by today …"

"Oh – I got his phone call. I don't know how that box disappeared because we put it in-"

"The safe?" Jason whispered after glancing at the bedroom door. "Dad … Jimmy's got the box."

"What?"

"He's got the box. He was looking at the pictures and he was … well … reading from the diary."

"How? By Google translator?"

Jason hunched his shoulders. "No. I saw his mouth moving as if he understands German." He hesitated wondering if he should say something. "Uh, Dad …"

Dad paused to wait.

Jason tried to say something – but something dry and strong seized his throat. Although his mouth opened, he could not say anything. Stuck in speech, maybe time, he tried to blurt it out again. Something else came out. "I … uh … got on the surfboard again today. Surfed for two hours."

Dad smiled, hugging Jason with one arm and messing up Jason's hair with the other hand. "It feels good to get back out there to conquer fear, doesn't it?"

Jason's smile broke again. He nodded.

"I'm proud of you, son. You're becoming a strong man."

"What's for dinner?" Everyone turned to face Jimmy. He looked as if he had not slept for a couple of days. His hair was disheveled, and his skin seemed to have whitened, and his eyes had darkened. However, Jason shuddered at his voice because it was no longer pleasant and easygoing, but rather tired … and angry. His energy and aura spread, slightly darkening the kitchen and dampening the good, positive, and warm feelings.

***

Usually in the morning, Suzanne woke up refreshed with new energy. Not today. The air seemed heavier, thicker, carrying an evil presence. It robbed light, joy, and rest. She wished Derek didn't have to leave so early. Worried, frightened, she trembled as she entered her boys' bedroom. The strange presence vibrated a low hum, pulsing like an erratic heartbeat. Looking around, she tried to find the eyes that danced all over her skin. It reminded her of summer camp when she was 15 and some boys were caught spying on her and some other girls. What was going on? Especially with Jimmy? Why was he sleepwalking? Why did he stare at the mirror for minutes, hours on end? He finally relented for some surfing today, although he still seemed out of sorts. Suzanne's distinct intuition or fear told her something evil resided in this room, and she worried it infected Jimmy.

She stared at the mirror. She squinted her eyes. She tried to look beyond it. A shadow jumped. It dashed from behind the bed. It settled in the shadow cast by the armoire. It was only in the mirror. Nothing moved behind her. It dashed again. The lights flickered. Unable to move, unable to think, she continued her stare. She jumped as the shadow moved again. It looked as if a man strode from the bed to the closet – but with only a silhouette. She heard him whisper. He stood behind her and clasped his dried, shriveled hands on her shoulder. A freezing cold dug itself into her flesh.

Her heart, fueled by a surge of terror, thumped so hard she heard it within her head. Horror warmed the blood in her veins, yet the terror made her skin cold. Despair darkened her eyes, or did they darken the light in the room. Feeling the hairs in her ears chill and tickle, she gasped, then lost the rhythm of her breath. Her eyelids got heavy and slammed shut. She heard him clearly. What language was that?

Her eyes shot open. There it was! Behind her. The grayish skin clung tightly to the emaciated body. Its long, sinewy arms clasped her shoulders. It had only three long fingers with a compatible thumb. Its large forehead tried to put the large, bulbous eyes in darkness. The long, dirtied teeth protruded from both the top and bottom of the lipless mouth. Instead of a nose, the creature had two large nostrils between the mouth and its eyes. Thin strands of long, dirty, stringy hair looked as if they barely clung to the scalp.

A scream caught in her throat. A few tears exploded through her eyes. They burned. She covered her ears as a bellowing, high-pitched wail made her cringe. Suzanne's eardrums retreated from the loud, icy wail. The soul within her withered as if retreating. She sat on the bed while shaking. Her fingers, her arms, even her skin vibrated.

"Hon," Derek said, "what is it?"

She gasped. The overwhelming dread seemed to make the house darker. "Derek," she whispered nervously, "there is something terribly wrong with this place. We should leave and find another house to rent."

"Sue, the State Department is paying for the place to rent. We're on their dime."

"We'll ask them to find us another place. Hell, we have money to pay for someplace else. Let's go. I can't describe why this place creeps me out. Jimmy is acting strange, and Jason is afraid of him. I've never seen the boys act like this. And I cannot stop shaking. It's gotten worse every day. And that box? How the hell did Jimmy …"

"I don't know, it seems strange to me, too. But I will get it and return it to …"

"You're not listening to me. To hell with the box, and the photos because I'm worried for us, and the boys."

Derek put his arm around her and squeezed tightly. Pulling her closer, he kissed her forehead. Usually, his warm skin and strong arms made her feel safe and secure. Most of the time his calm, bass voice soothed her anxiety. Not now. Almost crying, she shook her head. "Can't we just … go to a hotel on our own dime? I don't feel safe here."

He kissed her again on the forehead. She turned as their lips pressed. There was no passion or throw of desire, just a comforting, affectionate kiss. Closer to him, she could not understand why her body still shook. Another short peck and their foreheads met, and they stared into each other's eyes. Derek's fingers traced her eyes, her nose, and her mouth. As his fingers gently lifted her chin, he whispered, "Does that tickle?"

Often, she smiled when he did that. Most of the time, it did tickle. Usually, his hands were warm and inviting, but now they emitted a cold, dire uneasiness. Moreover, his voice would calm her every time – but now she felt Derek's words no longer offered the protection they once did. It seemed darker every day – even when the sun came out. She hugged him tightly as if to stop the trembling underneath her skin. Clamping her eyes shut, she took a deep breath. A tear trickled down her right cheek. Her voice quivered with uncertainty. Her nerves fired so fast, she could not keep count. They flamed, then froze. Next, they pricked her skin like needles, then deadened into a dull ache. She hated frightening things – even finding the movie, "Abbott and Costello Meet Frankenstein," scary. A few more tears streamed as she recalled the most frightening experiences of her life.

Do You Hear What I Hear?

The first occurred when her high school friends dragged her into that haunted house at the state fair. Even though it was an abode of trickery, false sounds, and silly people in hideous costumes, that event terrorized her mind. At night, her memories spewed the images of maggots on meat, arms reaching for her from the darkness, eerie sounds that reverberated continually, and deadly screams.

The other, the ultimate fright of her life, sprung up and slapped her in the face with a cold hand. The memory seemed much more powerful, poignant, and carried a fear comparable to a cold slab of hardened cement. At the age of seven, she found her little brother, Kyle, dead in the family swimming pool. She could not help him! She reached for him. She tried pulling the water closer with her hands, hoping it might drag his body closer. The water, so cold, chilled her skin like ice. She yelled his name, hoping he might wake up and swim to the edge. She cried for Mommy and Daddy, but they could not arrive in time. Daddy jumped in the pool and put Kyle on the pool edge. All she could do was watch him do CPR as Mommy screamed and screamed. The memory, palpable, returned with all the shrill sounds, the icy, vicious cold of the water, and the overwhelming sense of terror. She kept hearing "It was your fault." The voice, though, was her own, either as a child or as a woman. It whispered in her ear, over and over.

"Derek, please," her voice, quivering, on the verge of tears, "-we need to leave." She wiped a tear. "I'm hearing things. Voices. High-pitched noises. Tell me, please you're hearing them or that you believe me."

He sighed. She felt him shake. Sweat poured through his shirt – much like those nights he woke up with terrible memories from the Iraq War. Derek blamed himself since he was the pilot, and he often lamented over the two friends who died in that crash. He was trying now to be the rock, and the stable course. He hugged her tighter than ever before, as if to tame his own anxiety. "Okay. We'll start looking for somewhere else tomorrow."

Do You Hear What I Hear?

Leaving

Derek

Derek bolted his eyes open. The dream lingered – causing him to shake. Sweat drenched his skin, bedclothes, and sheets. It had the opposite effect he hoped for. Instead of blotting out the images in his head, they returned. Somehow escaping from his memory into his dreams, the helicopter crash replayed. It kept happening over and over. The roar of rotor blades chopping the air was deafening. Then, the small explosion triggered a small fire and smoke that filled the helicopter cabin. His men coughed and choked. Derek's eyes also watered from the invading smoke. Two, three, perhaps six alarms were going off. The stabilizer went out – forcing the helicopter to spin in the opposite direction of the rotor blades. Derek tried to get the stabilizer restarted. Unable to stay focused, he could not keep calm over the numerous, ominous sounding alerts. They beeped, chirped, whirred, and chimed all out of time into a clamorous and grating dissonance. Feeling dizzy he tried to set the chopper down with the yaw, but his loss of equilibrium put it down lopsided. The right lander tilted the helicopter on its side. Rotors hit the desert sand and rock, breaking into smaller pieces that went airborne. The fuselage slammed on its side. Derek jolted to a stop, as his straps held him in place. His head banged the inner hull, but his helmet provided the protection he needed. His straps, though, had hurt his torso, and possibly broken his ribs. Pulling his straps free, he slammed into the inner fuselage. His grunts were not the only ones that sounded. He hit the switch that would send a distress signal to the base. Standing awkwardly, he moved into the main helicopter section where his men, his friends, all coughed, wheezed, grunted, and moaned. Doing a headcount, he made sure all men remained inside. They are all accounted for, but two of them stared lifelessly at him.

Derek opened his eyes to get the last image out of his mind. He gasped, seeing the frightening creature for the third night in a row. It hovered in the corner, just above the dresser mirror. However, it seemed bigger, darker, and more frightening. What was it?

Derek's thoughts immediately went to his twin brother, Dan. He imagined Dan in searing pain, screaming at the top of his lungs. Derek covered his ears, somehow hearing the bellow stretch 5000 miles around the world. Glancing at Suzanne, he was shocked as she slept through the loud bellow. Did she even hear it? Was Dan really screaming?

Derek found himself home, alone in the basement. He loved playing pool with his sons and his brother. Usually, they were there watching TV, playing games, but now, he was alone. The room seemed bigger, longer, and more cavernous. It stretched before his eyes. Snapping back to true form, the furniture was missing. The pool table, the TV, the bar all vanished. It stretched again and as it returned, the windows blackened. Unable to see out, he tried to pry the windows open. He rushed up the stairs to the first-floor door. It was gone, replaced by a concrete wall.

Derek seemed to be whisked back to his Sao Paulo bungalow next to his wife. Feeling nauseated, shaking, and sweating, he tried to remember a prayer Father David taught him years ago as a choir boy. He clutched the cross around his neck and the words somehow returned to his mind. He

Do You Hear What I Hear?

whispered while keeping his eyes closed.

"May the Lord Jesus Christ be with me, that He may defend me; may He be within me, that He may conserve me; may He be before me, that He may lead me; may He be after me, so that He may guard me; may He be above me, that He may bless me, who with God the Father and the Holy Spirit lives and reigns forever and ever. Amen." He finished the prayer as he crossed himself.

With the terror vanquished, Derek opened his eyes. He stopped sweating. Calmed, his heart slowed, finding perfect rhythm with his breaths. His tingling skin relaxed and ceased shaking. He silently prayed again. All fear left, and somehow, he felt the loving acceptance of Jesus. It was not like the distant stories of larger-than-life Bible heroes, or an aloof Savior he could not comprehend, touch, or hear, but a gentle, soft voice. The love resembled what his wife offered every day: a commitment to accept him and keep him close to her heart.

A blunt force slammed across his face. Almost feeling as if his nose was broken, Derek was stunned and silent. Seeing tiny specks of light, and slightly disoriented, he took several deep breaths. Three loud bangs echoed through the tiny bungalow. He shook Suzanne's arm. "Honey. Honey, wake up!"

Groggy, she sat up as he turned on the lamp. Both shielded their eyes as Derek stood and put on his pants. He searched for a shirt and a few other things. "Honey, get up. Get dressed. Get a few things, then we're getting the boys out of here."

Three bangs echoed. The walls vibrated. The bangs circled, moving from wall to wall. The floors shook.

"Dad," Jason emerged in the door, also groggy, "-what's

the noise? What's going on?"

A vicious cold filled the room. An empty dread accompanied it. Their visible breaths fell to the floor. The banging returned. Every echo pierced their chests, froze their hearts, and hollowed them out. The lamp lights flickered – almost synchronizing with the booming sounds. Their eyes followed the dreaded sounds that circled them. Derek, Suzanne, and Jason moved tightly together. Sue pulled Jason closer while Derek put his arms around both. While he tried to share their body warmth, he mostly pressed against them for safety.

"Son, get dressed. Get your brother up. We're getting out of here."

Jason

Jason hesitated as the banging happened again – this time accompanied by the floor shaking. At first, he hesitated about separating from his parents. While his ears vibrated with every bang, his heart pounded intensely – almost yelling back at the menacing sounds.

Jason abruptly halted as the door in front of him slammed shut. He pushed the door. It would not budge! Pushing harder, he wondered why the door would not open. Terrified, he rammed it with his shoulder, finally opening it. A terrible punch landed on his stomach. He doubled over, trying to breathe but unable to find any air. He cringed as his skin burned where the punch had landed. A few coughs brought his breath back.

He turned on the lights and stirred Jimmy. "Jimmy, get dressed – we're getting out of here," he said while shaking his brother. Jason had to shake him a couple more times to rouse him from sleep. *How could he possibly sleep through all of this?* Another set of loud bangs echoed, and the lights flickered more. Jason retreated to a guarded position as items on the shelves and cabinets flew across the room. A couple of them grazed Jason's forehead and ear. Unable to think, panicked, all he could do was shake at the drawers going in and out and the lights flickering. He shook Jimmy harder.

"What?" said Jimmy, "-leave me alone. I wanna sleep."

"Dad said get up! Come on! Hurry!" For a second, Jason thought of dragging his brother outside naked, but instead grabbed some shorts, shoes, and shirts to get himself dressed.

He looked in the mirror. Jimmy's image behind him had spun around and lurched at him. Having a life of its own, the eyes turned a deep, ominous, fiery yellow. Deformities spread across Jimmy's - or rather the creature's face, trunk, and arms. As the hands reached for him, they were stopped by the glass from within the mirror. The image pounded from within the reflection, trying to get out. The glass froze. It cracked from within as taloned hands pounded furiously.

Jason's heart pounded with the same intensity. Drawers flew out shooting across the room. Desk lamps and other items followed – almost hitting Jason. The exploding fear tried to escape his chest and leave the soul behind. His skin tingled within, feeling like cold pinpricks from the inside. Still, he didn't want to leave without his laptop and backpack.

"Boys!" yelled Dad, "let's get out of here!"

Fuck my laptop and backpack, thought Jason as he shoved his phone and charger into his jacket pocket. He dragged Jimmy – half-dressed – to the living room out the front door, and to the rental car. Dad hurriedly started the engine.

Derek

"Honey," said Sue, "what happened to your face?"

"What?"

She turned on the cabin light to look. "Look at your face," she said while pointing his head to the visor mirror.

Derek gulped hard. Totally unable to talk, he could not believe what he saw. The bruise on his face was surrounded by reddened skin that resembled a three-fingered hand. The impact spread over his left ear, forehead, and also over his nose. A trickle of blood and a small scar was at the tip of each finger. Feeling it for the first time, it stung and burned - and had the scent of burnt salt. His skin, particularly his nose and lips, pulsated and swelled as a dull ache spread.

"Holy shit, that's …" His voice trailed as he scanned the rear-view mirror and saw Jason sitting next to … something. It resembled a large, winged creature with bulbous eyes. Drool fell from its jagged, uneven teeth. The skin was greasy, oozing some vile chemical that dripped off its skin. Derek glanced over his shoulder, seeing Jimmy.

Mom screamed loudly. The shrill noise reached Derek's eardrum – almost popping it. The noise felt like a punch. "Derek!" she screamed. "Jimmy's – "

"I see it, I see it. We're going."

The beast in the mirror bellowed a low-pitch howl, spraying drool all over Derek and Suzanne's faces.

Jimmy cried as his head twitched back and forth, rendering his face a blur. Burns formed on his arms and legs and sweat poured incessantly down his chest and back. All their screams became one overwhelming wail, mimicking an unholy chorus. Derek wished he could cover his ears, but all he could do was drive and repeat his prayer.

His heart ached, seeing Jimmy suffer, however, he did

not believe what he saw. His logic could not define what he heard, felt, or smelled. He only found a cold terror encroaching like a shark ready to attack. Rationality failed to describe the thing in the backseat, nor could it explain how it mixed with his son.

Derek pushed on the gas pedal more, making random turns. Turning up the road, he floored the accelerator, not sure of where he was going. Who was he going to tell? Who would believe him? Who would help him? Most people, even priests, would consider him mad. Derek turned sharp right, then counter-steered to keep the car under control. Instinctively, he turned left up another road. Which way to go? Which way to run? What would he do with Jimmy?

Something caught his eye. A church! Catholic, the structure was easy to identify. The large cross, the arching doorways, stained glass windows, and the high tower. He made a sharp turn and counter-steered but ended up in a skid. Without his seatbelt on, he bounced around the car – almost going to the passenger side. Somehow, he was able to hold onto the steering wheel to keep himself in the driver's seat. Remembering driver's education, he turned the wheel into the skid. The front and rear tires aligned, and he found some control.

Jason

Jason felt a phone hit him on the forehead, followed by a paper cup, a box of tissues, and something else. Slamming into the door, it felt as if it might give way.

Everything inside his chest froze. Jimmy no longer sat next to him – but rather some ugly, disgusting creature: wrinkled, leathery skin, a deformed head, chipped and chiseled teeth, and long, strong arms. A burning sensation seared Jason's skin as the strong, deformed hand seized his upper arm. Jason retreated from the hideous creature, somehow breaking from his grip.

The car jolted hard as it hit something. Glass broke on the rear passenger side. It fell into Jason's hair, bounced off his skin, and a few beads almost dropped into his mouth. Another sharp turn and Jason slammed hard into the left rear door. He felt a bone snap. Pain spiked and spread through his arm, shoulder, and collar. Dad, yelling some sort of prayer, veered the other way, throwing Jason onto the other door atop Jimmy. Again, he felt another bone snap and protrude through his skin. Pain receptors fired as he screamed.

Jason grabbed his seat belt as the car went off the road and bumped hard on the uneven terrain. He bounced several times while hoping to secure his seat belt. He hit the inside cab ceiling, causing him to bite his tongue. The car bumped from the left to the right, from the front to the rear. A sharp turn in one direction pulled him away from the seat and he hit Jimmy … or actually that thing.

There was a hard impact as the car jerked back to the left, and then to the right again. The force sent the left side upwards, pushing the car on its side. Jason slammed into the door. Jimmy landed on top of him. Beads of glass were thrown around. The insides of the car caved in closer to them. Dirt followed, along with grass. The car finally fell over onto its roof. Nothing moved. The horn blared as dust collected in the headlights. Despite fear and confusion, the chaos ceased as Jason was thrown into blackness.

Do You Hear What I Hear?

PART TWO: FLIGHT TO THE PAST
Remembering

Nathan hated the small seat. While his lean fame had plenty of shoulder room, his six-foot stature left him with no leg room. It was as if all airlines thought the average human being was only five feet tall.

The commercial jet leveled out at its assigned altitude. The chief flight attendant told everyone they could take off their seatbelt and use their electronic devices. Immediately smartphones and iPads lit up, capturing the attention of all ages. Nathan though, wanted to fully read the combined journals he had desperately searched for over the last six years. Changing to his reading glasses, he opened the old journal and studied the Germanic language. Although he was Polish, he knew how to read German, English, and Hebrew. He learned German, which he considered the tongue of the Devil, during his days in the Nazi camps. After his liberation from the camp, he moved to Great Britain where he studied English. Of course, as a Rabbi, he had to learn Hebrew – but was taught some as a child while growing up.

Then, the day happened when Yahweh let loose the demons of the pit into Poland: September 1, 1939. Nathan and his brother, Noah, were only five – but he remembered the day perfectly. Soon, businesses were outlawed and heavily regulated. Political leaders of cities like Warsaw, Katowice, Torun, and Nathan's home of Krakow had to bow to the Gestapo. He remembered Father working at the University as a Professor of Jewish Literature and History.

Mother was a maidservant to the mayor of the city – at least until she died giving birth to his younger sister, Nadia two years before the invasion. Nathan had trouble remembering her. Grandma was already living with them, so she took care of the children, raising Nathan, Noah, and their sister, Nadia.

Within a year of the occupation, Father was arrested for some unknown reason – and sent off like cattle in the dreary trains. Nathan recalled the awful smell of coal-fueled smoke that chugged Father away. Grandma was sent to the Ghettos, and she took care of Nathan and his siblings.

It was May 20, 1943 – another traumatic day he remembered perfectly. The sound of the gunshot echoed in his mind, penetrating the hands over his ears. Blood splattered from Grandma's chest as the Gestapo Officer gleefully shot Grandma. She tried to prevent the troops from hauling off her grandchildren. Nathan, Noah, and Nadia bellowed loudly, hugging her and begging that she would return to life.

Nathan cried as the memory dashed through the back of his eyes. Taking a breath, he pulled off his glasses and wiped the sweat off his forehead, as well as his tears. The flight attendant asked if he wanted something. He wanted some tea. Surely, they could make tea in flight.

Tears welled again as he recalled the trains taking him and Noah away from their sister. The metal wheels squeaked rolling over the tracks, pulling the large cars that resembled cages. They both reached for Nadia as she was drug away from her brothers. She screamed, kicked, and begged them to help. They, too, were pulled from her. Their eyes faded until Nadia disappeared into the chaotic crowd. He would find out that she died in Dachau with Father.

Thrown into the cars, Nathan and Noah swore they

would never leave each other. They remembered Father's fervency in prayer and hoped that he would save them. It was hard to move in the car because there were so many other children. One thing they noticed were the numerous twins – and a few triplets. Some were older, like 15 or 17, while others were as young as three or four.

As the SS guards slammed the doors shut, the children reached their hands and arms through the openings, crying desperately for their mothers and fathers. After a few minutes, the train pressed on, slowly clicking, and squeaking on the tracks, drowning out the wails of the children.

It was cramped. Nathan and Noah huddled in the corner with some other children and cried as a dire depression descended. Would they ever see Father again? Or what about Nadia? Father always told them to protect her. Would they be in trouble? As the smoke filled the sky, darkening the sun, the air stilled and fell upon them. The children eventually stopped crying and quieted, knowing the train carried them into misery.

As the sun retreated below the horizon, darkness fell and crushed their souls – as if their unanswered prayers to Yahweh were like heavy, blunt stones. Soon, no one cried, no one talked, no one moved. Twice in the night, Nathan and Noah found one girl and a boy dead. Both were crushed against the wall. At least twice, they both could not endure the excruciating pain of trying to hold their urine and let it flow – dampening their own clothes and the wooden floor. Others did the same. Eventually, the vile stench of human excrement mixed with the urine. Some children threw up.

Somehow, Nathan slept for a while, dreaming of life at home with Father, Grandma, Noah, and Nadia. It was interrupted by the railroad wheels grinding a high-pitched scream. Making it worse was the rising sun that hurt his eyes, taking away the wonderful dream that shielded him from reality. And then, he felt a huge, empty, dull pain in his belly. As the trains halted, he hoped there would be something to eat and drink.

The train doors slid open, and more Nazis Troops cajoled the children off the cars. Although tired and weak, moving around felt better. Then Nathan and Noah saw it: in the car, at least 20, maybe 30 children were dead. Their vacuous eyes stared straight ahead. The door slammed shut, failing to blot out the sight and memory of more dead children.

The soldiers steered the children along a dirt road. Nathan and Noah, as well as some other children, asked the guards for something to eat and drink. They also asked the men where they were going, but the men said nothing, staring straight ahead and holding onto their rifles. Perhaps they didn't understand the Polish language.

After a tiresome hike, the children reached a camp. It did not look welcoming. Boards made up the lower part of the fence, while the higher part of the enclosure was barbed wire. Dark wood was used to build the barracks. They had cracks and holes in the walls. Nathan hoped he and Noah could stay together.

"What is going on?" Nathan asked an older boy.

Probably 14 or 15, the older boy, along with his twin, looked at Nathan and his brother.

Somehow, Noah and Nathan spoke the same words simultaneously, as if their minds fused together. "Will they feed us? We are hungry."

The older boys leaned over to look Nathan and Noah in the eyes. They had short hair as if they had it cut off before

Do You Hear What I Hear?

getting on the train. Their chestnut brown eyes still had life, strength, and faith in them. They also looked fit – as if they played lots of football. The one on the right spoke. "My name is Erik, this is Elisha. Let's try to stay close together so we can help you." Finding their confidence alluring, Nathan and Noah stayed close.

They were taken to a building where the soldiers directed the children to specific cubicles. The signs, in Polish, said, "Remove clothes and stand still."

Separated from his brother and his two new friends, Nathan quivered. It was already cold, and he now had to strip. At least no one else could see him in this cubicle. Suddenly a loud blowing resonated in the building. A blast of warm air hit him, along with tiny pellets. They felt like rock salt but did not hurt. It did smell though. Afraid of the pellets getting into his eyes, he clamped them shut. He also kept his mouth closed and covered his ears. The odor was terrible, but he had to endure smelling it in order to breathe. At least the rush of air was warm, however it slung pellets constantly, forcing him to drop low for a breath. When will this stop? He wanted to put on his clothes and curl up in a bunk somewhere and dream of life again with Father and Grandma. After the longest time, the blowing and pellets stopped. Then, the artificial wind started up again. At least no pellets flew this time – and the stench dissipated. The doors opened and the military people came back, giving the children a new set of clothes. Still raggedy, and loose fitting, it was better than nothing.

The children were herded once again to a shared area. Tables and chairs were spread out, and they could smell something: food! Oatmeal? Maybe milk? Hopefully, water, too. Nathan and Noah did not care, scarfing it down. Nathan ate so fast his chest tightened as too much food gathered between his mouth and stomach. Once the food descended and cleared the path, he ate what was left.

Within 20 minutes or so, the children were rounded up again and guided to another building. In line, each child stood with their twin. Erik and Elisha stood about ten feet behind Nathan and Noah. It was comforting to know at least two people around them. Still, where were they? What was going to happen? Will they ever see Nadia and Father again? Nathan cried, thinking of Grandma dying before him. She bellowed loudly, clutching his ankle. He finally realized she would never sing to him again, kiss him on the forehead, and play games with him.

After waiting in line for nearly an hour, he and Noah entered a room. It only had a table, two chairs, and three men. One man stood at attention and nodded at the boys. "Boys, please tell us your name." He spoke Polish!

"Sir, what is going to happen?" Noah quickly asked. "Are we in trouble?"

"Boys," he repeated, "please tell us your names."

"Nathan Oberst."

"Noah Oberst. Will we see our father and sister again?"

"How old are you?" he asked.

Desperate, frightened, their minds became one, answering together. "Nine." They repeated the previous question with more angst and urgency. "Are we going to see our father and sister again?"

"What is your birthday?"

"March 10."

Noah, almost crying, changed his question to a demand. "We want to see Father and Nadia. Where are they?"

The man on the left stood while his friend wrote. The

one standing had a roundish head that was leaner on the bottom. A mustache covered part of his top lip. His eyes became friendly and alluring, and he smiled earnestly. Something did not seem right. Why did he not answer their questions?

"What is your father's name?" he said while dropping to eye level with them.

"Samuel," they both said. "And Nadia is our sister," whispered Noah. Their hope lifted. "Can we see her, too?"

"Do you not have a mother?"

Nathan took the lead. "She died giving birth to Nadia."

The stranger sighed as if he felt heartbroken. He hugged them tightly. For some reason, the boys reciprocated liking the embrace. The stranger almost wept. "I'm so sorry for the loss of your mother. It must have been so hard on the whole family."

"We want to see our father and sister – please." Nathan hoped the man would understand his sobbing pleas. His eyelids hurt from clamping them so tight. Not even Noah's strong hug could alleviate the dreadful melancholy that imbued their souls.

"I'm going to see what I can do," he said while leaning on his knees. Returning to the other side of the table, he sat, then reached for a sack. Both of his hands extended and opened, revealing chocolates. Nathan and Noah looked at each other, barely smiling.

"Is that for us?" asked Nathan.

He smiled at them. "Would you like some chocolates? It is very good." Nathan and Noah both devoured the chocolates. "My name is Josef. And I'm going to make sure you are assigned to my special barracks until we find your father and sister."

Stephen W. Scott

In Hell
(Auschwitz 1944)

"Don't believe him," said Erik. "He is the Angel of Death."

"He said he would find Father and Nadia," protested Noah.

Nathan moved closer to the older boy, finding the gumption to confront him. He certainly lied about the kind doctor. "You lie! He told us two days ago he found out where they are, and he is going to transfer them here."

"He's just telling you what you want to hear. He's a phony, evil man," tears flooded the older boy's eyes. His voice quivered. Over the last month, he had lost so much weight, he could barely stand. All the hope, confidence, and strength had vanished and faded from his eyes. "He let my brother die! He tortured him, cut him open while he was screaming for him to stop. The doctor smiled while he did it. I know it! I saw it!"

The words "you lie" repeated over and over by the younger children still infatuated with the kind doctor. Of course, they were better fed and were always offered chocolates. How could such a kind man do such a hideous thing? "You're jealous that he likes us more than you," said one boy. Another set of twins told him to "shut up" and a few threw small pebbles at him.

"Erik." The room fell silent. The boys all looked towards the calm, collected voice. The doctor stood before them, accompanied by his two friends – who never looked as friendly or inviting. Nathan and Noah did not like them too much. They never smiled.

In total silence, Josef stared angrily. For a change, he seemed upset, and stern. His voice, quiet and authoritative, remained calm. "Erik do not undermine my authority here," he said quietly. The way he said it chilled all of them. Fearful, the children stepped back.

"I know who you are," said Erik as he took a few quick steps. "I have seen it in the large room. You killed him with your needles, your scalpels, and your ..."

Josef slapped Erik. "Do not talk to me that way!" All the boys gasped and took a step backwards. Why did he do that? He was usually so kind and generous.

Erik, crying himself, held his stinging cheek. Cowering, his head dropped, looking down at the floor. Nathan and Noah moved closer together and stared at Erik. While angry at him, they hoped he would not be severely punished. However, his faith and confidence had waned. Nathan heard him cursing Yahweh. He should not do that. He should read the Psalms, or when Moses led the Israelites out of Egypt. Those should restore his faith. Or was it too long gone?

Josef raised his hand, calling his lieutenants over. One of them punched Erik in the stomach. He grunted and doubled over. The lieutenants dragged him by his arms.

"Children, go back to bed." Everyone remained still at Josef's subtle, yet fierce anger. An uneasy dread wrapped around the boys. A bitter cold followed. The stagnated air was the last layer to encircle them. Afraid, their skin chilled.

Josef left to follow the guards and Erik. What were they going to do to him? After a minute, the boys sneaked to the door and listened. No one was outside – at least they thought so. The door hinge emitted a long, yet quiet, squeak. The cold winter air rushed in, riding on the wind. All the boys, quiet, kept looking at each other. Erik was the surrogate big brother to all of them. Who would be the leader now? Who would warn them about which guards to hide from? Who would help them get a few extra bits of food? Who would try to protect them from the mean guards? Some of them cried. Others shook. Some of them retreated from the door into their barracks and pulled the tattered blankets over their heads.

Curiosity called out to Nathan and Noah, as well as three other sets of twins. They ventured outside. The lights in the big building jumped to life. As usual, they flickered and then illuminated the room. It was not a good light, seeming weak and ineffective. Dim, with a reddish glow, it appeared ominous.

Nathan led the way, goading the others to come along. Despite the chilly wind warning them to retreat, they continued. They all united in a small huddle. Moving together, their hearts raced, somehow warming their insides. Their breaths shot out quickly. A few lights from barracks lit part of the way, but corners hindered them from providing enough illumination. Hiding in the dark shadow, Nathan peered around one building. A guard sitting on the chair leaned back. His rifle sat next to him. He pulled his coat tighter, buttoned it higher and lit a cigarette.

Nathan scurried across the lit part of the compound to the cover of shadow. Breathing heavily, he and the other boys looked around to make sure they were not followed. Almost there, they darted across another lighted section. Noah was the first to climb the crates and boxes surrounding the outside of the main building. The others followed, quietly scaling the tall walls. Except for their short breaths, they made no sound.

Reaching the landing of the first tier, they moved towards the windows with the reddish light. It seemed the chilly wind blew harder up here. Fear tried to dissuade them back to the barracks, but curiosity called out to them louder, almost taunting and daring them to find out.

One of the boys, Stan, let out a quiet scream. His brother, Savan, covered Stan's scream. He, too, gazed at the deformity. Two girls, twins, were sewn to each other. It looked as if their backs or spines were combined into one. Their dirtied skin was pale. Their eyes of shock looked as if they might be dead. No, they blinked a few times. One of them cried. The other stared into oblivion. The crying twin blinked. Her lips moved. It looked like she said, "Help me." The girls' hair looked like a doll's hair. Cracks formed on the corners near their lips. The whitish skin had scars and bruises all over it. Their eyes had assorted colors, but it did not seem natural. Their setting changed abruptly. Shadows walked by. The lights flickered on and off much more – rendering the girls a blur. Their faces moved back and forth at incredible speed. Their elbows and shoulders tried to move, almost looking like a marionette on a string. Unfortunately, they could not stand.

Nathan and Noah retreated from the horrific sight and let out a muffled scream. Quickly, the other boys covered Nathan's and Noah's mouths. They peeked again, taking in the ugly deformity. Who did that? Josef? No. He couldn't. Surely a nice man like him would never do anything like that. How could he? He always wanted to give children candy and promised them if they would do what he asked for, he would always help them through times of trouble. He would talk nicely and never yell. He often knelt to look them in the eye.

Stanley motioned everyone to the window of another room. They saw a boy, alone, confined to a straitjacket, sitting in a corner, banging his head on the tile wall. His eyes, void of hope and identity, never blinked. His skin had no color, nor did his stringy hair.

As the boys scurried across the first landing, they noticed another room. Pressing their fingers on the cold glass, they looked intently into the dimly lit room. They gasped and let out a suppressed scream. Nathan instinctively darted his eyes away from the sight – but returned to see the monstrosity. He had to see it to believe it. A boy sat in a chair. His eyes had been removed surgically. Within the orbits of his eyes, a blank, dark chamber stared at nothing. Dark red blood stained the skin. Some inner tissue was exposed to the elements. Nathan could see a tear lining the inside right eye socket. Noah and Nathan cried for him, as well as themselves. Will that be their fate?

"Quit looking at it," said Stanely, "-and come over here."

Nathan took one more look at the boy below, then clamped his eyes shut, hoping to take the image from his memory. His teeth chattered. Taking a deep breath, he tried to calm his shaking, his crying, and his fear. Like Father always said, "When you're afraid, angry, or upset, take a deep breath and count to ten – maybe even 100."

The other boys had already gathered around the next window. There was Erik. He was tied to a chair. The perspiration was visible. His head moved around jerkily. Alone in the room, it looked as if Erik pulled on the restraints. The chair rocked. Would he fall backwards? Would that break the chair so he could escape? Nathan

Do You Hear What I Hear?

started to knock on the glass but stopped and withdrew from the window.

The lights flickered as Josef stepped into the room. The two other Nazi soldiers followed him. All the boys peered just above the windowsill as Josef stepped closer to Erik. A back-handed slap almost knocked the older boy over. He turned the chair 90 degrees to face a mirror. Josef secured Erik's neck, forcing him to look at it.

Curious, the boys stood a little higher to get a better view. A light mist fell on the floor of the room. Or did it lift? What? How could that happen? The two Nazi guards, looking afraid, took a few steps backwards. They clutched their guns. Josef, on the other hand, moved closer to Erik. Leaning, with palms on knees, he slapped Erik again. The six boys outside cringed. Part of them wanted to hide, but that part of them retreated. They felt the collective, burning curiosity of wanting to see rush through their minds.

The lights blinked repetitively. Between the shorter lights, the frightened guards abruptly left. Erik's head swiveled super-fast, rendering it a blur. Josef ... changed. Between some flashes, he stood a couple of feet taller. No, he was normal. He changed again. Brief glimpses of elongated ears, unusually long arms, and clawed hands. Turning to the side, between the flickers, the eyes glowed a hideous yellow. No, it was red. Josef looked normal again. Another flicker and the ugly skin tightened. The skin looked dried with several aging lines. Another flicker. Josef looked normal. Two quick flashes and he suddenly had empty orbs where the eyes once were. Another flicker. The mouth had pieces of flesh dripping from its teeth. Part of it seemed sutured. As it growled, hideous, uneven teeth emerged. The lights flickered a few more times, and something emerged from the mirror. White, winged, with demonic eyes and claws, it reached out and held Erik's head. Everything went dark. The lights returned. The creature opened its mouth and thrust it on Erik's head.

The spying boys all yelled as the lights went out. The blackout froze them. The lights came back on, startling them. Where was Josef? Suddenly, the hideous beast appeared, lunging at them. The mouth fully opened, revealing the sinister teeth. The skin, with many tight folds contracted, outlining the disfigured head. The empty eye sockets glowed red. The glass shattered. Large and small pieces fell around the boys as their frenzied terror exploded. They frantically scattered and climbed down the boxes as their hearts thudded erratically. Some of them cried while others yelled.

They jumped off the first landing, falling into a pen full of mud. The mire closed around them, trying to swallow them whole. Nathan and Noah held onto each other while Stanley and Sebastian tried to free the other two twins, Michael, and Micah. Escaping from the mud, the boys ran with no aim, no goal, or no end in sight. Where would they go? What would they do? How could they fight this thing?

Reaching their barracks, all the boys ran to their beds and pulled the torn blankets over their heads. They prayed. They shook as the terror kept surging. The desperation and horror bubbled, eventually pushing out some tears. A few minutes passed. Breathing tried to return to normal as the cold panic subsided.

"Boys, what were you doing out of bed?"

They gasped, wondering why they never heard the door creak open. A vile, salty stench rushed through. Nathan winced at the rank odor. Covering his nose, he realized he had to breathe the horrendous sulfurous scent. It almost made him gag. A chill joined – although it was still. Accompanying the cold was dark dread. Like the mud a few minutes ago, it surrounded him, trying to capture and drown him. Nathan's terror, in control, forced him to whisper sobs. Crawling across his skin, it felt like tiny insects were on the march. He could not think of a prayer, a psalm, or even a happy thought. The fear, so dark, prevented him from seeing the future beyond this moment.

Hearing some footsteps, Nathan peeked from underneath his cover. The silhouette stood. Not a man, it towered at least six or seven feet in height. Sinewy arms with talons at the end worked like the limbs of a bug. The large head only had a subtle reddish glow in place of its eyes. It huffed as if trying to find the boys by scent.

"Boys," saying it slowly, leaving a sibilance at the end, "you should not be out of your barracks. You should not have been spying on me." The words slowed and deepened. "You will pay the price."

Stephen W. Scott

The Pact
(Auschwitz 1944 – four months later)

Freezing rain fell, adding to the foul, sickening mud. It resembled a mushy, inedible stew. It seeped into the two boys' shoes, wrapping around their feet with a numbing cold. It passed through their shoes into the cold ground. Both crossed their arms, trying to pull their loose-fitting clothes tighter to provide warmth.

Heading towards the barracks, Nathan and Noah sought refuge from the rain, the mud, and the cold. Nathan kept thinking about Erik. What happened to him? Where did he go? Did that thing eat him? Inside, the intermittent rain echoed. The reverberation sounded hollow and empty, reflecting their despair and fear. Other twins huddled around a small fire. They all hoped it would last for the night. They fed some small and medium-sized twigs to the flames. They tried grass, dead leaves, and even some fabrics from the worn-out mattresses.

Nathan and Noah stared at the others held in captivity. Their misty breaths puffed out of their mouths and nostrils. Their jaws quivered. They shook, finding the flames losing to the vicious cold. Also, holes in the barrack walls let what little heat they had escape. Hope faded like the fire before them.

Michael, Micah, Stanley, and Savan pulled Nathan and Noah and huddled in a corner away from the other children. "What was that?" asked Stanley.

"I wish I hadn't seen it," Noah whispered.

"But what was it? The thing from the mirror!"

"It couldn't have come from the mirror," said Nathan.

"You saw it just as we did!" Micah's voice was closer to normal, almost frightening the boys. "It was like a ghost or a ... a."

"-demon," finished Stanley.

"And Josef," said Michael, "he is not human. He is not the man he pretends to be. He is evil. It is like he is the," he stammered searching for words. They all did, but Michael finished his thought, "the Angel of Death." They gasped, remembering the old folklore. Or was it history? Their parents talked about it at dinner, during chores around the home, and when hiding. The Angel of Death, Malakh Ha-Mavet. It was the angel who brought death upon the Hebrew people. He would dip his ghostly sword into poison and put it upon the doomed. Some believe it was truly Satan who came to steal God's Children from the face of the Earth.

"Maybe he is from the Darkness," said Savan.

"The Darkness?" asked Nathan. "Father was a Rabbi and a professor. He never spoke of such things."

"Rabbi Jeveski told us about the Darkness. Before Yahweh made the Heavens and the Earth, there was the Darkness that existed before Yahweh. It hid it in the seventh room of hell – the place for the wicked."

"This is crazy," said Nathan. "Josef is a man. He is an evil man, but just a man."

"Nathan, you saw it!" blurted Noah. "We all saw it," he said while looking around at the other five. "It was something from the pit. It was a demon of some sort. Call it the Angel of Death or whatever, it is evil. We felt fear. We saw what it was doing to those other children. Remember the twins sewed together? The ones with their eyes gouged out?"

He wept quietly. "What is it going to do to us? Let one of those creatures from the mirror loose to eat us, too? What are we going to do?"

"We pray to Yahweh. He will save us."

Savan interrupted Noah, "There is no Yahweh! Can't you see it? If there was, he would never let this happen to us!" Since his angry words did not help his despair, he erupted into sobs to purge his emotions, but the anger, sadness, and fear had a foothold that refused to give way. "He hasn't answered our prayers," he said, finally able to speak. "Why does God let these monsters take away our families? Are they doing the same to our parents?" He buried his face in his hands. "I just want to die. Just please, let me die."

Catching his lament, the other boys cried as well. Stanley hugged his brother.

Nathan finally looked at the others. Taking a deep breath, he whispered. "I admit it. Josef is something evil. But what are we going to do about it? Escape? We have no idea where we are."

"If we can escape," said Stanley.

Michael inserted himself. "We are not Rabbis. We are not men who know how to battle this thing. We certainly cannot throw rocks at it or set it on fire. Could we even shoot it? And how many things are in the mirror?"

"We saw it," said Nathan. "We know Josef is something not human. We know those things in the mirror are real. We all saw it. We must promise that if we can escape, we will find out what to do in order to stop it. It's up to us – because no one else will believe us."

Footsteps snapped them from their conversation. Three, maybe four men trudged marched towards the barracks.

Do You Hear What I Hear?

Their boots squished the mud, then slightly sank, before lifting out of the mire. They muttered the old language. The boys scattered, hiding in their beds, pulling tattered blankets and curtains over their bodies. A few even crawled under the moldy, decaying mattresses. Their desperation made the disgusting stench of urine and feces no longer matter to them.

Nathan and Noah hid together. Jaws quivering, they prayed to Yahweh. They asked him to strike the monsters that approached and turn them into chaffs. The shadows of the barracks crisscrossed, never allowing a full view of the creatures that wandered in like scavenging vermin. They came up the rickety steps. Their footsteps thudded on loose and decaying floorboards. They stopped, looking around like lions searching for prey. "Children, where are you hiding?"

"Yahweh, please make them go away," whispered Nathan. They gasped as the hand came down on Nathan's shoulder. He screamed as the strong hand picked him up. His feet tried to run, but he dangled over the floor. It was the monster that grabbed him! The gray and black hat tried to hide those eyes. The gray uniform was decorated with medals, with two bolts of silver lightning on his collar. A winged, crooked cross was on the uniform. The man's sharp, lean jawline turned to the left, putting his profile into a deep shadow. As he turned back into the light, he smiled. The disguise did not fool Nathan. He tried to wriggle away from his shockingly strong grip. He screamed and kicked his feet, hoping the arm might tire and let him go. The monster dropped him but kept his strong grip on Nathan's wrist. Cold rain fell on him as he was dragged across the ground. The miry mud and filth spilled down his shirt, pants, and shoes, chilling his already cold skin.

He begged in his native tongue to let him go or perhaps have mercy and not hurt him. Pulled across the compound, he noticed some other children scrambled inside to find a place to hide. Nathan was pulled inside the warm, dry cabin. It felt nice, but right now, he would prefer the outside cold, wet mud to whatever was in store for him. More cold showers? Electric shocks? More needles in his arms and legs? Abject terror not only triggered his tears but also caused his heart to shudder.

Slammed into a chair, two other Nazi henchmen used leather strips to secure his wrists to the arms of the seat, and his ankles to its legs. He pulled at them slightly, just like the other times. Tight, unable to move, he thought of trying to tip the chair over, hoping it would break. However, a cold, callous hand pushed his forehead into the back of the chair. Some cords now put his head in a vice-like grip. Unable to move, Nathan could hear his own heart thud. It almost hurt. Biting his lip, he looked at the monster.

The uncaring beast knelt, pulling Nathan's left eyelid. Nathan tried to wriggle but froze as he saw the tiny stick coming towards his eye. His heart sank as it froze. Everything inside him tingled, like cold pricks. The little stick was propped between his eyelid and the bottom of his eye socket. Nathan struggled less as the creature did the same to his next eye. The chair was turned to face a mirror.

Forced to look at his own image, Nathan almost did not recognize himself. He had become so gaunt. His arms and legs were like twigs. He desperately wanted to close his bulging eyes, but the tiny plastic sticks prevented it. The discomfort forced him to forget the cold mud that still oozed down his shirt and pants leg.

Helpless, panicked, his breaths erupted out of rhythm –

sounding like the staccato of a railroad car. Desperate for some control, Nathan sucked in a huge breath, held it, then let it out slowly. His respiration slowed, along with his heartbeat – helping them coordinate the proper rhythm. After several short breaths, he was able to calm his breathing. His eyes, still scared, relaxed. The calmness spread. His hands and arms stopped flexing. Eventually, his legs, too, relaxed. What was he staring into? Why did he feel so calm? Even his mind ceased its continued cries to run. Tears stopped flowing.

His reflection broke free. The facial expressions relaxed. Their eyes turned from terror to hate. An evil grin spread up one side of his mouth. The eyes narrowed. A subtle orange-red glow simmered. The muscles in the arms and neck relaxed. Taking short, relaxed breaths, they became quiet.

Meanwhile, Nathan's jaw shook. Terrified, he wanted to close them but couldn't stop staring at the evil image within the mirror. His breaths burst in short spurts. Tears streamed from the corner of his eyes. However, the reflection had none of those elements. It stared back quietly.

The image opened its mouth and bellowed a horrible scream. Nathan wanted to cover his eyes and ears. The noise was deafening. It leaped from the chair in the mirror and rush at him. The glass somehow knocked it back. The reflection continued to scream while pounding on the inside of the glass – as if it tried to escape.

"Stop it!" He screamed the words so many times, he never understood why Josef was doing this. What was the purpose of this torture? What was the reason for the terror? It made no sense. It did not fit into his idea of the world. It was so full of fear and uncertainty. Such a life gave him no love and no hope.

It emerged in the first reflection. White, dead skin was pulled tight around the head. Sickening, twisted, pointed ears seemed to grow. The eyes were a black, empty abyss. A moth flew out of one socket. Another one escaped, along with three more. Ugly, deformed insects flew out of the other socket. The mouth tried to open, but stitches of flesh draped vertically, preventing the jaw from fully opening. The sutures opened, showing blood-stained fangs. A herd of cockroaches crawled out of its mouth. It bellowed some low, hideous scream.

Nathan heard something whisper in his ear. Unable to hear it, he shifted his eyes and saw its reflection standing next to him. A hot, stinking breath draped across his face. His gag reflex stifled Nathan's screams. The carrion stench had a similar smell to that of the barracks: rotting dead meat, urine, and some feces. It screamed in his ear, this time releasing a biting cold on his skin.

No. It was not a hideous creature. It was the Nazi Doctor. No. It changed back to a vile creature. Suddenly, bat-like wings spread behind it, darkening the room. A dark hood lifted around the head, hiding the face. In the mirror, it was the Nazi again. Next to him was the demon. They switched places. Once, twice. What was this?

The mirror fogged. Starting at the corners, it spread. Carrying a frigid cold with it, the mist covered more of the mirror. Part of it froze. A few cracks developed. The lights flickered and burned out. Nathan screamed.

***

Nathan, curled up in a ball trying to warm himself, stared at the door. The wind hit the barracks hard. The walls offered little resistance to the brutal cold. The chills found their way in. Nathan's feet and hands felt numb. He experienced no emotion. He merely existed with no identity, person, or will. He gulped, trying to find the will to remain alive.

A ringing echoed in Nathan's ears. Hypnotized, he had no thoughts or feelings. He only stared at Noah. Hearing whispers, he tried to understand them. What did they say? What did they want? The ringing got louder. His head hurt. The ache throbbed, almost syncing with his heartbeat.

The door bolted open. The blast of freezing air chilled Nathan, as well as the other boys. A Nazi soldier held Michael and Micah by their shoulders. Exploding into the air were the boys' grunts, screams, and cries. Both had bandages wrapped around their heads, covering their eyes – and they sobbed incessantly. The soldier dropped them to the frigid floor.

Nathan rushed to the boys and rolled them on their backs. Michael and Micah both bellowed in pain. What happened? He tried to pull the cloth away from Micah's eyes. Did Josef hurt them? How? Nathan and Noah took the bandages off - revealing Michael and Micah's eyes had been removed. In their eye sockets, only bloodied and sutured flesh remained. Nathan fell back at the sight, not having any idea how to help him. "Michael! Micah!" Nathan had to yell over the boy's screaming. "What happened?"

Stuttering through the pain and crying, Micah clutched Nathan tightly. "Josef – cut them out. It hurt. It hurt. It hurts so bad. Oh, God. Why?" Micah's voice faded into loud sobs.

"Why did he do that?"

Still yelling, wailing, and stuttering, Micah somehow got out his words. "He … he … he … said that … he didn't want me looking anymore – so he cut them out."

Nathan turned to Michael and pulled away his bandage. Nathan lost breath. He could see what Josef tried. The mad doctor had placed Michael's eyes into Micah's eye sockets. The sutures, uneven and obviously done in haste, had blood on them. Some of the blood had caked and dried near the corners of the eye sockets, resembling dried tears.

"Micah? Micah?" Michael yelled louder. "Nathan, what's wrong with Micah?"

Nathan already noticed the chest flattening. A tiny breath jumped out, misted, and fell back into Micah's mouth. Nathan shook his shoulders. "Micah! Micah, wake up!" Michael sat up and felt for his twin's body. He shook the chest, also yelling for his twin. Soon, both boys' voices merged into a desperate, loud bellow. "Micah! Wake up!"

Do You Hear What I Hear?

The Escape
(Auschwitz, 1945)

Nathan's eyes flooded quietly with tears. Warm, they slowly streamed down his cheek. His huffs, still quick, mixed with a few grunts as the pain still vibrated from his lower back. It hurt so much. He grunted ten or twelve more times, trying to put the throbbing, numb, and stinging pain into retreat. It dissipated some – but not completely.

Nathan focused on Noah's lifeless body. Blood stained his back. A surgical scar – or rather a hole had been opened. Nathan touched his back and felt the sutures that had been sewn into his back. He now had his dead brother's kidney. Nathan turned his brother's head and cradled it. It looked as if he slept. Nathan felt nothing. Strangely, his tears poured like a silent waterfall. A huge part of his soul died. It had already been dying for the last few years. Every day, another part of his being froze and numbed – robbing him of life. He never thought a soul could drown. Little by little, the small holes grew and pulled him closer to death. It changed him. He hugged his twin, whispering to him. "I will miss you. I will find Father and Nadia, I promise."

Looking over his shoulder, he gasped at the sight of Michael. He did not breathe. His chest remained still. Nathan had been Michael's eyes for the last year – guiding him to the latrine, to the mess hall, or the sessions. At least Michael had never been plagued with the visions in the mirror. Or being able to see the Angel of Death. He never had to look at the camp, or any of the other victims. At least his blindness freed him from those gruesome images that kept eating at Nathan and the other children.

Nathan realized something: He was almost alone. It had been two years. Now at the age of eleven, most of his friends from the barracks were dead. Some died in their sleep. Several committed suicide. Nathan remembered waking up to find that Stanley hung himself. His body was swaying back and forth, dragging his shadow across the barracks. Most deaths, though, were at the hands of starvation, disease, or awful experiments. Dysentery, Typhus, and the Flu claimed many lives. The doctors did try to help – but only for the sake of keeping subjects for their experiments. Or did they die before their hearts stopped beating? Most of the children wandered in a stupor around camp. A few tried to escape. Some were shot. There was a huge pit on the east end of the camp. That's where the bodies were. The horrendous stink had lost its repugnance. Nathan had acclimated to it. Was a mass grave fitting for his brother's death? For him? What if Father and Nadia were both dead in a mass grave as well?

A cold hand dropped on his shoulder. The doctor dropped to a knee and looked Nathan in the eye. "I am very sorry for your brother," he said quietly. "But you should know that you have always been one of my favorites."

Still at a loss for words, Nathan stared at him blankly. His soul, so exhausted, could not even muster any hate. Fear waned to utter despair. Defeated, he watched Dr. Mengele open his hand and revealed chocolate. Nathan, for the first time, shook his head. "No thank-you, sir."

The doctor's smile faded. At that moment, a shadow, probably from a cloud, passed over them. The image was lost in a silhouette. The doctor's shadow grew. Shoulders spread with elongated arms. Talons extended from his hands. A hideous head tilted, revealing a subtle red glow where the eyes should be. Ears grew pointed. The mouth had a vile stench that rivaled the excrement and dead bodies. Nathan, used to seeing the Angel of Death's true form, turned, and walked away.

***

Hearing the jet noise, he emerged from the reverie. No. He had been sleeping for the last … two hours? He double-checked his watch. The memories were still vivid. They were probably more powerful than the day he married his wife, Rebecca, and the day his daughter, Nadia, was born. He missed them both. Rebecca died seven years ago in her sleep. Nadia married a fine man, but she got fed up with her father's obsession with finding the "Angel of Death." She found his tales of the supernatural insane. In fact, her husband, a physician, tried to have Nathan committed to an insane asylum. Hopefully, if he could find the ancient evil, and find a way to confine it back to the pit, he could give up his quest and reconcile with her.

Nathan cried. His heart ached. Suddenly he realized his heart fluttered again, not keeping time with his body, mind, and spirit. Disjointed, he gasped. He leaned forward – reaching for the pills in his jacket pocket. No. Immediately, his heart returned to a normal pattern – like a drum, keeping time for a band. Leaning back in his seat, he relaxed … a little.

Nathan's recollections turned to his liberation. It was about three weeks after Noah and Michael had died. First, Russian troops arrived. Although dirty, bloodied, and stern, they reached down to the children and hugged them. The children reciprocated, finding actual smiles and true friendliness. Their touches were warm, caring, and loving. Even better, the kind men offered the children real food like cooked meat, vegetables, and baked bread. The Nazis only had soup, stale bread, and dirtied, raw vegetables. Many of the children were surprised to see these grown, strong men cry at the monstrosities committed: the results of experiments, the mass graves, and the vile conditions. Some vomited – scaring the children. Were they that ugly and reprehensible to these soldiers? Some of the soldiers boiled with such anger they hung or beat the Nazi SS and Kapo personnel to death. Loud gunshots echoed through the camps as many Russian – and eventually British and American troops – instantly executed those Nazis. The deafening shots did not just hurt their ears, but the deepest part of their spirit.

 He spent a few weeks in a hospital, getting attention to his wounds, receiving nourishment and regaining his coordination. He rarely spoke, thinking of everything that happened: starvation, degradation, torture, experiments, the hideous creature. Receiving help, his strength returned, along with his hope.

 After the hospital, some French and British orphanages took in the children. Although most were Protestant and Catholic, the Jewish children welcomed the loving acceptance. A Scottish family eventually adopted him. Nathan smiled, recalling the kindness and love Mother and Father gave him. He also felt it from his adoptive brother and sister, but he never found the connection with them as he did Nadia and Noah. Now, he had outlived them all. The only remaining family members included an adoptive niece and nephew, and his own daughter – but they all thought he was crazy. His smile faded, feeling alone as he did in the Nazi Death Camp.

Do You Hear What I Hear?

Nathan sighed and read more out of the Angel of Death's journal as the plane descended towards the place he heard so much about but had never visited: the United States.

Stephen W. Scott

PART 3 – HOMECOMING
Unseen Home
(Albany, NY)

Jason quietly walked by the gentle tug of his cousin, Justin. He was born the same year as Jimmy, but Justin was born four months later. All their parents called them the triplets – even though Justin had a thicker build and was about a head shorter than Jason and Jimmy. He also had broader shoulders, and more muscle on his compact build. Strangely, his voice had not changed yet.

Jason bumped his arm and shoulder into the door frame. He grunted. His broken clavicle and dislocated shoulder had mostly healed, but those areas were still tender. His leg, although freed from the cast, still had a boot and a lot of physical therapy ahead. It was difficult enough navigating through the new blindness in his life.

"Let me turn on the light. Just a few more steps to …"

"I know," Jason snapped, interrupting his cousin. "And I don't need the light." The anger faded. He sat on the bed and loosened his tie. Two things still worked on his eyes: the eyelids, and the tear ducts. The lids closed while more tears lifted.

It had been six weeks since his family died. Their bodies arrived a week ago. That was the first punch of reality. The second punch was the funeral. The reality felt like a sharp sword pushed through Jason's chest – bringing all the pain and regret. Mom, Dad, and Jimmy were gone. Even if his eyesight had been preserved, he still would never see them

Do You Hear What I Hear?

again. He did not know who to miss the most. Dad? Mom? No, Jimmy. He was the one person he was closest to. They could always talk. They could always joke. They could always laugh. They knew each other so well, even more so than Mom and Dad.

"Can I get you anything?" Justin asked.

"No." His words, caught deep in his throat, were barely audible. It was as if they were caught in a black hole of loneliness.

Justin stood there for a minute, feeling awkward. Jason could tell – by hearing his cousin's breathing and sensing slight movements of the air. What was he doing? Looking at him? Mocking him? Revulsed by the scars on his face? Feeling pity?

"I ... uh ... I'm going to my room ... for a while."

It was quiet. Somehow, Jason could tell that Justin remained. His nervous breaths told everything: the sadness and the awkwardness of not knowing what to say or do. Jason hesitated and took a breath as if the words were trapped in his throat. Should he say something? If so, what? Jason whispered, "Justin, please don't go." Jason's voice cracked, matching his soul. "Don't leave me alone, please." He cried lightly. Feeling the bed move, he knew Justin sat across from him. Afraid and ashamed to lift his head and acknowledge him, Jason took a couple of deep breaths. He cried harder, bellowing sounds of anger, fear, and depression.

At that instant, for some reason, the light of reality broke through his blindness. Mom, Dad, and Jimmy were not on a trip, nor were they with Grandma and Grandpa. They were truly gone, never coming back. Although his sight was gone, he would miss them in other ways. He would never hear them laugh on Christmas morning, or cry during a sappy movie or television show. He would never hear their voices talk, cheer, or scold him. He would never feel their touch on his shoulder, receive a hug, or get an unwanted embarrassing kiss from Mom. He could never share the waffle breakfasts Mom made or visit the Pizza Warehouse with them. The unexplainable pain pulsated through his skin, muscle, and bone, attacking him with intense emotions: fear, anger, sadness, doubt, and despair all merged into a deep, agonizing bruise. It swelled through his whole body.

Tears seeped and beaded heavily down his cheeks and curved under his jawline. Instinctively his eyes clamped shut as if he tried to hold them back. They were warm, attempting to cleanse and heal his horrible wounds. Too weak, they failed. The pain in his chest was so hard to describe. Maybe a heart that would not beat properly – or perhaps a rupture that spread through his stomach.

"I miss them," he said quietly. "I miss him so much. I just want to talk to them – especially Jimmy. I want them back. I want them back so bad." He wondered if Justin could understand his words that drowned in his sobs. "I should've died with them."

Justin moved next to him and wrapped one arm around Jason. "Don't say that. You're alive so be grateful." Justin stammered as he cried, too. "You can still talk to them. I'm sure they can hear you. And now you're here with me and my parents. We'll take care of you."

"Why did I live? I should've died. Why did I live?"

The awkward silence allowed Jason to find control over his lament. "Maybe to be the brother I've never had."

The words triggered more crying.

"I mean – I was always envious of you and Jimmy being

brothers. I'm still here. I'll be your brother. Maybe not look like you – because you do look like a shithead."

Jason had a brief laugh. It was yanked away by the flood of tears. After the brief respite, they fell again. He sniffed his nose, desperately wanting that smile back. "You look more like a shithead than me – you little runt."

"How would you know since you can't see me anymore?"

"Well, you certainly smell like a shithead." A few more laughs subtly pushed his mouth wide for a smile.

"I have an idea," said Justin. "I know this is going to seem really lame and really gay, but I think I can do something to cheer you up. And it's perfect. So just relax and listen."

"You're not going to kiss me, are you?"

"No, shithead. Just listen." He opened something, likely a book of some sort. Justin spoke slowly. "In the first frame, he stands atop a church in his dark red costume while the rain pours down. He's listening to the streets. The second frame, his head turns sharply, and he thinks, 'I hear his footsteps. Yes, that's him. He has the exact same arrhythmia I heard at the courthouse.' The third frame, he jumps off the church. The next five frames, he uses the sound of the raindrops to locate the ledges and statues to grab, push off, flip, and drop safely to the pavement …"

Dinner

Jason found a smile, thinking of the Daredevil comic Justin chose to read – wishing his senses heightened like the blind superhero. Like Matt Murdock, his senses had changed dramatically, giving him a sharper awareness of the world around him – although they were nowhere near Daredevil's mythical ability.

Over the last six weeks, a whole new world beyond his sight had announced its presence and attached itself to his remaining senses. Jason could smell the different aromas of food Aunt Janie prepared. He was not too sure of the sauce, but it found its way into his nostrils, tempting his palate much more. A distinct aroma of baked bread – likely rolls basted in butter – forced him to smile.

Jason's brain was working overtime to heighten his other perceptions. His hearing sharpened to where he could hear a whisper. Hearing Samson's breaths, Jason reached to pet his seeing-eye dog. He wondered if he might be able to hear a person's heartbeat like Daredevil can in the comics. His heart ached. Jason could never see that show again or see one of those Marvel Movies with Captain America, Iron Man, Thor, and Hulk.

Uncle Dan and Aunt Janie whispered, but to him, he could hear it easily. "According to Mr. Presley," said Aunt Janie, "we should look for a therapist for Jason. He said the trauma of losing his sight is just as shocking as losing his parents and his brother."

"Well of course," said Uncle Dan, "-you don't think I

figured out that one?"

Her voice stood on edge but remained a whisper. "Don't be snippy with me." Her voice softened. "When are you going to start looking for one? He needs to get into therapy as soon as possible."

"Hey," his whisper stiffened, "-he wasn't the only one who lost anything. I lost my brother, too, and can't stop thinking about it and never being able to talk-" Uncle Dan's voice trailed, stifled by the hurt.

The whispers overlapped with each other, trying to redirect any personal responsibility of their own to each other. The pleasant aroma of food faded as Uncle Dan wept. Jason, uninterested, sighed and dropped his head. Some tears spilled, as if a deep reservoir existed inside, always replenishing the supply. How did his body produce an endless supply of tears and snot? Did they come from his soul, the pop or water he drank, or from something else?

Aunt Janie's whispers prevailed as Uncle Dan's retreated into a whimper. "Honey, I'm sorry for your loss. I really am. I lost my brother-in-law and sister-in-law, too. And remember, I lost my little brother when I was only 21."

Jason's head turned. He never knew that. He thought he knew his aunt and uncle so well – but he had no idea she had a little brother.

"-but Jason needs you and I to be the strong ones. It's been six weeks since he got back. He's doing therapy for his arm and collarbone and now his leg; he also needs it for his mind and spirit. We have got to get on this."

Jason sensed Justin sat next to him. Could Justin hear? No. He was already eating. In fact, he talked between bites. "Mashed potatoes are at nine o'clock. They're great." A few bites. "Come on, eat, man. Try the chicken. It's at six o'clock." The references let him know where his food was – but Jason had not fully acclimated to a clock setting yet. He had used digital all his life.

Finding his fork and knife, he carefully found his chicken and started cutting. Taking a bite, his sense of taste whisked his attention away from his aunt and uncle. This was another sense that surprised him. His taste buds noticed the smallest details and he could now tell how much salt, sugar, or spice was on a particular food. The chicken was marinated in a delicious sauce. As to what kind it was, he was uncertain, but his mind clung to the rich taste.

Uncle Dan and Aunt Janie sat down at the table. Jason sensed their apprehension. *What? Going blind gave me ESP as well?* He picked up so much: fear, embarrassment, confusion, anxiety, and sadness. After swallowing, Jason decided to ask them. "So, when will I start seeing a therapist?"

Both slightly gasped. They both feigned being cool and unaffected, but he could tell they were searching for the right words. The difficult silence lasted for only a second. "I keep forgetting about your incredible sense of hearing."

"It's not my fault," Jason said quietly.

"You're right," he said more pleasantly. "I'm sorry. I shouldn't have said that." He hesitated. "It's just that ... I'm mourning, too. Your dad and I were close – like you and your brother. So, I know exactly what you're going through – at least about losing Jimmy."

Jason almost wept until Uncle Dan reached across and pulled him closer with a one-armed hug. Comforted, feeling closer to his uncle, Jason hugged back and whispered. "Thank-you. I'm sorry you lost your brother. I forgot."

Sitting correctly, moving fully into the seat on his chair,

Do You Hear What I Hear?

Jason suddenly felt Aunt Janie grasp his left hand and clutch it tightly. "Honey, we're going to help you. I'm setting a goal: we will find a therapist for you a week from Friday. Okay? I can't even imagine what you're going through. Especially not being able to see."

"Well, I can still see in my dreams."

Uncle Dan emitted a "hmm" while eating.

"Wow," said Justin. "I never thought about that."

"Yeah. It's weird, but when dreaming, I can see." His smile faded as his description continued. "It's mostly Jimmy, Mom and Dad, you guys, and a lot of friends, too. Memories of surfing, baseball, movies, and ..." He recalled a common image too distant to fully comprehend. Cold, dark, sinister, it seemed to be related to ... something.

"And what?" asked Justin.

Quiet and embarrassed, his mind tried to stretch for something tangible, but only a shadowed, faint memory existed. "I'm not sure. It was ... something ... scary. But I'm not sure where it's from."

"Well, I hope you see me tonight in your dreams, cuz."

"That'd be a nightmare to see you, shithead," Jason quipped back.

"Jason!" He forgot Aunt Janie's disdain for name-calling, much more for profanity. "We are a family and don't talk about each other like that."

"Me and Jimmy, I mean, Jimmy and I did it all the time. Mom didn't mind."

"This house belongs to your uncle and I, so we don't talk that way at the dinner table."

"Okay," he said, "I'll just call him a shithead away from the dinner table."

Uncle Dan and Justin laughed out loud while Aunt Janie

somehow stifled her laugh. She had to cough to do it. "No. I don't want to hear it in my house."

"Okay." His response was accompanied by a subtle eyeroll. He took a few bites, hearing the plates and silverware chink. He could hear them chewing and breathing through their noses. Jason recalled his aunt and uncle's whispered conversation, and a burning question pushed out his throat. "Aunt Janie ... you had a brother?"

Justin gasped and dropped his fork. Uncle Dan barely whispered "Oh boy" right after swallowing a bite. Aunt Janie seemed to choke on a bit of food. She swallowed and took a deep breath and paused for a few seconds – although it seemed like a few minutes. What was she going to do? Slap him? Yell at him? Knock his plate off the table and tell him to clean it up? He quivered, regretting his curiosity. Why bring it up? It was obviously very painful for her. He heard her voice crack. Was he older or younger? Did she blame herself? Was it suicide?

"Yes, Jason," her voice stammered a bit – as if it fought to answer his question. "I did. His name was Bobby."

"Was he younger or older?"

"He was ten years younger than me." She took a deep breath. "I was 21, and he was eleven. Unfortunately, at that age ... I had a ... drinking problem."

Jason sensed she was fully crying, but still coherent. "He was with me, and I was driving ... and I ..." Some sobs lurched out. "I wrecked the car." She sobbed some more. "And he was killed." She paused. "And it put a huge rift in my family. My sister, Jenny, has barely spoken to me in nearly 20 years." Her voice trailed into oblivion again for an uncertain time. It returned quietly. "Excuse me." She got up and left the table.

Do You Hear What I Hear?

Embarrassed, Jason sighed at his lonely thought: *I'm such a shithead.*

A New Family

Justin knocked on the door. "Jason?" He peered into the dark room. "Why are you sitting in the ..." Embarrassed, his voice faded. Mom always said, *"Just because you have a thought does not mean it needs to come out of your mouth."* Dad told him, *"Think before you speak."* Justin finally understood. He could not imagine going through the trauma of blindness – much less losing his family.

Jason's fingers pushed across the book, taking in the words. He sighed, backed up, and tried again.

Justin, about to blurt out a question, thought about it. Yes. The question was safe. "How hard is that? Reading Braille?"

"Some letters are confusing," he said quietly. "C and B are close, and W is sure weird. I have to feel not just the bumps, but the flat part as well. I like it when I can guess the word based on the first four to five letters." He got quiet for a minute. "It's frustrating to learn this. It's like learning to read all over again." The shadow of Jason's head fell into his hands. His voice was muffled. "I can't do this, Justin." He cried. "It's too hard. It's so hard. It's not fair." After a few seconds, Jason's lifted his head. The tears stopped.

Justin, unsure of what to do, remained still. Afraid to say the wrong thing, his mind scrambled for any words to comfort his cousin. Something inside bubbled quietly. Words illuminated his mind and formed. His mouth worked with his lips, tongue, and jaw. "Tell me what you need, and I'll try to help."

"I gotta do this on my own. You can't read this shit. It's almost like a foreign language." It seemed as if he had to search for the right words as well. He cried. "This happened so fast. I don't know what to do or where to begin."

Justin decided his words were meaningless. Nothing he could say would help. Instead, he hugged Jason by the shoulders. "I'm here, man. I love ya." Again, he wanted to ask him to play some video games or binge something on Netflix – but stopped himself. They would upset his cousin.

Some words came to mind, but Justin had to take a deep breath, think, and let them out slowly so he could hit the target properly. It reminded him of aiming an arrow on a bow. "I ... uh ... don't ... like ... have any idea what it's like ... for you. I'd be so lost without my parents, you know." He stammered. "And going blind ... I can't imagine that. I don't know how I'd handle it. I'd be pissed, too." Justin needed to say something else, or should he just be quiet? No. "Hell, I'd be so scared I'd shit my pants. But you can't stop. You gotta get this Braille thing down. Remember when you guys were learning to surf? How hard was it to balance yourself? But you kept doing it – until you could shoot across the water between waves like a pro. So ... I can, like, listen to you, and keep you going. Okay? But don't quit. Don't stop. You'll get it."

Jason let out a few breaths, which staved off his emotions as well as his tears. "Okay. Okay. I won't stop." He nodded to reiterate his words. "Thanks, Justin. I really need you right now." He sighed. "I can't see anyone. I can't see the waves on a beach again, or a cool sunset, or those awesome mountains. I can't surf again. I love surfing so much."

Realizing how much Jason lost, Justin hugged his

cousin again.

"I can't see those cool Marvel or Fast and Furious movies – or Point Break."

"You've seen it a hundred times," said Justin. "Besides, that movie's lame."

"Listening to your opinion would be a waste of time."

Justin grinned and laughed quietly as Jason said the line just like the bad surfer dude in the movie. "I need you, too, bro. I mean ... maybe we could use your blindness to meet girls. Have you thought of that?"

"I'm not a sideshow. I'm not to be exploited." He grinned. "Except to meet girls." A brief exuberant smile faded. His head dropped. "Justin – I ... I can never see a pretty girl smile again."

"Well, maybe there's Braille porn?" Justin wished he did not say that. His levity dropped. Again, he tried to imagine life without seeing a pretty girl. Sure, he could hear their voice, feel their skin, touch their breasts, but never experience the sight of a beautiful girl smiling. Perhaps some of the girls at school would prefer a blind guy. They wouldn't be judged by their weight, their curves, the size of their breasts, or looks in general. On the other hand, a lot of guys at school would benefit if girls could not see them, either. Of course, an obnoxious personality is perceived in other ways as well.

"Well," Justin wavered, "I can warn you if a fat, ugly girl is trying to kiss you. Also, you will see better than most guys. Your dick won't rob your brain of its blood so you can think better. Think about it: you've seen plenty of breasts – but one day you'll get to touch them – and I'm sure that's so much better."

"I guess you're right."

Do You Hear What I Hear?

Justin liked to see his cousin smile. "You have to listen to a girl, and you better listen well, or you could be fooled by a guy. You can still touch their skin – but then again that could get you detention and charges filed against you. You can smell them – and that's your best bet because us guys stink a lot more than girls. And – if you give into cannibalism, you'll know which one tastes better."

He protested amidst the laughs. "Okay, enough with the blind jokes."

"And when you get married to some fat chick, there's nothing to curb your arousal."

"Get out of here, shithead."

"You could have a great career as a football referee, or an umpire."

Samson barked slightly, as if protecting Jason. Or was he laughing, too?

"Get out of here." As Justin's footsteps faded with distance, Jason laughed hard from his stomach, his chest, and shoulders. He had not laughed this hard since – the smile disappeared. He had not laughed like this since Jimmy was around. A peaceful, contented smile stretched across his face. Justin was becoming like Jimmy. He never thought about the closeness he shared with a cousin – which was like having an extra brother.

The serene silence changed as something did not seem right. His skin chilled and his stomach knotted as he sensed strange eyes gazing at him. His throat was constricted painfully as he heard a cold whisper tickle the hair in his ears. Usually, he could decipher them, but these were too faint. Standing, he concentrated on the noise but could hear no laughter, no footsteps, or anything else. Apprehension seized him, stiffening his whole body.

Samson's bark caused tension in his arms, legs, knees, elbows and neck to convulse violently. Samson's bark turned to a whimper. "Shit! Samson, be quiet." The dog let out another yelp, startling Jason a second time. "Samson, heel," he said while moving closer to the door. Suddenly, his dog seized Jason's shirt tail and pulled him backwards. The dog refused to relent, growling while pulling on the shirt. Realizing his dog was trying to drag him away, Jason stepped back, slightly tripping over something on the floor. Falling on the carpet, he flinched. "Who's there?" he whispered. "Uncle Dan? Aunt Janie? Justin?"

The cold presence caused his skin to shiver. Nervous, his fingers, toes, and legs shook. His hair moved as a weak, warm, disgusting gust of air hit his face. It was familiar, but still foreign. Part of him wanted to run, yet a deeper part wanted to stay still. He relied on the latter as Samson came back and stayed close to him. The dog barked several times, then got quiet and let out a subtle growl.

"Jason ..." Aunt Janie's voice dripped with concern. "- are you okay? How'd you fall?"

The anxiety diminished. "I don't ... I mean, I tripped on something while backing up."

"Well, why don't you turn on the light ..." her voice quieted abruptly. "I'm sorry, honey. I forgot. I shouldn't have said that." Samson let out another few barks and growled. "What's wrong with Samson?" she asked while hoisting Jason to his feet.

"I don't know. He just started barking – but I don't know why." Jason's hands found Samson and rubbed his fur. Samson whimpered. "What is it boy? What happened? What'd you see?"

"I get a freebie on the lights comment since you're

asking a dog 'What happened?'"

Jason grinned. Smelling his aunt's perfume still clinging to her skin, he imagined her face from the past. Why was it that whenever he remembered someone, he thought of them smiling? Aunt Janie's thin lips stretched wide, and her blue eyes glowed. Those eyes, small and determined, radiated confidence and empathy. Her light auburn bangs barely touched her eyelashes. Her jawline, taut and sleek, still allowed the smile to stretch sincerely. The memory of her face faded as darkness encroached. All he had now was her voice.

Jason remained quiet for a couple of seconds. "Aunt Janie ..." he hesitated, worried he might upset her. "I'm sorry for bringing up your brother. I was just curious."

She kissed him on the cheek. "It's okay," her voice trembled. "I need to deal with my guilt and pain."

"You haven't talked to your sister in 20 years?"

Her breath disappeared. Jason guessed she nodded, forgetting he could not see.

"I'm sorry," he whispered. "I guess you really miss her?" He remained quiet for several seconds. "Aunt Janie," he gulped, "I really miss Mom and Dad. And I really miss Jimmy so much."

"I miss them, too, sweetie." Aunt Janie's warm arms wrapped around his torso. Her hands possessed healing as she clasped his shoulders and rubbed them. She finished by kissing him on the forehead. Usually, such stuff would embarrass him. For some reason, though, he now liked it.

"Aunt Janie ... I love you." More tears gushed as he hugged her back, knowing she was his mother now. He held on tightly, as if his life depended on it. Jason couldn't believe how helpless and alone he felt. Usually, Mom would embarrass him, often testing his patience. Yet, he missed it: her voice, her sternness, her impeccable order, and organization – and even the grammar corrections.

"I love you, too, sweetie." She caressed his face, running her fingernails across his eyes, nose, and down his scars.

"Aunt Janie … am I ugly? The scars? Did they...?"

"No!" she interrupted quickly. "Not at all! You're becoming a handsome young man – both inside and out." She gently touched the scars near his eyes and followed them down his cheek and to the underside of his jaw. "They are noticeable, but they're like battle scars, making you look strong and tough. They don't detract from your handsome face."

Sure, Aunt Janie had to say he was handsome – just like Mom. Still, he felt comforted and smiled.

After she left, he stripped to his boxers and crawled into bed – taking notice of the changes he had experienced over the last several weeks. Jason could perceive tiny differences in the surface of different woods, carpets, or tabletops. He could detect when other people were in the room as the air expanded. It seemed he was more sensitive to temperatures as well – noticing cold and heat much easier. While he struggled reading Braille, he found he found it much more engaging as his mind focused much more on reading. Jason remembered things he read in Braille much more than using his eyes on a page.

The sense of smell amazed him. He could tell if someone had not taken a bath or shower in the last 12 to 24 hours. He noticed distinguishing scents of genders, and different aromas of cologne or after-shave. Jason could even distinguish the different smells of skin and hair. Although he was unsure which was which, he noticed different odors of grass, trees, and flowers.

The sense of taste exploded as well. For the first time, he could taste the difference between Coke and Pepsi. Dr. Pepper was too much for him – as well as mildly loud sounds. For a change, chips became too salty. Spices, even mild ones, were much more noticeable. When he could see, sometimes, a smell became so pungent, he could taste it. Now, it happened more often. For the first time, Jason noticed how much the senses of smell and taste worked together.

He sensed the air displaced, and the light tread of feet on the wooden flooring outside his bedroom. A masculine smell that mixed aftershave and sweat reached his nose. Hearing the steps made him realize it was not Justin, but a taller, heavier presence.

"Hey, buddy," Uncle Dan said quietly, "-can I come in?"

"Sure." He could still picture Uncle Dan's face, especially since it was exactly like Dad's: a long, thin, bald head accompanied by a long nose and a very thin crown of hair. His eyes, serious and tough, still had humility. His voice, too, was also like Dad's: quiet, tough, with a slight rasp.

"I ... uh ... wanted to thank you for apologizing to your aunt. That was the right thing to do. I really appreciate it."

An uneasy, thick quiet surrounded him. Awkward, unsettling, Jason could not think of anything to say. All he could do was gulp and shift away from Uncle Dan as far as possible. He already felt bad about making Aunt Janie upset. Who knew such an innocent question could have provoked such emotion?

"You're a good man," said Uncle Dan as he patted Jason on the shoulder. He also hugged Jason and kissed him on the forehead. "I love you. I miss them, too. So, we gotta take care of each other, okay?"

Jason felt like retreating for some reason. Sure, Dad hugged him and kissed him on the head, too, but his uncle now doing it seemed a bit strange. Of course, the whole ordeal seemed weird. Six weeks ago, he could see. Six weeks ago, his parents were alive. So was Jimmy. It all happened so fast – as if glancing skyward for a second and missing the receiver catch a pass for a touchdown at a football game.

"Good night, son," said Uncle Dan.

Jason sighed – then slightly smiled realizing Uncle Dan called him 'son.' His head dropped sadly. He could not understand how he could feel happy and silly at one moment – then, within a few minutes, break down into tears. "Uncle Dan … I miss Jimmy so much." His voice got lost as the latest barrage of tears exploded. "I want him back so bad." Unsure if he got the last part out past his sobbing, Jason repeated it: "I want Jimmy back so much - and it hurts."

Uncle Dan immediately hugged him. It was tighter than Aunt Janie's – as if he tried to expel the painful feelings in Jason's chest. "I know, I know," he whispered. "I miss your dad in the same way. I want to talk to him so bad. We were just as close as you and Jimmy - so I know exactly how you feel."

Was Uncle Dan crying, too? Jason always thought his uncle, like his dad, was tough. Neither of them smiled fully. It wasn't a lack of humor, or because they were not happy, but they both forged a strong restraint. Perhaps military training – and growing up as military brats trained them to be disciplined and rigid. Both smiled, but it was never a full

Do You Hear What I Hear?

smile stretching across the whole face. That's when their dark eyes brightened with color. Those moments, like now, were when Uncle Dan showed his true humanity. He rolled Jason's shoulders tightly. While Aunt Janie's hands were soft and warm with healing qualities, Uncle Dan's were strong and tough – as if they were protectors who shielded him from fear and doubt.

Both sighed a few times to let the sadness fade. "Good night, son."

A brief smile spread across Jason's face. It vanished fast as he heard the light switch click off. While it made no difference to his sight, he sensed the room's lack of light rob him of any joy. Reaching down, he felt Samson's fur and rubbed it. The dog whimpered, then licked Jason's hands. Did Samson try to comfort Jason with affection, too?

Just like every night, once alone, he started feeling the left side of his face. Two scars, most likely hidden by his long bangs, ran vertically. One was next to his nose, the other at the outer eyebrow. One of his fingers traced his left nose and nostril, perceiving the missing pieces of flesh. He traced the other three scars – two of which descended from his eyes, forming perfect grooves for his tears to flow down. The third groove, just beyond the left eye corner, ran down his cheek to his maligned earlobe. A part of it was missing. His fingers spread, finding the low scars (also three) running his lower face and jawline. His pinky traced a wound on his lower left lip. *I'm blind and ugly.* The thought kept repeating itself. *They think I look like a zombie or something, but they can't say it.*

Jason's feelings mounted an attack. Alone in the dark for the rest of his life. The abrupt change. The people closest to him were taken away. The disfigurement. The pain surged from his chest. The waves he liked to surf felt like an angry tide slapping within. They surged higher – finally escaping through the only exit they had: his eyes. Tears did not just flow, they gushed relentlessly, and hard. It seemed as if they tried to drown him every night. He heard Mom's voice, and Dad's voice, as well as Jimmy's. They whispered together, although just below his threshold of hearing.

It finally broke through: Jimmy's voice. He could hear it as it caused both joy and sadness at the same time. Confused, he tried to discern what his brother was saying. Was it really him? Or perhaps just memories from conversation? However, all thinking stopped as the emotions continued to purge. Again, he knew he would cry himself to sleep.

Falling to a level between asleep and awake, the voice became clear. Although soft, Jason thought he heard Jimmy.

"Jason, he's coming for you."

Do You Hear What I Hear?

Justin and Jason

Jason heard a couple of bumps. It sounded like someone – likely Justin, hitting the wall or the door frame.

"Jason," said his cousin, "can I borrow your cane?"

"Why? You're not blind."

"Today," Justin said proudly, "I am." He suddenly yelped as if he tripped or hit something. He coughed.

"What'd you do, shithead?"

"Damnit," Justin grunted, "I racked myself," he grunted again, "on ... maybe your footboard." He coughed.

Jason turned to Justin's voice. "What are you doing?"

"This morning, I thought that I needed to learn what it's like to experience your world," Justin said after a few breaths.

Jason hunched his shoulders. "You mean experience the world of sanity, right?"

"No shithead," Justin said laughing, "I put on a blindfold and I'm keeping it on all day to see ... or rather not to see ... what your world is like."

Jason's laugh emanated through his stomach and chest. "You're crazy."

"Come on. Just let me borrow your cane."

"I need my cane."

Justin sighed. "Well, can I have Samson?"

"He's my service dog."

Justin remained quiet for a split second. "Sic 'em, Samson. Sic Jason."

"Justin – just take off the blindfold. You don't have to

do this."

"No. I'm going to do this today. By the way I'm also giving up looking at online porn ... at least for today."

"Just to remind you – your dick is at six o-clock," Jason said while grinning.

Jason was amazed how Justin stuck to it. He almost tripped down the stairs but regained his balance. He learned how to use his hands to guide himself.

Breakfast was a little sloppy. Justin tried to listen to music on his smartphone, but he had no idea how to find the music list he wanted – especially since his phone wasn't designed for the blind. He finally figured it out. "Siri – play Alice Cooper Mix 1."

"Congratulations," said Jason.

Going shopping had a unique twist – mostly done by Aunt Janie when having Jason and Justin trying on jeans.

"Mom – these jeans don't feel right – and why aren't there any pockets?"

"Because I got you girls' jeans."

"Mom!" It sounded like he retreated to the change room. "Mom!" he said again, "where are my jeans?"

"Oh, I've got them out here."

Jason, surprised at Aunt Janie's mean streak, laughed.

"Justin," said Aunt Janie, "are you going to take the blindfold off?"

"No. I promised Jason I'd finish today blind."

Once back at home, Justin kept sighing. "I keep wanting to play a video or watch something on Netflix – but I can't if I want to stick this through."

Later, he asked Jason to help him try and read in Braille. He learned what his name felt like, then followed something new Jason typed up and connected to the Braille sensor. It read the text and made the bumps for him.

JUSTIN IS A SHI...

"Hey!" he said as they both erupted into laughter.

"Okay," said Jason, "let me walk you through this next one."

JUSTIN IS THE BEST COUSIN.

***

Justin smiled, thinking about his blind experiment yesterday. He hoped that would help Jason feel better.

However now, he concentrated on the workout. His arms churned, lifting the dumbbells as fast as he could – losing count within a minute. He just wanted to do it until he became exhausted. Sweat beaded out his pores and dripped down his arms, chest, face, and back. Strangely, he liked it. His heart raced, pumping more blood to his muscles that broke down with a burning sensation. Those muscle fibers would grow back firmer and stronger. He kept it up, until he could not curl them anymore. Exhausted, he let out one huge huff, then put the dumbbells on the floor. Looking at his mirror, he grunted hard while flexing his biceps. The sweat glistened the curves on his biceps, outlined his shoulders, and made his chest stand out. He turned to the bathroom mirror and lifted his arms up again. He turned back to the door mirror and put his hands behind his head to show off his biceps and triceps. He turned back to the bathroom mirror.

It lurched at him. It tried to push at the mirror from the other side. The hideous thing's breath fogged it from within. The face had burnt scabs and pieces of flesh peeled away from the face. The black eyes stared angrily at him. Its mouth stretched wide open, revealing fangs from both the upper and lower jaws.

Justin's wide eyes somehow blinked. The image vanished. It was too late as the horrifying image buried itself inside. It sank deep into his soul, keeping his heart racing with red-hot blood. A wind within his chest erupted, swirling violently like a tornado or thunderstorm – grabbing debris and scattering it everywhere. Shock froze him for a half second, but let loose the second half, causing him to flinch, lose balance, and fall to the floor. His breath became visible.

Scrambling to the wall, Justin grabbed his crucifix, held it tight, and said a prayer repeatedly – just as Dad told him to do whenever he felt scared. However, it felt much more like a serious dread that trickled through his mind and heart. The room darkened, and the air stilled, carrying a musty smell. Quivering, Justin closed his eyes and continued to pray. The stirring inside lost momentum. The perspiration lessened, his heart relaxed, and the chilled skin started to warm. The swirling eddy inside his chest broke apart and became a peaceful, refreshing breeze.

Justin recited the prayer three more times. Relieved, he took a huge breath. It provided the final brace that set everything back together. Aligned, feeling stable, Justin finally decided to turn out the lights and pull the covers up to his neck. As his eyes closed, he heard a scratching sound.

***

Jason's eyes exploded with sight. He could see again. He was surfing. Gliding across the wave, droplets of water fell over his head and dripped on his shoulders and chest. It felt refreshingly wonderful. He reached back, cutting the wave with his hand. The wave collapsed and water fell over him, knocking him into the warm ocean. He looked up to see the underside of the wave bubble white and race towards the shore. Breaking the surface, he spit out the salt water that got into his mouth. Smiling, he looked for Jimmy. There he was, still riding the wave.

Jimmy's eyes leaped forward, blackened, then receded into black holes. His skin wrinkled, shriveled, and darkened. His mouth shortened as the lips disappeared and hideous fangs protruded through his gums. A sinewy blackness swirled – forming a hole over his mouth so dark, it resembled an abyss. A hideous, low-pitched scream reverberated – hurting Jason's ears. The sun instantly dropped below the horizon. Or did it just vanish behind some clouds?

Jason gasped heavily. Although his eyes opened, darkness emerged, losing sight as he woke up. His chest heaved so fast, it almost hurt just like his throat. Disgusted by the drenched sheets, he yanked the covers off and sat up. Jason took deep breaths and let them out slowly, trying to push away the invasive terror. His panic faded into nothing.

Something icy laced the hairs in Jason's ears. Somewhere between tingling and tickling, the annoying sensation pulled him from sleep – ending the pleasant dream. Maybe Jason still slept – or perhaps he still lingered between sleep and consciousness.

Sitting up in bed, he analyzed every noise he heard: Samson's breathing, the heater pushing warm air through the ventilation, and the slight buzzing of the vents from changes in the air pressure. A weak clicking noise tapped along the baseboard.

Subtle vibrations ran across his skin. Like the steady surf that crawled on the ocean surface, it felt cooler and pressed light. It tickled his skin with a touch of electricity – not feeling evil but rather bizarre. Rolling across his lips, and sinuses came the hint of a sneeze that hid in his nostrils.

Whispers passed by his ears. Did they call out his name?

"Justin," Jason whispered, "are you here?" Something did move to his left and circled. It faded to nothing – indicating it had no physical being. What? Another distinct voice barely lifted to an audible level. "Uncle Dan?" No. It sounded like Dad. "Dad? Are you trying to tell me something? Disappointment followed the dissipating voice. "If that's you, Dad, please talk to me. Please. I really miss you." The angst hit his chest, knowing Dad would not come back.

Somehow, he wasn't startled as something gently stroked his hair. Gentle fingers – more likely fingernails, ran through his thick hair. Catching a whiff of perfume, he recognized Mom's scent. Some tears lifted like a slight overflow from his eyes. He tasted one of them that trickled over his lips and landed on his tongue. Closing his eyelids, he tried to use them as a spillway to stop the flow. Falling gently back to bed, he turned to his left side and opened his eyes, wishing so hard to see the formation of shadows in his room, and perhaps the face of Mom and Dad.

He heard Jimmy. The voice, although weak, barely lifted over the whispers. Although he could not decipher the whispers, Jason no longer wept. His crying lurched angrily. It hurt – not just in his eyes, but his whole body. Even his chest sobbed. After a few minutes of purging the emotions, Jason sighed heavily. "Jimmy – I wish I would've died with you."

A low growl spread from Samson's throat. Drawn out, angry, it remained constant. It simmered – then erupted into a small bark. Another growl bubbled for a long minute – followed by another bark.

"Samson," Jason got out of bed and used the snarling to guide him. Samson, a German Shepherd, did not let his guard down, maintaining a defensive posture ready to change into an offensive one. Sensing the dog's warmth, and hearing the guttural growl, Jason dropped to his knees and pet his friend. "Shhhh," he whispered, "Samson, be quiet. You'll wake up everyone."

Samson turned his neck. The canine whimpered slightly, then breathed heavily, flooding Jason's nostrils with a foul odor. The dog turned his head, lowered it, and let out a guttural roar. Jason continued to pet his dog to calm his guide and protector. Samson relented, now only breathing heavily.

A blast of cold hit Jason. A ringing, or rather an annoying buzz vibrated in his head. He shivered as perspiration drenched his skin. It felt like cold pins pierced his pores. The air stilled, reeking of dead, decaying meat. The whispering returned. It was several voices, meshed and rendered clear words dissonant. The voices, the ringing all ceased – fading into silence.

Samson's paws pattered on the wooden floor then scraped the outside of a door – which was probably Justin's room. The panting breath again changed to a low growl, and the subtle barks returned.

The fierce cold permeated the wooden floor. Jason sensed the soles of his feet chill as the frigid temperatures leaped from the floor into his body. The cold wrapped around his head. His ears chilled as if exposed to a harsh northern wind that barreled across the snow.

Instinctively, he reached for one of his canes in the corner. He swung it back and forth as he traversed the floor to his seeing-eye-dog. Reaching down, he clasped Samson's collar. "Boy," he said while pulling the dog, "what's gotten into you?" His words were intermingled with a couple of grunts. The dog would not pull away from the door, scratching it with his canine claws.

A long, painful creak emanated slowly in front of him.

***

Justin stirred. Jerking awake, he took a deep breath. Shaking, he realized the unsettling dream was merely a phantom in his mind. However, what was the dream, and how did it agitate him so much? He heard scratching. It emanated from his door on the other side. Turning, he caught his darkened reflection in the mirror. No – it was much more as the silhouette had height, reach, and … glowing eyes? Turning on the light, Justin relaxed seeing his reflection. How could that be? A second ago, it looked like something else. *You're seeing things*, he told himself. He turned off the light. Again, the mirror image grew into something that did not match his stature.

The light ignited, revealing a hideous humanoid creature standing in the mirror. It had deformed, scabrous, gray skin, and its long arms had large taloned hands. At the fingertips were long, razor-like fingernails. The hands pressed from within the mirror. The mouth opened, revealing a set of fangs. Pieces of flesh and blood dropped from the jagged, uneven, and sharp teeth.

Panic captured his mind, freezing him still. Unsure of what to do, he stood still as his mind scrambled for a solution. Run? Hide under the bed or in his closet? Yell for Mom and Dad? Suddenly he heard a long, painful creak as his door opened inward. He sighed – recognizing the low shadow, the fast breath, and the pattering paws. "Samson," he whispered. "Thank God." He laughed. "I mean, thank dog." The anxiety let go, allowing Justin to relax.

"Sorry," said Jason, "-but Samson's acting all weird."

Leaving the light off, Justin got on the floor to pet Samson, too. The growls subsided, and now he just whimpered. "What is it, boy?

"He's crazy – that's what," said Jason. "He woke me up. But that was good because I had a real creepy dream."

"I was having one, too." His mind tried to recall the frightening aspects of the dream. "But I don't remember it."

"Mine was about Jimmy – but it was so ..." he looked for the words to describe it, "frightening. He looked hideous and deformed. He yelled at me, too. But ... I don't remember it too well. All I remember is that I somehow knew that it wasn't really ... him. It's kinda like one of those TV shows where the good guy has an evil twin, and people can tell it's not really the good guy. Like when Dex dressed like Daredevil and pretended to be him, but Karen knew it wasn't him."

"So, you don't miss the fake Jimmy?"

"No." Jason shook his head, reiterating his statement. "Actually, I vaguely remember something like that when we were in Sao Paulo."

"What happened there? You've never told me about what happened. Dad's confused about it, too."

Jason sat on the floor in the hallways, still petting Samson. He thought blindness would help him concentrate and remember things. It didn't. The memories were there, but fuzzy and unclear – like static on a walkie-talkie or a ham radio. Just barely out of reach, he tried to concentrate but found nothing. Just faint images that were too disjointed. It was like a puzzle with only half a frame, partial corners, with too many missing pieces. "I think there was something in the ocean that scared the crap out of me. And weird things were happening – but what? Jimmy was acting strange, too." He sat quietly for a minute, listening to Samson and Justin breathe. He imagined Justin, sitting shirtless, and curling his lips. Justin always did that when he was unsure of what to say. If he was correct, Justin would follow that with two sighs. Jason smiled hearing Justin let out the two breaths. "You know, the weirdest thing was … going blind. And I keep asking myself, 'Why'd I go blind?"

"Blunt trauma."

Jason scoffed. "I mean … why?"

"I don't know. I can't imagine that. It's gotta be tough. I would think it sucked, too, if I went blind. I mean, would going deaf be any better? I'd hate to think of what it would be like to be in a world with no sound. You can't hear music, or the sounds of people laughing, or the sound of a dog."

"I can never see a sunset on a beach again. I can never see a hot girl in a bikini … or less."

"I'll do the looking for you."

Jason found a little laughter at that thought but then spoke the inner thoughts that bothered him over the last few weeks. "I can never see a cool movie again. I can't watch a football or hockey game ever again. I can never see … faces again. Eyes, head movements, and gestures." He hesitated. "But do you know what I wonder about the most?"

"What?"

"Why did I live? Why did Mom, Dad, and Jimmy all die? I got to live, but in the dark for the rest of my life? I just don't get it. Why did I live and everyone else die?" Jason let out a sigh that faded into dead silence. "Justin, I should've died."

"We've been through this before – remember? Don't talk like that. Be grateful you're alive."

"That's easy for you to say." Jason's voice cracked.

"You don't know what it's like."

Justin's voice lifted from a whisper. "Okay – I don't know what it's like. I get it. But wishing you died with them sounds so ... scary. I want you here. And Mom and Dad want you, too." Justin's hand clasped Jason's nape, pulling him closer. His voice cracked. "Don't talk like you wish you died. Talk to me. Talk to Mom and Dad – but don't talk like you don't want to live."

Embarrassed, comforted, and calmed, Jason nodded as tears traced his jawline, curved under his chin, and trickled down his neck. He had not felt this close to anyone since Jimmy was alive. "You're right. I'm sorry. It's just that it doesn't make sense."

"What in the world does? I mean – it seems like every other week there's a shooting somewhere. And then there was that kid ... I forget his name ... who killed himself at school last year?"

"He was at home."

"Well ... we knew him, and he went to our school. And what about that freakin' pedophile the police caught last month. He kidnapped that girl and raped her and left her for dead. And remember that mission trip from two years ago in that lame country? Honduras, I think? Remember all those orphans whose parents were shot by rebels?" Justin sniffed. "You have us, but those kids didn't have anyone. Even I forget how lucky we are."

Jason found a little perspective. "I guess you're right. I guess it's not so much the blindness – but rather the questions." Jason noticed how quiet Samson had become. "Well, I'm going back to bed."

"Yeah, me, too."

Jason stopped abruptly – then turned toward his cousin.

"Justin," he paused, started to say something, paused again, then finally blurted a whisper. "I love you."

"I love you, too, man."

The hinges creaked but stopped when Jason whispered again. "Justin," he worried about the question, "do you hear … voices or whispers?"

"Sorry. No."

"'Night." Jason used his cane to help himself stand while gently pulling Samson's collar. He found his way back to bed and pulled the covers tight. On his side, he thought about the conversation with Justin. It stuck with him perfectly: word for word, line for line. Alone, he tried to make sense of the pieces of his life – especially the most recent ones.

Sounds in his room, although soft, helped him relax. Samson's breaths had a rhythm. The clock quietly ticked. The ventilation pushed through the vents. Jason felt the pleasant warm air on his ear and cheek. Pulling the blanket up to his head, he felt his eyelids flutter. Relaxed, at peace, his ears found a faint whisper. It sounded like Jimmy. What was he saying?

Seeing School

The images of Mom, Dad, and Jimmy faded into black. Jason's eyes opened. Reality returned, crushing him. He cringed, realizing they were gone – like his eyesight. Why couldn't he stay in that dream? His family was alive, and he could see. Every morning, his throat tightened as if the emotional pain tried to strangle him.

Jason quickly turned his head as he caught a whiff of Samson's breath. His dog made a quick bark, then licked Jason's cheek and ear. The wet, sloppy tongue tickled, causing Jason to laugh. Maybe Samson did that to cheer him up from the painful awakening.

He moved to the shower; he turned on the spray and stepped inside. The warm streaming water woke him up. He enjoyed the sensation of water beading down his arms, torso, and legs. After scrubbing his body with soap, Jason shut off the shower and stepped out.

"Jason, honey, hurry up so I can get you to school on time."

Terrified, he backed away from the door, cringed, and covered himself. His skin shriveled, and his head fell in shame. "Aunt Janie? What are you doing? Don't do that! It's embarrassing."

She sighed. "Look – I've changed your diapers, gave you baths when you were infants, and I watched you, Jimmy, and Justin run around this house naked when you were toddlers."

"Close the door!"

She closed it, but he still felt mortified. So, what if she saw him naked as a baby and a toddler? He was a teenager now. He was fourteen and still felt awkward and embarrassed about his body. He cringed at the one thing even more humiliating: when Mom walked in on him masturbating. That was a nightmare. At the time, he was only twelve. Ashamed, Jason felt as if his face was red for two days. He could not look her in the eyes. Did she have disdain for him and think he was a demented pervert or something? He thought she forgot about it until Mom had him in the car. She apologized and added it was normal for boys to do that. It was adding insult to injury. Who talks with their mom about jacking off? Eventually, Dad talked to him as well. That went better – because Dad was a guy.

Jason returned to the present moment, remembering he would never hear their voices again. He would never see their faces. He would never get one of their hugs again. He could never have that awesome chocolate cake Mom made. His embarrassment faded. He dried, put on his boxer shorts and a t-shirt, then headed to finish dressing.

Stepping into his room, he felt shame as Aunt Janie tried to stifle her laugh. "Aunt Janie, please. It's not funny. You didn't knock. Mom knocked and if there was no answer, she'd wait." For the first time, he truly felt vulnerable. Although his hearing had heightened to new levels, as well as his sense of smell and touch, he truly felt handicapped. Yes, he could read Braille better, and he knew where different foods were on his plate. His smartphone was now compatible for blind people, he had a dog, he had a cane, and he wore glasses, so his permanently dilated pupils did not freak anyone out. However, he could not know when someone saw him naked. He felt his face blush – as well as

Do You Hear What I Hear?

his ears. He sighed, almost crying when Aunt Janie let out a small laugh. "Aunt Janie, please. It's not funny."

"Oh, I wasn't laughing at that."

He wanted to believe her but didn't. She was laughing at him – probably for having a short penis.

"I was thinking of a time when I was embarrassed. I was a little older than you and I went with a bunch of friends to a new water park that had been built. There was a huge water slide that was probably 50 or 60 feet high. It was scary. Very scary. But after my friends did it, I tried it and when I slid into the pool at the base ... well ... the force of the water ripped off my bikini top."

Jason let out a slight chuckle.

"And I had trouble finding it." She laughed. "Of course, it wasn't funny at the time. Especially when this one boy I liked, Kevin, found my top and told me to come out of the pool to get it. I freaked out so much and refused to come out of the pool. He and my friends ran off, leaving me there with only my bikini bottom. Then I got more scared when a lifeguard comes over and told me I need to get out of the pool because others were waiting at the top to come down. I cried telling him what happened to my bikini top and that my friends ran off with it. He laughed, but feeling humiliated, I kept crying. He got a towel to cover me and helped me retrieve my bra." She had to take a huge breath to get control of herself. "Oh, God – I wanted to kill them. They never let me hear the end of it."

Jason found himself smiling as she told the story – and he finally let some laughter escape. "So did you ever go up on the huge slide again?"

"Oh – no way in hell would I ever do that again. Even when I wore a one-piece swimsuit. I always cringe and laugh now. So someday, you will, too."

"Did you ever get to go out with that guy, Kevin?"

"Yes. We went out a few times until …" Her voice, laced with regret, faded.

"Until ... when? What?"

She faltered. "Until we … had sex. Then he dumped me."

Embarrassed, regretting his question, Jason sighed. "I'm sorry he did that. He shouldn't have."

She whispered. "Don't ever do that to a young lady, okay?"

"I won't."

She pushed his bangs back like Mom used to do. "And I'm sorry," she said. "I guess I forgot how sensitive young men can be in front of their relatives." She whispered. "I've caught Justin naked, too and he freaked out much more than you did."

Jason relished the thought of his cousin getting the same treatment.

"And I once caught him … doing things that boys do."

Jason grinned, recalling the time Mom caught him. "Mom caught me once. God, that was so humiliating." Somehow, he laughed at that embarrassing moment.

"Now come on. We gotta get you to school." She handed him some jeans, socks, shoes, and a sweatshirt.

He did like the school – mostly because it was not as large and crowded as his old school was. It had to be so nobody would trip over another student's cane or dog. At first, he worried about getting to class, but Samson guided Jason with ease.

First period was English. Mr. Daniels was also blind, so he knew exactly what the students had to deal with. Today

Do You Hear What I Hear?

they had to read out of a book. While there was an audio file, the kids were required to follow along with their Braille books. That was the best way to learn Braille. It was some book called "Fahrenheit 451." It was also weird because at his old school, kids begged for a movie about the book – but that was not possible here. At least he found reading much more engaging now.

Second period was History. Mrs. Masterson could see, which made her a better monitor of the students. She could tell if they were reading or not. She could always muster up a polite conversation about government, history, or geography. Just like English, Social Studies requires a good imagination.

Science was the third period. He had to work on a paper about photosynthesis. For this, students had to use their laptops. Keyboards were universal, so he and the others had to learn how to use them efficiently. Fortunately, he had a keyboard that had raised images on the individual buttons. Other kids had Braille keyboards. They had special software to help spot typographical errors as well as grammar errors. Those warnings came over the laptop speakers, or actually their earphones. There was also a computer Braille extension that made indentations for every word or number in any given text.

Lunch was good. At first, he sat alone, eating the food Aunt Janie made for him. It was a special plate using the areas of a clock. Soon, though, he made friends. However, he had no idea what they looked like. He had to go by their voices and scents. David was easy to find since he did not like to take a shower. Timmy used Irish Spring, whereas Aaron used the Axe Body Wash – the Apollo scent.

Their voices also played a huge role. Ray, being

originally from Texas, was distinctive as he had a southern accent. Drew's voice was smooth, like a radio DJ and it flowed with such optimism – as if he could accomplish anything. Timmy had a slight Irish brogue, which is probably why he used the Irish Spring soap. Of course, Marla and Susan were easy to detect because they were girls – although Susan had a lower pitch and a slight rasp. Jason found it sexy.

These were his new friends. He told Uncle Dan and Aunt Janie that these friends helped him see in the dark. He wished he knew what his new friends looked like. One way to find out was to use your fingers to trace their face, outlining their eyes, nose, lips, and jaw. However, Jason did not feel comfortable enough to let anyone do that with him – nor did he feel comfortable to outline any of their faces. All of them admitted it takes a lot of trust to let someone do that.

They also had different perspectives on blindness. While Timmy and Marla went blind, it happened at an early age. Ray and Drew were born blind – always living their lives in the dark. On the other hand, Susan could see to a certain extent – picking up light and faint images – but was legally blind as to reading signs and books.

A question hanging in the back of Jason's mind kept irritating him – like an annoying mosquito bite. It was something his therapist told him in his first session last week. "Uh, guys, my therapist told me that … over time … my dreams will fade into nothing. I was wondering – how long does that take?"

Their conversation faded into a difficult silence. It scared him … likely as it seemed to scare them.

"Well …" said Timmy, "I went blind at the age of seven,

and I think around the age of 12, I was blind in my dreams, too."

Marla interjected. "I heard the longer you're able to see, the longer you'll be able to see in your dreams. I went blind at the age of eight and somehow had seven years of visual dreams," she added. "And I think seven years out is the longest someone will last before their dreams go dark."

Jason sucked in a huge breath, worried about the final darkness where he would no longer be able to see even the memories of Mom, Dad, and Jimmy. The anxiety tightened his heart and forced it into a subtle fearful rhythm. "Thanks," he whispered. "I just needed to know."

The bell snapped Jason from dreading the day – or rather night – of full darkness. He had to focus on today – something else his therapist and Uncle Dan told him. Two more classes awaited.

The day was not done without some sort of creative class. Jason fluctuated between two things that sparked his interest. One was making ceramics. Most guys like auto mechanics, carpentry, or electronics, but Jason preferred creating pottery and other similar decorations: vases, basins, and table décor. Right now, he was still learning the diverse types of clays and their uses, and how to use his hands better. It required attention. Going only by the touch or feel of the clay, he had to make sure his fingers did not press too tightly, or too lightly. They also had to learn how to turn it into a shape.

The other was making podcasts or audio recordings. That was the project for today. A couple of days ago, Jason met with Marla and Tom over the Internet by using Skype. It was part of their English Project on "Fahrenheit 451." Each of them adjusted their microphones and recorded it.

However, their laptops only recorded the individual talking into it, leaving out the other two. Jason learned from podcasting that this is the best way because people tend to talk over each other. This way, he only had to deal with one voice at a time. He pulled Marla's and Tom's tracks from the cloud drive and aligned the three. Now it sounded like a conversation. He just had to edit or scrub his peers talking over each other. He could go to the separate track and scrub the little part that tried to talk over their peers. Jason also scrubbed the "ers" and "ums," the few times they coughed, sneezed, or said "shit," "damnit," and the "fucks." Fortunately, the laptop used audio commands from the program to help him find the tracks with his mouse and perform these tasks.

He also had to remove background noise. Marla's heating vent kept going off, so he isolated the one sound and scrubbed it. At one point, Tom's little brother barged in and interrupted the talk. Later he would lay out another track and lower the volume considerably so they could have background music.

On his own track, Jason had to deal with Samson's agitation and barking. The dog would not stop for several minutes. Sometimes Samson whimpered, other times he growled – but it was mostly barking. There was too much good material his classmates discussed, so he did not want to scrub all of it. Isolating the background sound, he prepared to scrub it. However, as he listened to the barks again, he noticed another background sound. What was it? He isolated that sound and turned up the volume. The mysterious noise beckoned him, piquing his curiosity. The strange sound distorted at high volume, so Jason had to do some tricks to isolate the whisper. Maybe some radio signals or music from a nearby Bluetooth spilled into his track. No. The words were angry and vile. They were short, curt, strong, and threatening. What was it that upset Samson? He had to raise the volume again to hear it clearly. Hearing the voice, he wondered what language he heard.

Mirror, Mirror on the Wall

Justin took a huge breath. His fingers shook as an icy anxiety wrapped around him. His eyes darted everywhere, somehow knowing strange eyes glared at him. It reminded him of the time Peri McFarland gazed at him, moving her eyes up and down. She grinned and raised her eyebrows at him. Her leer made him feel uncomfortable.

"What are you doing?"

"Undressing you with my eyes," she winked at him. *"You looked very good in that skimpy swimsuit at practice yesterday."*

He laughed, hoping to dispel the awkward feeling. Strangely, her lustful gaze and comment filled with him with pride, although an embarrassing shame followed.

However, while Peri's comment and stare made him nervous and embarrassed, the invisible eyes left apprehension, and a ghastly fear.

Justin found a more comparable memory from the fifth grade when three bullies circled him, wanting to beat him up. Nerves mounted, his heart raced, and his skin tingled. Thank goodness for Jason and Jimmy helping him. However, this bully was intangible. Or did it exist in the first place?

Almost crying, he pinched his nose to quell the weeping. It didn't work. After a few breaths, he stopped crying. He thought of sleeping in Jason's room. No, he could deal with it and sleep on his own. Crossing himself and praying pushed the shaking horror back – albeit lightly.

Do You Hear What I Hear?

Justin heard the creak on the wooden floor as he moved to the bathroom door and shut it tightly. Usually, he kept it open in case he had to pee. However, the last few nights he woke up and could see something. The sinister reflections were terrifying. Last night, he closed the door, but he woke up and found it open. This time, he put a 25-pound dumbbell in front of the door. He thought of the hideous, sunken, oval eyes that looked sad and depressed. However, the orbs had a sinister red, sometimes yellowish glow. Its deformed hands pressed against the inside of the mirror. Justin wanted to take it down, but the mirror was imbedded in the wall.
Sighing, he wondered if he should tell Mom and Dad. No. They had seemed tense over the last week. They had enough to deal with taking care of him and his cousin. Besides, they might think he was crazy. For some reason, he almost cried – but why?

Lying in bed, he pulled the covers tight. He turned out his light and started a quiet prayer again. After he said "Amen," he crossed himself. He exhaled. The edginess ebbed. Taking a few deep breaths, he clutched the crucifix on his necklace. He closed his eyes, hoping to find good rest and sleep.

Finding himself out of bed, Justin shook his head. He stared at the mirror. For how long? When did he get up from bed? Why would he do that? He glanced at the clock in his bathroom: 6:30. He was up that early on a Saturday? How come he didn't remember any of his dreams? Breaking free of his stupor, as well as the ringing in his ears, Justin stepped back.

A shadow passed behind him. He looked around. Back in the mirror he saw a dark, hideous creature behind him. The head bowed. It had dark, mangled hair. The arms, covered in flaking and peeling skin, suddenly contorted. It sounded like the clicking noise of a bird. The arms stretched long. The talon-like fingers reached for Justin. He spun around to face it. It disappeared. The dank, wet breath air blew across his skin and pushed Justin's hair back.

Footsteps. He spun back around. Nothing. Samson appeared. Justin's whole body cringed. Holding his chest, he laughed. Justin smiled, dropped to a knee, and pet the dog. Samson seemed to enjoy the rubbing behind his ears, neck, and back. The dog yawned, somehow signaling Justin to yawn.

Samson stopped panting as his ear folded back and lowered his head. A subtle growl escaped his throat. Justin stood and backed away as the growls erupted into a series of short barks. Had Samson gone mad? Did he not like something about Justin? "Samson, it's me, boy. You know me." He wanted to reach down and pet Samson more, but the German Shepherd's growl startled him.

The growl turned to a whimper as his jaws lunged at Justin's leg. Afraid, Justin backed against the vanity. The dog's teeth caught the hem in Justin's boxer shorts. "Samson!" Panicked, he started to yell for his parents or Jason but stopped when he realized Samson was yanking him backwards one step at a time. Out of the bathroom, Samson yanked once again, and Justin fell to the carpet.

The dog ran to the bathroom door and started growling again. More barks emanated from the dog's throat. Justin stared into the bathroom. The lights flickered somewhat. At first, they were like a reactionary blink – as if something got in someone's eye. No. The way the lights flashed angrily. His skin tingled as the hair on his arms stiffened.

Another presence made itself known. Startled, Justin

held his chest when he saw Jason come into his room. "Samson," Jason's stern voice did not stop his dog from barking. "Samson, come here now!" His dog finally came to him. Jason folded his cane and knelt to pet him. "Sorry, Justin. I don't know what's into this dog lately."

Justin finally stood. "He was trying to pull me out of the bathroom. And growling and barking."

"I know. He's done that with me a few times. I'd hate to trade him for another service dog. He seems like part of my family now. Doncha, boy?" Jason smiled while petting the canine. Justin also rubbed Samson's fur – focusing behind the ears. Samson's head dipped to that side and grunted as if he liked it. His coat was almost perfect for a German Shepherd with the correct ratio of brown to black fur that easily identified him during the day and gave him cover at night.

"Uh, Jason," Justin hesitated for a second but continued petting Samson, "-do you get the feeling you're being watched? It seems like there's something else here. And sometimes I see things in the ... in the ... well ... in the mirror, or in the corner of my eye. I was staring at that thing," he pointed to the mirror, "for I don't know how long. It felt as if I was hypnotized or something – and I hear this ringing in my ears, get headaches, and feel cold."

"I'd sure get a headache and a ringing in my ears if I saw you, too. Admit it – you're ugly."

Justin whined, almost crying. "Come on, shithead. I mean it. Sometimes I think I'm imagining things – but I'm feeling more spooked about it. I feel so ... sad and hopeless a lot. Nervous. Shaking." Justin's voice teetered towards being childlike, retreating from the deeper voice on the other side of puberty. "Please tell me you feel it, too."

A low-pitched howl exploded – forcing Jason to cover his ears. The blast blew his hair back, and the horrid breath drove him to reel. Another howl carried an eruption of drool that splattered on his face – even some getting into his mouth. A disgusting nausea replaced the fright that suddenly exited his body.

"What the fuck just happened?" Justin's whisper was barely audible.

"Did …" Jason gagged, trying to spit out the invading slobber. "Did you … like … see anything?"

"No. But it hurt my ears, though."

"Mine, too? Is there drool all over me?"

"Sure is. It's on me, too. This shit's disgusting."

Jason heard his cousin turn on the water. Justin handed him a warm washcloth.

"Here, so you can wipe yourself."

Jason followed Justin's footsteps out the door, down the hall to the edge of the upstairs.

"Mom! Dad!" yelled Justin.

"Yes, son?" Mom asked him. "What is it?"

"Did you hear that?"

"Hear what? Samson's barking?"

"No," Justin, "the other thing."

"Son," yelled his dad, "what other thing? Other than Samson, we haven't heard anything. Tell Jason to keep that damn dog quiet." The commanding voice echoed off the walls, dissipating fast.

Justin stammered. "Uh, never mind. I think I know what happened."

Both boys retreated to Justin's bedroom. "What should we tell them?" blurted Justin. "This shit's freaking me out – but they're going to think we're crazy."

Do You Hear What I Hear?

Jason stuttered and his volume waned. "Look, maybe," he stopped, realizing no idea came to mind. "What if we …" His voice trailed. "I just can't … think." After rubbing his forehead, Jason whispered. "Justin …" he paused, "I hear voices and whispers a lot. Can you?"

"No. But I hear footsteps, scratching on the walls. I'm seeing weird shit. And I can't shake this god-awful feeling. I'm shaking. I feel cold. It's like my skin is shrinking and I often feel like crying for no reason. I'm nervous and scared a lot. I don't know what the hell is going on."

Jason shrugged his shoulders, took a deep breath, held it, and let it out slowly. Justin did the same. Their dads always said when they feel scared to use that breathing method to calm down. At the tenth breath, Jason felt the anxiety and angst fade. "I feel better," he said.

"Me, too," added Justin. "Still – we better tell Mom and Dad."

***

Usually, he would devour his mom's mashed potatoes and gravy. Justin just looked at it – poking it with his fork. Not even the idea of her lemon pie seemed appealing. He forced himself to have a bite of the mashed potatoes and gravy, but the wonderful taste eluded him. There was no joy. Even the cold vegetable salad, which he liked, did not satisfy his hunger. He took a sip of the water. His mouth dried. It opened, then froze. What would he say? He tried to speak again. No. He finally blurted out – although quietly. "Uh, Dad, Mom … I … er … need to tell you … something."

His dad stopped eating and looked at him. A stranger might think Dad was angry or uncaring, but Justin knew it was his straight, matter-of-fact face. He was in the Air Force for ten years, along with Uncle Derek. Both saw terrible things and put up a wall to protect his family from those awful things. Justin did not push it, nor did Mom. They knew Dad and Uncle Derek could always talk. Justin, though, wondered how hurt Dad must be after losing his brother. Mom, too, lost a brother. Unsure how he would react to such a loss, Justin hesitated. He knew Dad cared and would listen. He'd also try to help and protect him. Justin wished he could be as tough.

"What is it?" asked Dad.

He could tell Dad's softening voice he sought to understand and help. He could talk to Dad about anything: girls, hunting, baseball. Justin almost smiled at the thought, but something stifled the openness tonight. Suddenly his throat constricted within. It felt like a slight pressure. It only paralyzed his voice box, and not his breath. The icy, intangible grip pulled harder. It slowly released him. Justin tried again. "Well, it's … uh … it's." Again, the icy grip returned, squeezing tighter. What was going on? The grip loosened. Justin sighed. "Never mind. I'll tell you later."

Dad hesitated, looked at Mom, then back at Justin. "What's going on with you boys?"

"Dad, never mind. Maybe I'm not quite ready to talk about it."

"Sweetie," said Mom, "please talk to us." She gently clasped his wrist, finally bringing some warmth to Justin's ever-cold skin. "Honey – you're shaking like nothing else. And why are your hands so cold?"

Justin quivered. "I … uh … well it's that …" The tight, cold grip on his throat clamped tighter. Why couldn't he say it?

"We want to help," said Mom as she squeezed his hand tighter.

Justin looked at Mom. The dark looming figure towered behind her. It cast a shadowy outline that grew large wings. Pieces of the darkness swirled around her. Could she not see it? Could she not feel it? Its yellow, piercing eyes appeared to stare at him – then at Dad. He couldn't see the veiled creature, either.

"Justin," Dad's voice became harsh, "what's wrong, son? Please tell us."

The images disappeared. Did he imagine that? Or were they real? He closed his eyes, doing the trick of holding in his breath for ten seconds, then letting it out slowly. He did it a second time. "I'm sorry," he stammered. "Maybe I'm not ready. I'll talk to you guys about it … later." His voice trailed.

"Please, do," said Dad. "We really want to listen and help you."

Dad and Mom glanced at him periodically until Justin finished his meal. He quietly went up the stairs. Jason followed.

"Why didn't you tell them, shithead?" muttered Jason.

Justin snapped, but only in a whisper. "Why couldn't you? I tried but … something … stopped me."

"Did it feel like … something grabbed your tongue … and set it on fire?"

Justin hesitated. "No. It was like it grabbed my voice box, turned it cold and squeezed it. I kept trying to say something, but it hurt so bad. It felt like I couldn't breathe." Finally crying, Justin let all his emotions out – but quietly. "This is driving me crazy. I don't know what to do."

Even Jason sounded on the verge of tears. "I don't know, either. But we gotta tell them."

Justin dried his few tears and looked at his cousin's

shadow from the downstairs light. "Jason, can I sleep in your room tonight?"

Jason's arm somehow found him, wrapped around Justin's torso, and pulled him closer. "Anytime."

Do You Hear What I Hear?

Dan and Janie

After dinner, every night – Dan stared at the dresser mirror. He also did it at work, and other places. Earlier today, he almost crashed as he kept looking in the rear-view mirror and did not pay attention to what was in front of him. At work, he would go into the restroom and after relieving himself, he'd stare at the mirror for minutes on end. The mental state broke when coworkers came in. Every time, his tense colleagues winced, sighed, and left. They seemed to be on edge and avoiding him. Were they sad that he lost his twin? Or did they fear him? The latter seemed more likely.

Dan heard a ringing in his ear. It seemed to become louder, higher pitched, and more irritating. What was happening? At times, it felt as if something pulled him into his reflection. The hair in his ears tingled. His blank mind idled. Thoughts of his brother, his sister-in-law, his parents, his son, and wife, were all cast aside – as if something kept wiping his mind clean. His eyelids dropped. He jolted them open.

Startled, his chest froze. His eyes fixed on his image that now sneered at him. The eyes had a subtle, silverish glow. Evil escaped from his sinister eyes like acidic water from a sprinkler. The image flickered. His head changed to something inhuman. Decayed flesh, rotted teeth, sunken eyes with pieces of skin dangling over orifices, the nose cut and sunken.

"Honey," said Janie, "are you okay?"

Dan's stupor vanished. The high-pitched noise silenced

and the hair in his ears stopped tingling. Whisked from his reflection, he stood from the seat and closed the closet door. Shaking his head a few times and grunting, he had to force his identity, personality, and will back to reality. Shivering, he hugged himself, trying to keep his skin, joints, and muscles under control. "I'm sorry, honey," he replied, "I guess I'm just overwhelmed." He wept lightly. "I miss my brother. I miss my sister-in-law. And we have Jason now. I try to be strong, but I feel sad a lot." Afraid of not being manly enough, he turned away from her face as he cried more. "I thought I had grieved properly – but ... I want to talk to Derek so bad."

Janie pulled Dan close and tugged his chin to face him. Seeing the tear in one eye, she used her finger to wipe it away. She kissed him. Using her hands to cradle the back of his head, she pulled him closer. "I miss them, too." She kissed him a second, then a third time. "I know exactly what you're going through. I'd do anything to get my brother back, too." She kissed him, then they locked eyes and smiled.

"I love you," Dan whispered. He turned towards the bathroom.

Something tugged Janie's wrist. She felt an intense cold sink into her arm, up her shoulder and into her chest. Bobby! Brain fluid and blood stained his skin just below one ear. The left arm and leg were deformed, as if broken limbs had not been re-set properly. The clothes were torn and caked in heavy blood. Some teeth were missing. One eye was wide open with blood dripping like tears. The other eye partially rolled up. His mouth moved up and down, but she heard nothing.

Janie, breaking from her mirror image, yelped. Cold

tears chilled her skin like a waterfall in high mountains. She closed her eyes as Dan rushed to embrace her. "Honey! What is it? What's wrong?"

"Dan," she said, "please tell me you saw him. Please tell me you saw Bobby in the mirror."

"Honey," he whispered, "I didn't see him – but I believe you. I've been spooked, too." He looked up as if peering through the ceiling into Justin and Jason's room. "Maybe that's what's going on with the boys. Perhaps they're spooked, too."

She huffed small visible breaths for a minute. The cold bit her skin, making her jaw quiver. Feeling the warmth of Dan, she drew closer as he wrapped his arms around her. Comforted by his strong embrace, she sighed, then clasped his shirt under each collar bone and pulled him closer. Her arms, hands, and shoulders were now wrapped up in his arms, giving her the security she longed for.

"Honey, what is it? Did you see him again?" he asked. "You're shivering." He pressed tightly, trying to squeeze the fear, the ugly feelings, and the cold out of her. The sound of her crying cut into his chest, diminishing his identity and strength. "Honey, calm down. I'm here for you." He kissed her a few times and rubbed her limbs. "What's happening to us? We need to figure this out together.

Janie cringed. Usually, the touch warmed her and made her feel secure, loved, and fully accepted. Now, they seemed impotent, and distant. The chill sank deep into her muscles, bone, and organs. Her heart shriveled as it beat irregularly. The stomach tightened, shrank, and moved closer to her spine. What was happening? Weeping, she tried to think of the old prayer the Methodist Chaplain taught her while she spent time in jail after her DUI. What was it? Janie took some deep breaths to calm her racing mind. Finding a few random Scriptures, she focused on them.

> *"In my house are many rooms. I go to prepare one for you."*
>
> *"I am the bread of life. He who believes in me will never hunger."*

The anxiety dissipated – like a tide that lost strength on a deep ocean. A few more breaths, and the uncertainty was gone. Janie's stomach stopped shaking. Warmth returned to her heart, stomach, and lungs. How does Scripture provide such comfort and hope? So many people liked to use Bible verses to justify their own behavior, judge others, and puff up their egos. Right now, she found its true purpose: to comfort and restore hope. Janie was United Methodist before meeting Dan – and she converted to Catholicism. Still, she knew the founder of Methodism, John Wesley, had a high regard for Catholicism and other branches of the Christian faith.

Enough of the intellectual facet of her faith. She desperately needed the visceral element of Christ. She knew in her head that God loved her. But it was rare to feel that love in her tummy. She smiled, thinking of Mom telling her, *"Do you know Mommy and Daddy love you? Do you feel it in your tummy?"* Janie smiled, recalling that wonderful feeling in her tummy when she felt and knew Mom and Dad loved her. Nervous stomachs knot, grumble, and turn cold. A tummy that felt love was open, warm, and even seemed to dance. She wished the love of Christ was more prevalent in that manner.

The lights were off, so they got into the bed, pulling the covers tight. She felt his warm body behind her. Dan's strong arm draped over her left side and still pulled her close. She

Do You Hear What I Hear?

smiled hearing him whisper one more time: "I love you, honey. Goodnight." He kissed her shoulder, again embracing her as if wanting to meld with her essence.

Both closed their eyes, and focused on each other: their touch, warmth, eyes, skin, strength, and faithfulness. Relaxed, they listened to the tranquil sounds: a gentle rain on the roof, the fan, the clock's ticking, and their breathing.

The light rain did not exhibit any anger or fear. No thunder emanated from it. The rain fell at the proper pace: not too much to flood, nor too little to be of no use. The tower fan swiveled back and forth, cascading a shield of cool, refreshing air over them. The clock's ticking matched their heartbeats, then provided a cadence which hypnotized them into a sweet, blissful sleep.

The last sound, their breathing, slowly synced into one breath. Inhaling and exhaling at the same time, Dan could not discern where he existed apart from Janie. When they first met and fell in love 20 years ago, he thought they were close, but every year they took a step closer – forging a deeper intimacy and strength. They were separated for two years as he did two tours in Iraq, but when he returned home, the two grew even closer than before, knowing each other more intimately. Then Justin was born, and they encountered the struggles of raising a child: waking up at night, robbing them of their sleep, and forging new worries – both real and imagined. These new stressors became stronger, harder, and more oppressive. In turn, those obstacles made them stronger – not just in themselves but also as one. In that struggle, they found a stronger, deeper commitment to each other – and they grew as better parents. Now – they faced a stronger challenge with taking care of Jason. Derek wondered how his nephew was doing right now.

***

Justin's eyes opened. Rolling to his back, he looked up at the darkened ceiling. He heard Jason breathing peacefully – at least for now. Earlier, after turning out the lights and lying down for a while, Justin heard his cousin crying. What was it? And should he say something? Ask Jason what was wrong? Or just let his cousin cry through all the confusion and pain by himself? Would he embarrass Jason if he asked? Justin cried when he heard it. He pretended to be asleep. Was that wrong?

Justin's eyes, adjusted to the dark, looked around at the room – finding it ironic that Jason could not see it. He only knew the room by his other senses of sound, touch, and smell. Justin thought about Jason "being able to see in his dreams." What was that like? He went from seeing in his dreams to being in the dark when waking up. He wondered if he could adjust to such a dramatic change as Jason had. He needed to help Jason – to fill in for Jimmy and be a brother for him. Of course, growing up together, Jason was like a brother – and Jimmy, too. Justin felt an opaque pain. It was hard to describe – much less locate where it resonated. Barely numb, the pain fluctuated between his chest and stomach – or was it in his spirit?

A cold chill wrapped around Justin. Even with his blanket, it was freezing. He wanted another blanket – a thicker one. He kept the quilt tight around him while standing. He whispered a cuss as his large toe grazed one of the foot legs of Jason's bed. Reaching the door, he thought of just going back to his own bed for the night. No. He hated the anxiety of being alone in his room at night with all the weird things happening. Still, he needed the thicker blanket.

The dark hallway seemed longer. Did it stretch? Of

course, he could only see the different, misshapen shadows. Some of them leapt over the mirrors and pictures hung on the walls – as well as the thin table. One of them was between Jason's room and Justin's room, the other between Justin's room and the office room at the end of the hall.

Why was there a light on in the office room? The weak illumination tried to grow beyond the crack between the floor and the door, but the darkness squashed it. Justin froze in his tracks as the door slowly swung open – emitting a long, thin creak . The light outlined a dark figure. "Dad?" Justin whispered. "Dad? Is that you?"

Heavy, metered footsteps crossed the floor. The closer the footsteps approached the harder Justin's chest thumped. The dread, like a hand, seized him and squeezed – causing his heart to fall into an unusual rhythm with loud, unusual beats. Like a drummer who had no rhythm, the beat was erratic with unusual emphasis on certain hits. A cold stench spread through the hallways. Justin wanted to close the door yet couldn't because he had to verify if this event was real or not.

Samson growled subtly and let loose a few low barks. While he was grateful for the protective dog, Justin worried this was something Samson could not fight. Justin's eyes darted back and forth and up and down the hallway – trying to find something ... anything. He gasped, seeing something in the mirror above the hallway table. The steps passed in front of Justin's room as a large shape, darker than a shadow, started to grow. The steps quickened. Dust, outlined from the light of the end office room, kicked up from the floor with every step. The hideous shape burst into a full form that resembled a man.

Justin's cold skin surged with fright as his heart

exploded and his muscles spasmed. Screaming, he slammed the door, locked it, and fell on the bed. "Something's out there!" yelled Justin. "Something's out there!"

"What?" asked Jason as he bolted awake. "What is it?"

Justin watched the doorknob turn. His eyes widened as a cold gap hollowed out his chest. He and Jason screamed as the door shook violently. Terror exploded, turned into panic, and circled them. In a frenzy, unable to think, their only reaction was a horrid, painful, and panicked yell.

***

A cold dread sprang up. Icy fingers clasped around Dan. It disturbed his dreams, turning them into dark, frightening images, loud and abrasive sounds, horrible pain in his joints, a vile smell of carrion mixed with excrement, vomit, and blood spread in his mind. It felt like a cold, scabrous, scaley blanket wrapped around his body, pulling him away from Janie. It was not fear that exploded, but rather a chilling terror that spread from his fingers and toes to his chest and head. His heartbeat thudded louder with each thump, as if trying to break free from his chest. His stomach felt the thuds as well, shimmying within as if amplifying the foreboding sound. A sound reached into his slumber and tried to break him free of the sensations. It resounded a second time.

Screams triggered a spasm that leapt from his chest to his arms and legs. Every muscle flexed as if given an electric shock. Something upstairs rattled violently. A text alert sounded. Dan grabbed his phone to read the text from Justin: *"Dad, someone's inside the house."* Another text followed. *"I'm n jasons room."*

The screaming stopped. The door stopped rattling. After several seconds of quiet, a metered step – almost like a military march – treaded upstairs back and forth. The heavy steps pressed on the wooden floors, emanating not only the steps, but also creaks on the floorboards and deep moans in the floor beams. He texted back. "Lock your doors and stay in your rooms."

He jostled Janie awake. "Honey ... someone's upstairs."

She yawned. "The boys?"

"No. Something else. I'm calling the police."

Stephen W. Scott

911 Call

Yawning, Roger took off his headpiece, stood and stretched, trying to wake his muscles, bones, and tendons. He looked forward not only to his shift ending at 6:00 a.m., but more to the end of his time on the 10:00 p.m. to 6 a.m. shift. Every other month, the 911 personnel would change. He would go to his favorite shift, the "A" shift which went from 6:00 a.m. to 2:00 p.m. Those on the "A" shift would move to the 2:00 p.m. to 10 p.m. slot that was the "B" Shift. That one wasn't too bad. Most operators, though, despised the "C" shift, often dubbed the "Shit Shift." That's when most of the weird calls came: the people who are stoned and want the police to catch the person who sold them bad drugs, the mentally deranged person who hears voices or thinks the CIA or FBI is watching them, and the ones who were upset they got the wrong order at a drive-through. At least those were not truly insane calls like shootings, stabbings, fights, terrible crashes, or medical emergencies. Those calls could stress out a person – even a seasoned first responder like Roger who formerly worked as a firefighter paramedic.

How long had it been? Five or six years? He thought about it. Robyn was nine when the accident happened, and she'll be 15 in April. Six years – give or take a few months. He came to the 911 Center after the accident that crippled him. Roger was strong and liked working. As a firefighter paramedic, he knew the skills very well, how to stay calm and focused during an emergency, and to calm frantic victims of fire or trauma.

Do You Hear What I Hear?

As a fireman, he respected fire – never fully hating it, loving it, or fearing it. Flames sometimes put out another fire. At other times it ravaged homes, businesses, cars, memories, and hope. Too many people took fire too seriously and feared everything about it, while others (mostly younger people), did not take it seriously enough. Either way, fire would burn someone who could not find the place between love, fear, and hate. The middle spot was respect. You respect fire in the ways it hurts and the ways it helps. Once a person finds respect, they realize that anyone can get burned by it. It never discriminates between race, socio-economic background, or sexuality.

Disease did the same. People had no respect for disease since antibiotics, Flu shots, and vaccines. Now, many diseases had returned because people feared the cure and thought they knew everything about it. The Internet did that. Now everyone thought they were an expert at everything.

Roger took a sip of his coffee. Of course, he had to lightly stir it. His favorite thing to do was hold the warm mug in his hand and trace the lip of the cup with his thumb. He would inhale the sacred scent as if breathing incense. Then, he took a sip to relish the taste.

The beeping noise yanked Roger from his trance. "911, how may I help you?"

"I think there's an intruder in my house," said the shaky voice. "He's upstairs walking back and forth, up and down the upstairs hallway. My son and nephew are up there!"

"Sir, how do you know it's not them?"

"Because they texted me from upstairs and are scared out of their minds. And my nephew's dog won't stop barking."

"Okay, sir, I am dispatching the police to your location."

Roger quickly held his hand over the scanner and felt the braille formations that revealed the address of the caller. Using the notches on the keyboard, he easily determined which key was which and typed in the address for law enforcement. "Sir, I'm sending the police now. Right now, I need you to stay put. Do not put yourself in danger. Does the intruder have a gun?"

"I don't know. I have one."

"Stay calm, sir. If you choose to use your firearm, you want to be sure it's not your son or nephew."

"Shit," said the distraught man. "I don't know what to do. I can't stop shaking. Nor can my wife."

Roger's ears perked at the man's voice, finding confusion, fear, uncertainty, and panic. "Take a deep breath, sir." Using the notches on his keyboard, he made sure his fingers were in the correct position before typing – or rather pounding – the keys as if it would encourage the police to arrive faster.

The caller breathed heavily in a short, rhythmic fashion. "I'm going upstairs. I have to protect my boys."

A feminine voice gasped. Was she crying? He heard the wife whisper, "Please, Dan, don't go."

"Janie, I have to. I need to help the boys."

"Sir," said Roger, "please be careful. You're best to remain hidden from the intruder. And you could accidentally shoot your boys. Please do not act rash."

It sounded as if the bedroom door opened. His ears picked up more things: a dog barking, loud footsteps, and a loud, echoing banging noise that caused his sternum to vibrate. The thuds sounded eerie – almost ominous. They reverberated through the house, the phone line, and his ears. The presence sent a chilly anxiety through his chest.

Do You Hear What I Hear?

Somehow, it added darkness to his already blinded eyes. Roger's fear dissipated. "Sir? Sir?" The loud thuds continued, competing with the dog's barks and the heavy footsteps. Those steps were the only rhythmic element. It sounded like a march. "Sir? Can you hear me?"

"I can hear you." It was a desperate whisper.

The thuds emanated a deep bass that shot through the phone line and into Roger's chest. His heartbeat matched the metered loud bangs. A deep chill pierced his skin, leaving behind an icy tingle. The resonance, like eels or worms, slithered into his bones, weakening them while disturbing his soul. Roger had to take a few deep breaths and let them out slowly to get rid of the anxiety.

Something else garnered his attention. Underneath the loud noises, something subtle, yet present, stayed in the background. Whispers? Having an idea of what they were, he focused on them. What were they saying? He upped the volume and focused on them. Although his ears had adapted and became strong, they still had some damage resulting in Tinnitus. It was a casualty for many first responders because of being around sirens so much of their careers.

Roger wiped the sweat off his forehead. After drying his hand on his pants leg, he wondered why he felt so tense. Taking a few deep breaths, he held each one for several seconds. After the seventh or eighth one, the uneasiness waned – mostly.

"Can you see that?"

Roger stammered. "Uh, sir ... I can't ..."

Dan spoke louder but kept it in a whisper. "Oh, my God." The voice faded.

"Sir – what is it that you see?"

Dan's scream burrowed into Roger's ears. He pulled off

the headset as three or four gunshots followed. Then ... dead silence. What seemed an hour extended for a few mere seconds. "Sir? Dan? Are you still there?" He asked again and a third time.

"I'm here," he said, letting out a few huge breaths. "I'm alright. I think that's the police downstairs."

"Does anyone need medical attention?"

"No. But we're all scared shitless – that's for sure."

Roger heard something else. The whispers returned. They tickled the hairs in his ears, gently tapping on the tiny bones and eardrums. His ears reached out. There it was again. Roger tilted his head to listen intently and dialed up the volume. What language was that?

Do You Hear What I Hear?

Faith and Doubt

Jason put on his sunglasses and stepped outside. The wintry blast hit his face – almost numbing it. The weather turned sharply colder two days ago, not letting loose its grip in upper-state New York. The wind slapped his face again, almost knocking him back in time to experience the pain of recent memories.

He pulled the stocking cap tight, then tightened the drawstring of the hood. Using only his cane, he found his way down the sidewalk. He waved it back and forth, occasionally tapping the ground to make sure there were not missing sections of pavement. Samson did not accompany him, nor did anyone else. Aunt Janie would freak out if she knew he was out on his own. In many ways, Aunt Janie was very like Mom: overprotective and doting.

Compelled to get out on his own, he wanted to walk away from the house, even if it was just for a few minutes. Without conversation, he could think, process, and make sense of the last three months. People passed on both sides, going in both directions. He felt the air move, and a few thick-sleeved arms nicked him. Somehow, he could tell that they turned their heads and noticed him. He heard bits of conversation from the pedestrians. At one point, Jason wondered if his hearing picked up their thoughts.

"Poor kid."
"What happened to that poor boy?"
"Does he need help? Should I offer him some?"
"Oh my God – his face is hideous."

"Where's his dog?"

Jason felt surprised by all the emotions within – as well as his thoughts. Even though the tragedy happened nearly three months ago, it seemed like last week. Things happened too fast: moving in with Uncle Dan and Aunt Janie, losing his sight and his family, and going to a blind school.

He made a turn to the right. Using the sound of chirps at a crosswalk, he knew when to navigate the intersection properly. He did it two more times, along with another turn to the left, and then another to the right. The temperature dropped. He must be in the shadow of a building – and he had a good idea which building it was: Saint Matthew's Cathedral. The cane guided him to some stairs. He used the handrail embedded into a stone wall along with his cane to climb the steps. Finding the door, he opened it and stepped inside. The warmth immediately refreshed his chilled skin, allowing him to pull off his hood and stocking cap.

Memory helped him recall the images around him: the stained-glass windows that depicted stories of the Bible. The altar, and the choir section, majestically situated next to a large organ that bellowed every Sunday. He heard a bit of conversation among men, women, and children.

Jason heard footsteps approaching. Turning towards the presence, he knew it was one person or another. Instantly, the aroma of perfume along with the displacement of air told him who it was.

"Jason! It's so good to see you." A soft feminine hand touched his shoulder.

He found it amazing how he could "hear" a smile from someone as they talked. His mouth widened as well, although it was brief. His lips could not relax, and were somewhat taut, but he managed to be polite to his favorite nun. "Hi, Sister Catharine."

"What brings you here by yourself?"

He tried to think of something funny to say – but not in a smart-assed way. "My cane and my feet, Sister."

"You are such a witty boy. And so handsome. And you've adjusted so fast. If wasn't a Nun, I'd-"

"I know. You'd love a son like me." He imagined her face from memory. It was a little ashen from being inside the Church quite a bit. She also had light brown eyes. He had seen her without her habit but could never remember the color of her hair. Her face had fattened some – but no more than a normal woman who was pushing 40 or 50. He wanted to ask her how old she was, but Mom always told him "Never ask an older woman how old she is." Yet, being blind, it was much harder to tell – except with much older people who often had worn raspy voices.

"What can we do for you? Father Nelson will be conducting the Eucharist in about an hour. Do you wish to talk to him beforehand?"

"No, ma'am. I just wanted to … think and … and I guess – pray."

"Sure," she said while gently grasping his arm. "Let's go to the prayer room."

Jason felt a bit insecure, considering the doubt he felt. His cheerfulness faded as he looked down. He stammered. "I … I want to go by myself, Sister."

She hugged him gently and he returned the hug. He held onto her for a brief second and he took a deep breath – maybe hoping to capture a bit of her peaceful spirit. Sister Catharine was more than a nun. Her presence throughout his life had molded and shaped his heart, mind, and spirit. She taught him, Justin and Jimmy about the Bible and the life of Christ.

Jason wanted to believe in the Resurrection of Christ, and the life Jesus lived – but its existence seemed too far from his identity as a regular kid.

When Jesus was 14, was he girl-crazy? Did he wrestle with other boys? Did it hurt if he got racked in the balls? Did he wake up with boners? Did he laugh at a good joke, or punch someone who annoyed him? Did he ever get disappointed or sad? All that seemed difficult to comprehend.

In the empty prayer chapel, Jason knelt at the altar. He crossed himself, wondering if his prayers reached the true ears of God? Or did they just fall back on him as empty weights that crushed his soul. Sister Catharine explained the saints had doubts, and she shared her doubts as a child, an adult ... and even as a nun.

Again, all he thought of was his parents and Jimmy. They had so much fun together. All the vacations to Thailand, Sydney, France, and Jamaica, the Sabers and Bills games they attended, and playing games like Monopoly and Trivial Pursuit. The Christmas and Thanksgiving dinners felt close and distant from him, delivering joy and pain at the same time. The memories, like a double-edged sword, jabbed him, like him picking at a scab or pimple on his skin. He ran his fingers down the scars and his damaged ear. Deformed, blind, and alone – his heart wrenched on itself, allowing some tears to lurch free. Why didn't he die with them? He knew it was wrong, but Jason somehow found a deep regret for not dying.

He tried to stop crying, but that hurt. It was easier to let his tears loose.

The faded whispers returned. Although the voices had faded, Jason wondered if those were memories of Dad,

Do You Hear What I Hear?

Mom, and Jimmy, or did he hear their real voices. Unable to tell, he resigned himself to the fact they were taunting memories. His prayers froze as his emotions pushed out a waterfall of tears.

Mission

Roger inhaled deeply. "Is this the place, Nat?"

Natalie, his sister, gently touched his shoulder. "4322 West Hickory Road. Are you sure about this?"

"I have to find out," he said, holding his cane in front of him.

"Daddy," said Robyn, "this is weird. I don't wanna go in there. They're gonna think we're crazy."

"Pumpkin, I have to find out. They could be in danger."

The bells sounded inside. Within a minute, the door opened. Robyn's tension faded seeing the two boys about her age. Both had sandy-brown hair. The shorter one had broad shoulders and a nice chest. His bangs were long, partly in his eyes that had a boyish quality, but still showed strength. The other one (maybe his brother?) stood a few inches taller and was skinny, but not lanky like some boys. His face was thinner than the other boy. His hair, long and thick, parted on the right. She noticed his eyes: more man-like, less round and … dilated. They resembled a blank screen. She noticed a few scars on his face – although they were not heavily distracting. Glancing down at the dog next to him, she gasped. What were the odds? She gasped. "You're blind?"

"I'm blind?" He turned to the other boy. "Hey! Why didn't you tell me I'm blind?" he said while grinning.

Robyn slightly blushed while palming her face. She chuckled for a minute. "I'm sorry for being stupid."

"It's okay," he said. "I'm Jason, this is my cousin,

Justin. He's stupid – but not sorry at all."

Robyn's dad interrupted their laughter. "I'm Roger Paden, I'm a 911 operator and I took your parents' call two nights ago. Are they home? Can I talk to them?"

Jason took the lead. "Aunt Janie, someone's at the door." Within a few seconds, she appeared. "This is the 911 operator Uncle Dan spoke with the other night, Roger Paden. That's his daughter and this is ..."

"I'm his sister, Natalie."

Janie's perplexed look beamed into a wide smile, although Robyn found it a bit phony. Her eyes were a unique shade of blue, and her short hair was somewhere between brown and blonde.

"Oh, thank-you so much," Janie said nervously. "I must admit being embarrassed by the whole situation. We are so sorry. I hope we are not in trouble since the police could not find any evidence of an intruder. And my husband panicked and shot three holes into our ceiling." She let out a quick laugh. "Oh, please come in." She turned her head, "Dan! We have company!" Turning back to Roger, Natalie and Robyn, Janie used a smile again – except it was used like a mask to hide her discomfort. Uneasy, she waited for Dan to enter.

Dan walked into the living room, looking tired and distracted. "Dear – this is Roger Paden, his sister, Natalie, and his daughter, Robyn. Roger was the 911 operator you spoke with the other night."

Dan started, looking as if he had a headache, or was walking in a brain fog. His head swiveled back and forth a few times. After rubbing his eyes, he sat, coughed, and rubbed his head. "I'm sorry," he whispered, "I'm not feeling too well." After rubbing his temples, he looked at the operator and for the first time realized he was blind. The cane was obvious enough, but he fixated on the dark sunglasses. More awake and focused, he leaned forward. "What brings you here? We aren't in trouble with 911 – are we?"

"I know there was someone walking outside in the hallway," said Justin. His more boyish tone emphasized the fear. "It was like someone marching up and down the hall. I heard the boards squeak and moan."

"I heard it, too," Jason interjected after Justin. "I promise you we are not making this up. My dog, Samson, was spooked. He was barking and-"

Roger raised his right hand over the cane, "Wait, I'm not accusing you of anything like that. If 911 was going to press charges, the city would send detectives and police – and from what I understand, there is no history of your household using the 911 system. I am here because I have another concern. And it's ... going to shock you. I really don't know how to approach this, but I hope you will listen and have an open mind. But before that – I do have a few questions. First, can you explain what happened?"

Dan recounted the story, somehow getting through his brain fog. "We were feeling very spooked that night – kinda like you know something's going to happen, but you're unsure what. Or waiting for that jab of pain from the dentist injecting the needle in your gums. I kept staring at the mirror, for minutes on end ..."

"It was almost an hour, hon."

Dan turned to Janie. "That long?"

"Yes."

Dan turned back to Roger. "Anyway, we went to bed. I had trouble sleeping at first. I've been overwhelmed lately. A few months ago, my twin brother died in Sao Paulo – along with my sister-in-law and my other nephew. We took

Do You Hear What I Hear?

Jason in – as in my brother's will. Something you put on paper you never think would happen until it does. As you can see Jason's blind now and it's up to my wife and I to take care of him, see to his new special needs and ..." Dan sighed and shut his eyes for a quick second. "It's hard to adjust. All our lives were upended. But, back to the story: I had finally fallen asleep and then I heard a loud banging. When I woke up, I heard loud footsteps. My son and nephew texted me, and that's when I called you."

"I relistened to the call," he said after emitting a few dry coughs. "First, I am curious if you can describe what you saw?"

"It was ..." he thought hard as if the memory was difficult to grasp. "It looked like a man not fully there. Partially. Maybe like a blurred photo with a ... greenish haze. I remember he looked at me and – then he cast this creepy sneer. That's when I fired my gun."

"Can you and your wife lead me upstairs? I'd like to get a feel for the area and maybe explore some possibilities. Natalie, I might need your help." As he stood, he turned to his daughter. "Robyn, pumpkin, stay down here with the boys."

***

As the adults walked up the stairs, Justin poked Jason with his elbow. "She's beautiful and smokin' hot," whispered Justin. "You be my wingman."

Justin moved next to Robyn. "They could be upstairs for a long time. Time enough for ... "

What was his shithead cousin doing? It sounded like he tried to take her hand, but perhaps she yanked it away from him. It was followed by the sound of a hit. "Get away from me you sleaze. And don't you be touching me, or I'll nail you in your balls to the floor before you'll know what they're good for."

Jason failed to hide his grin, liking how Robyn could put Justin in his place.

Justin, undeterred, tried his incredibly phony apology. "I'm so sorry. Can I take your coat? Your sweater? Your bra?"

Jason, irritated, raised his cane sharply in front of Justin's face. "Justin – shut-up, stop being rude, or my cane goes down your throat until it pokes through your asshole."

"I'm only kidding," he whined. "Can't you take a joke?"

Jason wondered if his cousin had been looking at computer porn too much. However, Jason realized he missed looking at hot, naked girls: their breasts, legs, butts were magnets for his eyes when he could see. Maybe going blind was better for him in that regard. "It's not a joke to be rude so shut up." At this time, he really missed Jimmy. He would be a little obnoxious, but not so rude and insensitive. Jimmy always backed off when Jason was talking to a girl and left them alone. Sighing, Jason shook his head. "Now, get out of here so we can talk. And if I hear you again or if Robyn tells me you're listening and watching, I'm going to sic Samson on you."

Justin sighed and moved up the stairs. He whispered, but Jason heard it. "Jason and Robyn sittin' in a tree…"

Jason sat on the couch. Robyn sat next to him. Embarrassed, shaking his head, he sighed. "My shithead cousin is so retarded. I'm really sorry."

"It's okay," she said while clasping his shoulder. "He's kinda cute, but too bad his personality kills everything. But don't worry, I know where to kick the little runt."

Jason enjoyed the clasp on his shoulder, so much so he

smiled. "He'd probably see that as a come-on. It's like all the blood in his brain rushed to his ..." he stopped himself from saying "dick" to her. The last thing he wanted to do was upset her. Fortunately, Robyn laughed – something Jason liked hearing. Her voice was soft and soothing. For a girl, her voice was low, but not manly. He didn't like girls who talked with a high pitch because it sounded as if they were pretending to be dumb. Where do girls get the idea boys like dumb girls? He wanted to reach out to her but did not want to invade her privacy – and he had a slight fear of her father. Jason wondered about the color of her eyes, her hair, and her skin. Was it pale for someone who was inside, or slightly tanned like a girl who enjoys the sun? How was her nose shaped – as well as her eyes? Justin did say she was beautiful.

"Wow! I love this house," she said looking around. She stood up, pulled him up by the hands and twirled. "This living room is so large. I love the echoes and the carpeting and the decorations."

Jason grabbed his cane and used it to point at the fireplace. "Okay, this reddish-brownish stone was cut ten years ago, and it took six months to get it right for the stacking. The masonry took another six months and the chimney itself is 25 feet tall. The lights in the ceiling in front of it have to be changed with a long pole that only my uncle knows how to use."

He pointed to the couch. "This plush, brown couch was custom-made and cost $5,000. The rug underneath us was hand-made and has the emblems of 25 Indian Tribes of Northeast America." Taking a few steps forward, he pointed to the chairs. "These four chairs in a semi-circle were purchased by my Aunt Janie at the JC Penney's home store on clearance for only $200. She always brags about that deal. We have that island a few feet back which is the partial barrier to the kitchen. I helped Dad and Uncle Dan put in that really fancy tile about five years ago. We also helped install those granite counters."

"It's like you can still see."

"In my head, I can." He pointed to the left to the large TV screen fastened to the stucco wall that had a shade of light brown. "And my uncle and dad had us watch a bunch of cool movies like old black-and-white monsters like Dracula, Frankenstein, and the Wolfman. Aunt Janie and Mom could never stomach those old movies."

"Where does that go, to – the backyard?"

The hallway between the kitchen and the TV wall was set at a 45-degree angle. "Again, Justin, Jimmy, Dad and Uncle Dan and me all installed that wooden floor. God, that was fun. It didn't seem like it at the time. That's the dinette," he said pointing to the tables. "And yes, that's the backyard where we all shot baskets and tossed the football and baseball around." His smile abruptly stopped. His chin dropped. "I really miss those fun things." His eyes shut for some reason. Maybe to indicate his sadness? Was he still grieving? "I miss playing ball, watching those movies, looking at all the sad Indian paintings, and sitting outside in the back looking at the cool colors of the trees during fall." He sighed. "I'm sorry, I should be talking to someone else about it – like my therapist."

"It's okay," she whispered. "Let it out."

Although feeling sad, he somehow smiled. He had not really talked about stuff like this with his aunt and uncle. Why was he telling someone he met a few minutes ago? They barely knew each other. "Thanks for listening. I've talked to Justin about some things, but he often has to make some sort of joke. Jimmy could listen without doing that. I really miss him."

"Who's Jimmy?"

Jason hesitated but told the story quickly to prevent him from hurting too much. "My twin-brother. He died in Sao Paulo – along with Mom and Dad. It was in a car wreck. That's how I lost my sight. Sometimes I wish I had died with them. I cannot understand why I lived. Or why I had to go blind." Embarrassed, his fingers wiped a few tears away.

She clasped his elbow. Her hand slid down his forearm and her fingers gently clasped his hand. Her touch felt wonderful as Robyn's skin was soft and warm – triggering a smile.

Something sweet resonated in the air. Catching a whiff, he found particles emanating a pumpkin like odor. How did that work? With the hairs in his nose? Or through something else in his olfactory senses? Sometimes smells warned him if food was bad, or if cleanliness was lacking. Of course, smelling things like shit would warn him of possible diseases. Aromas enticed him to delicious food. Others warned him of gas leaks from a propane grill or a gas-powered unit. However, at this moment, he focused on that perfume … and the soap she used, along with the shampoo on her hair.

"So that's why your dad calls you 'Pumpkin.' Because of your perfume?"

"No – I wear pumpkin scented perfume because he calls me 'Pumpkin.'" She giggled quietly.

"I really like your laugh."

"You're really cute."

His smile widened more. Then it faded, remembering he

had no idea what she looked like. Justin said she was pretty, but Jason wanted verification. At the same time, he felt drawn to her. For some reason, he felt as if he could talk to her about anything and she would just listen. He shrank back, hoping she wouldn't notice a bulge in his pants. Weird. He had not even thought about sex and his body had this biological reaction. Why was that? Instinct? Or just the thought that someone finds you attractive?

She gently tugged his hands to lead him back to the couch. "So how long ago did all this happen?" she asked.

His exuberance faded – or rather changed to sadness. "A little more than three months ago." He could not tell if the sadness changed to confusion, or if both emotions battled for dominance at that precise moment. "I just can't remember … what happened in the house, or why Dad was driving us away that late at night? Or … I don't know. I just wish I could remember."

"It's probably best you don't,"

"Maybe." He wanted to shift attention away from his sadness. "So, how'd your dad go blind?"

"In the line of duty. Daddy was on the fire department. His station was working a car wreck, then another drunk driver hit them." Her voice faded. "The crash made Daddy blind, hurt another firefighter, and killed Uncle Ronnie."

Jason's mouth dropped open. "Your uncle was killed?"

Robyn hesitated. Was she crying? "He was Dad's best friend – so he was an adopted uncle."

"That was six years ago. But he refused to be a victim and went from Fire and EMS to 911 operator."

"What about your mom? She didn't leave him because of the accident, right?"

She let loose a sigh laced with pain. He sensed her

mouth frowned by the voice – which slightly faded. "She died when I was five. She had pancreatic cancer." Robyn remained quiet for a moment. "So, we've been through a lot. Aunt Natalie, that's Daddy's sister, was going through a divorce and decided to move in with us to help take care of him after he went blind. She and Lucas are great."

"Who's Lucas?"

"My little cousin. He's ten. He's with his dad right now."

"Oh." He hesitated for a second. "I'm sorry your family's gone through so much."

Her voice sprang with life. "Daddy is a rock. He learned about Stoicism in college. He's always talking about it and how we have to be resilient and realize that terrible things will happen and that you have to take control of the things you have in your control." She giggled again. "Are you like that? Strong, resilient, and able to take control of your mind and emotions?

His smile faded. "I don't know. I sure hope so." He thought about telling her how he sometimes will find a place to hide and just cry – like he did at church recently. No. That was his secret – the one he wanted to keep to himself.

***

Roger trudged up the stairs while listening to Dan and Janie talking. His right hand alternated between using the railing and the wall as a guide up the stairs while his left hand held onto Natalie. He prepared for the standard questions: "How did you go blind?" "How long ago was that?" However, he was surprised to hear one he never considered: "Can you give a man and his wife any tips on raising a nephew who recently went blind?"

"All I can say is give him time and space. Remind him

to take control over the things he has control over: his emotions, his actions, and reactions, and remind him there is still a world he can experience. He still has his remaining five senses and teach him to use his insightful sense."

"You mean four other senses, right?" suggested Dan. "Unless I'm missing one."

"Ears also provide our sense of balance. And there is emotional sensitivity. That is picking up on people around you and how they feel. For example, I can sense you two have relaxed about me and accepted me. And I could sense a little fear and uneasiness in your wife when I told her who I was."

"And remind him he has people who love and care for him," said Natalie. "Just like Robyn, my son, Lucas, and myself all care for Roger. But don't do too much for him – or that will cripple him. Has your nephew tried to use his blindness to get out of some things yet?"

"Not yet," said Janie. "But I'm sure we will see it eventually."

"Don't let him," said Natalie. "It's very common in people who go blind, although Roger never did that."

Reaching the top of the stairwell, Roger let go of Natalie's hand and unfolded his cane and used it as his guide. A vibration emanated from the door on his right. His fingers pressed on it, feeling a heavy cold. It slithered through pores, his skin, then dug into his muscles, tendons, and bone. Something tried to push him away. He cringed at a fetid stench. Strange whispers tickled his ears, leaving an empty thud resonating in his mind. The rhythm pounded like a heartbeat. All the sensations coalesced into one force. He took a deep breath. "Whose room is this?"

"That's our nephew's. Jason."

Roger pushed the door open. The dead stillness of the air had a slight smell. It was not of sweat or dirty clothes, or uneaten, molding pizza – but more like a carrion stench of dead rodents. "Do you all smell that?" he asked.

"I don't," said Dan "-do you, hon?"

"Nothing."

"I can't smell anything," added Natalie, "-but Roger's sense is very heightened."

Roger shushed them as he moved closer to the smell. His cane met the wall – or the corner of the room. Sniffing, he noticed the odor becoming a bit stronger. It reminded him of working an EMS call where the patient had a GI bleed that mixed with his bowels. The smell caused his whole body to wretch and back away. Breathing through his mouth did not help – and it triggered his gag reflex. His eyes watered. "Do you all smell that?"

Footsteps moved backwards. They all grunted, coughed, and gagged. "What the hell is that?" asked Dan.

"Oh my God! That's disgusting." added Janie.

Natalie pulled his arm. "Roger, I can't stand it. Let's get out of here."

Unable to tolerate the rancid stench, he conceded and followed Natalie. "Oh, God – that is bad." He retreated hastily. "Let's visit your son's room."

"This way, please," said Dan.

While their footsteps lead the way, the firefighter traced the wall with his hand, feeling the textured drywall. He tried to listen for any supernatural voices as the couple and Natalie remained quiet. He heard the door open. Inside, Roger swiveled his head back and forth trying to hear something – anything. His ears only found the couple's light breathing, along with the slight swaying and minute steps on the rich, thick, wooden floor.

His elbow bumped into the door frame. Even 15 to 20 feet away, he could still smell traces of the reeking odor. Turning, Roger stepped into what seemed to be the bathroom. Footsteps echoed slightly – until his foot stepped on a slightly crumpled towel. His hands dropped to the marble sink. Imagining a mirror in front of him, he remained quiet and recalled his own vision in the mirror for a split second. It had been too long, and he could not hold onto the memorial images in his mind. He had forgotten over time what he looked like – as well as Robyn, Natalie, and his wife. It was strange, though, he had never seen his nephew, Lucas – nor the people he was with right now.

In the bathroom, the presence felt stronger, leaving a trace of trepidation and uncertainty. Or was it despair? Unable to truly feel it, Roger could not tell. It seemed like angry, fearful eyes examined him, burning holes in his skin. Pores opened, and the hair on the back of his neck stood as if static electricity stiffened them. "Do any of you feel anything? Uneasiness, fear, or maybe …"

"Cold," said Janie. "It's suddenly very cold in here."

"I feel it, too," added Natalie.

"I feel as if we're being watched. It's been happening more lately," said Dan. "Mostly in my room."

"I get that sense, too," said Janie. "It's like someone is always watching me. I can't stop thinking about … something that happened a long time ago." Her voice trailed into a sob. "I'm edgy, cold, I can't stop wondering what's happening to my son, my nephew and…I can't talk to my husband." Janie cried.

Dan took a step towards her. "What? How could you mean that? I'm still the same person. Nothing's happening to me. I'm fine. I'm just worried like you."

Her voice immediately overlapped as she let the frustration through. "Dan you won't stop staring at that mirror. It's like you're hypnotized or something. Last night, you looked at that damn thing for nearly 30 minutes, zoned out. You barely look at me, or talk to me, and I feel alone. I ask you a question and you barely glance at me or ignore me altogether. Sometimes, you look like … you want to hurt me." Sobs distorted her last words. They returned like a group of firecrackers igniting. "What the hell is wrong with you?"

"Honey," Dan gasped as if he did not know what to say. "I'm sorry. I know you're edgy and so am I – but we gotta keep together. You have to believe me that I will not hurt you."

Roger felt uncomfortable. He didn't like being around married couples breaking down or fighting. Thinking about Heather, he sighed. The void in his heart dropped into a bottomless pit, hollowing him out. He recalled the day she died in the hospital in front of him. As a paramedic, he had to fight the instinct to render care: chest compressions, intubation, and an IV to push in epinephrine.

Dan and Janie's voices faded. Did Natalie try to say something to him?

Roger clenched his eyes shut to find that strength in himself, and he tried to think of Jesus on the Cross. Praying for a sap of strength, something surged in him. He took a deep breath as a cool, refreshing rush of air filled every limb, nerve ending, bone, muscle fiber, tendon, and artery. Finding peace, he let out the breath, then inhaled to find a deeper serenity.

"Calm down please," he said softly. "Calm down,

please." His voice remained peaceful, not harsh like many first responders used in emergency situations. Roger never understood why anyone would think yelling "calm down" to someone suffering a gunshot wound, heart-attack, or some other sort of trauma would work. Again, he spoke, finding serenity and authority within his request. "Calm down, please."

Janie and Dan's voices faded. Natalie touched Roger's arm. "I think," he said, "whatever this thing is … is feeding off our stress, and emotional hurts. Take a deep breath. Count to ten and pray. Focus on God … or Budha, Thor, Apollo, or whoever you think is God."

Whispered laughs pushed out the entity. "Can you take me to your bedroom? After that, I might be able to figure something out and help you understand what's going on." Somehow, he sensed their trust and realized they all nodded. "Remember," he said quietly, "if you feel distressed, close your eyes, imagine God, and pray."

Dan and Janie led Roger and Natalie downstairs to the master bedroom. The stagnant air possessed an eerie vibe. Completely still, Roger could not feel any ventilation and caught the whiff of a musty smell. Something dripped on the back of his neck. Something grabbed his wrist and pulled tightly. His arm stretched as a brute force locked his shoulder in place. Stretched to the max, Dan's grunts turned to bellows. Something howled at him. The noise was so loud and horrific, it made him wretch. The stink spread over his face. The entity let go and pushed him to the floor. "Shit. Shit. Oh, fuck. This hurts."

"Roger!" Natalie's desperate voice stretched as she dropped to the floor next to him – rubbing his guarded shoulder. "What happened? Are you hurt? How bad is it?"

Do You Hear What I Hear?

Again, he alternated with grunts, and curses. Desperate, he clutched Natalie's hand, hoping it would soothe the bubbling anxiety in his chest. "Nat," did you hear that? Do you hear what I hear?"

She stammered. "I didn't hear anything." He heard her cry. "I just saw you being attacked ... by nothing." Natalie hugged him while crying.

Roger's head turned towards the couple huffing to his right. "Did you two hear that?"

"Mr. Paden, we didn't hear anything, either."

Although sore and tired, he used his cane to regain his footing. "I'm sorry to ... scare you – but I think this is worse than I thought. Worse than ... 'The Last Jedi.'" He slightly laughed, lamenting that it was the last Star Wars movie he saw before his accident. He wondered if they would agree – or get the joke. Despite a short laugh, Roger's hand clutched his chest, hoping to calm its agitation.

"Over here."

Roger heard the whisper.

"Over here."

It was first to the left – then shifted to the right – and returned to the left.

"Over here."

Confused, Roger shifted his head position to isolate the sound. "Everyone – do you hear that?"

Although stymied, whispered "nos" surrounded him.

"Roger ..." Natalie's voice cracked. "It's looking right at me."

Dan and Janie's rapid breaths exploded. Janie whispered. "I ... see ... I see it, too."

"Me, too," Dan said between shaking breaths.

"What is it?"

Natalie's stammering breath hindered her voice. "It's in ... it's in the ... mirror."

Roger listened. He sniffed, catching the whiff of something hideously disgusting. He flinched and took a step back. "Nat, do you smell that?" No response. "Nat." An uneasy quiet fell over him. Malevolent eyes glared at him, circling him. Roger turned around two, maybe three times. Cold, his hair stood erect. It felt like a subtle surge of electricity during a dry winter day that shocks the fingers when they touch a light switch. "Natalie – can you hear me?"

He heard her gasp – along with Dan and Janie. The three breaths tore the presence away. Or did it just decide to leave? Unsure, he reached for Natalie. She wasn't there. A hand fell on his shoulder. "Natalie? Dan? Janie?"

Dan, Janie, and Natalie all yelled as the hand on Roger's shoulder grabbed him. The touch felt like cold, rotting flesh. Talons burrowed deep into his skin as the grip squeezed. He yelled as pain erupted from the touch. The stabbing pain resonated from his shoulder, his upper arm, and traveled to his right hand. It also delivered a burning sensation that pierced his skin. Falling to his knees, Roger instinctively tried to pry the invisible grip but found nothing solid to touch. In that second, an overwhelming sense of dread surrounded him and contracted. Finding no retreat or solace, an explosive fear surged. Fear quickly followed.

All the elements: fear, dread, chills, and pain were vanquished in a second. Roger, wincing from the pain, felt a serene calm. He heard them: Dan and Janie, and even Natalie had joined them.

"...hallowed be Thy name. Thy kingdom come, thy will be done, on Earth as it is in Heaven. Give us this day our daily bread ..."

Do You Hear What I Hear?

Roger joined them to finish the prayer.

Immunity

Roger grunted as his sister pulled his shirt over his shoulder. The deadening pain vibrated in his shoulder blade and shot down his arm to his biceps. It seemed worse, settling near the underside of his forearm near the elbow. Another pain stung and stabbed at the same time – comparable to when a patient high on PCP stabbed him with a switchblade. Hot blood seemed to bubble and seep through the gashes. His soul, though, took the worst beating. It felt cold, as if ice crept from the inside-out.

"Roger, are you okay?"

"Quit asking me that. For the umpteenth time – I'm okay." He instantly regretted the snap at his sister. A few deep breaths released his anxiety, although the fading pain still remained. Gently, he clasped Natalie's hand. "I'm sorry, sis. It scared the hell out of me more than anything."

"What was it? Do you know what it is? What can we do?" The desperate voices of Janie and Dan overlapped with each other as the questions flew. "Can you help us? Should we move? How do we fight something like this?"

Roger put up his hand. "Whoa – guys. I'm not an expert. I just have the hearing to help me. A lot of this is guesswork. Theories. Hunches. Trust me it's like finding your way around in the … dark." He smirked at this choice of words. Immediately, his seriousness returned. He stood, turned towards them, and shook his head. "Moving, I seriously doubt, will help. Often, stuff like this is attached to someone in the home. Have any of you experienced a traumatic event or been traveling lately?"

"I have."

Roger turned towards the young voice. It seemed stuck between being a boy and a man – and right now it sounded more like a frightened, unsure, quavering child. He tried to imagine the boy's face: sadness and fear likely filled his blinded eyes.

Recalling his own trauma and loss of sight, he compared the two journeys. The biggest difference was a grown man like him had already dealt with adversity and suffering: witnessing terrible tragedies both from fire, disease, and blunt trauma and watching adults, children, and even his own wife die. On the other hand, this boy had been thrust into darkness and lost his closest family members instantly. He did not have the maturity, adversity, or strength to deal with such dramatic change.

Standing in front of the voice he heard – Dan used the last location of the boy's voice to reach out. Natalie guided one hand, while Robyn guided the other to Jason's shoulders. He heard Jason sniff, and Roger smelled the boy's tears.

"I try not to think about it," said Jason, "but it's all I can think of." His quick gasp helped the boy regain his composure. "I can't see anymore. I can't do the things I once loved to do. My mom and dad are gone – and I really miss my brother. I want my life back."

"That's not going to happen," Roger said in a whisper. "I know it hurts like nothing else, but you have to take your life back. And people telling you to 'get tough' or 'move on,' is going to piss you off to no end. They don't know what it's like to experience what you're going through. And I have some bad news for you: your world will get darker. Soon, the images in your dreams will dim and eventually disappear. Then you're faced with the darkness in yourself. Just don't shut off the people around you." Roger hugged the boy tightly.

Jason

Jason pulled him tighter than anyone else over the last couple of months. He felt a deep connection with the stranger who had keen insight and understood the difficult adjustment. Sure, physically Jason was able to navigate in the dark, but emotionally, Jason felt overwhelmed. It was like being knocked off the surfboard and swallowing a mouthful of seawater as a wave rolled over him. This was not a therapist – but a person with almost the exact same journey. He was on the same path and suffered the same losses as he did.

"I want to know why. What's the reason for this?"

"I hate to tell you this," said Roger, "but there is no 'why.' It's simply there. We all suffer in some way or another and you're experiencing so much of it right now. All you can do is take control of the things we have control over: our own choices, actions, and reactions – and more importantly, hold onto these wonderful people around you – and hold on tight."

For some reason, Jason felt the words penetrating his soul and soothing his feelings. His sadness retreated first, then his anger, and finally his fear joined the other two. The three emotions were the storm creating a choppy, angry surf that now seemed to flatten. Finding the peace that eluded him for so long, he found contentment. "Thank-you," he whispered.

"Jason," continued Roger, "I need you to understand something right now: something dark may have latched onto you. And these supernatural beings will strike all of us at our weakest points: our prejudice, hatred, fear, sadness, and anger. They will exploit you and your family to no end. Can you tell me what happened in Brazil?"

It seemed as if a light penetrated Jason. Although he could not see physically, the light grew inside his mind. Lighting up corners subtly, it was not too much to reveal everything at once. It shined like a small flashlight, going over those dark corners. In one area – he saw Mom. His memory reconstructed her face in the shadows as a cold breath misted out her mouth. He heard her crying between pained breaths. He called out to her. "Mom! Mom! Can you hear me?"

"Jason" she gasped, "where are you? I can't see you, but I can hear you." She stuttered.

"Mom – I can't see you in here, either. I can hear you – so walk to my voice."

"I can't. I can't. I can't. I can't do it. It'll see me."

His anemic flashlight swept from left to right, trying to find her silhouette. "Is Dad in here, too?"

Mom's voice stuttered amidst some crying. "Yes, but he … but he …" Her voice broke into sobs.

The flashlight within his mind – perhaps the deepest pit of it – scanned the old, dark place to find Mom. Instead, he found worn, dusty, and old bookshelves lined with aging books. He noticed the titles on the spines: friends, family, 2008, 2009, 2010, 2011, Grandma dying, surfing with Jimmy.

Anticipation jolted within his chest as he caught sight of Mom's silhouette. He knew it was her. Wanting to rush to her, he took several hasty steps.

"No son! Get away. Don't get any closer!"

Desperately wanting a hug, a touch, Jason stood. "Mom? Where's Jimmy? Where's Dad? Are they here?"

"Jason," whispered Mom as she pointed, "it's got your father and brother."

His head turned, following his dim flashlight. It went across some beat-up wooden furniture, metal tables, surgical tools ... and the tattered red flag with the emblem of an eagle, with a tilted, winged cross underneath it. Underneath it, he saw the wet, scaly, rough flesh. Aiming his beam higher, Jason realized it slept against the wall. Its large head, with a medium snout, jagged teeth, and pointed ears. Jason's light outlined the cold, misty breath expelling from its nostrils and mouth. Shocked, Jason could not move. The demon used its wings as padding between its body and the brick wall.

As his faint light dropped, he then saw it: scraggly light-brown hair. Matted, long, it draped across one eye. The visible eye stared ahead, uninterrupted for the longest time. It blinked – and then the mouth twitched.

Startled silent, Jason realized who it was. "Jimmy?"

"Jason ..." Jimmy's voice, rough and weak, hesitated. "Help me. It won't let me go."

"Son ..."

Jason shone the light on Dad who sat next to Jimmy. Both were naked. Something like tendrils had wrapped around them, almost fusing with their skin.

"Son," Dad's voice, although weak, spoke much clearer and with more strength. "Get away. Get away. It's got them, too."

Jason realized the bulbous, rounded pieces of the demon were ... children. Heavy streams dripped out of his eyes without any sobbing. The children deformed, sick, and

Do You Hear What I Hear?

starving, all cried. So full of despair, Jason felt sick.

He wondered how he could help Dad and Jimmy. Taking a few steps forward, he stopped when Dad lifted his maligned arm and whispered angrily. "Son, no. Please don't. It's strong."

"Jason," said Jimmy, "please don't leave me."
Jason took a few more steps until he tripped over something. Hitting the floor, he coughed, causing dust to stir up from the ground. Shivering, he found his flashlight and focused on what he tripped over: a book. He brushed away the cobwebs and dust to find the title: Sao Paulo Trip. Desperate to remember the trauma, he opened it.

A dry, eerie gust of wind blew across his face, blowing the pages over and over and over. Somehow his eyes caught every word, every image, every conversation. He only needed a glimpse as his eyes worked, taking in everything as if downloading files onto a computer. At the same time, Braille indentations spread across all his fingers. Somehow, he understood all of it.

The wind stopped as the book and the shelves disappeared. Standing, his tiny flashlight revealed a standing mirror. He jumped back at the sight of his own reflection. Sighing, he relaxed, then stared deeply at his darkened image.

He heard a whisper to his left. He glanced as it faded.

Looking back at the mirror, he stared at his glowing eyes again.

He heard a whisper to his right. It, too, faded as he looked back at his reflection. He put his hand onto the mirror. It felt cold – although a thin layer of dust provided some insulation.

He screamed as the reflection's hand jumped through

the mirror and grabbed his arm. A biting cold jumped from the icy grip, freezing his fingers, his palm, his wrist from the inside. The cold spread as he tried to pull away. Now it flared with pain – feeling like spikes driven into his skin.

The thing tried to pull him in, but he resisted. It now took a form of its own: huge, disfigured, its scaly skin was decaying into cold dust. The mouth, more like a cavern, had rows of jagged teeth. The deafening scream sprayed a disgusting slobber on his face. Jason kicked, pulled, wondering why he could see all this when he had gone blind just a few months ago. Freeing himself from the grip, he fell backward, and everything went dark.

Do You Hear What I Hear?

Waking Up

"Jason! Jason! Can you hear me?"

Jason tried to sit up, but the ghastly fear had him shaking, cold, and it felt like tiny insect creatures crawled on the inside of his skin. They dug deeper, refusing to stop. Wishing the feeling would leave, he clenched the air above his chest – trying to slow his heart and breathing.

"Calm down." Mr. Paden's voice, calm and collected, soothed him. "That's it. Think of something pleasant – like a nice song, or a touch of a nice warm blanket, or the smell of baked bread – or a hot girl in a bikini."

Jason slightly laughed.

"You had some sort of seizure." Mr. Paden's voice sounded worried. The firefighter's hands danced over Jason's head, face, shoulders, torso, and legs. Mr. Paden talked with Natalie who did the observations. They took his blood pressure. What? Did this guy take his emergency medical kit everywhere he went? Is that what firefighter paramedics and 911 operators do?

"I feel better now." Jason tried to sit up.

"Jason – can you tell us what happened?"

Jason hesitated, trying to process the experience. The darkness, the images of his parents were more than memories or images. The creature's touch, smell, and sight left their impression, causing him to shake. A frightening doubt stirred like a violent whirlpool in his chest. What was in those books he looked at? How did he read it so fast? How did he suddenly remember everything?

Partially sitting up, the memories returned like a heavy tide. "I remember now," he said while standing. "Uncle Dan, I can remember everything: the stay at the house in Sao Paulo, Dad, Mom and Jimmy all in the car." A trace of sadness rushed into a melancholy waterfall. Tears almost lurched through. "Dad was trying to get us away from ... something. It was taking over Jimmy, but none of us knew what it was. And it was after me, and Mom, and Dad." He continued while more tears bubbled from the corner of his eyes. "But I don't know what it was." His eyes burst open – but no light could enter to form a picture. "At night ... I can hear voices. Not just the ... creature after us ... but others. I think the voices are ... Jimmy, Dad, and Mom."

"You're hearing them? How?"

"I don't know, Justin. I just am."

Roger interrupted. "Yes – that's what happened to me. After I went blind, my sense of hearing intensified so much, I could hear supernatural voices – probably ghosts."

"I can't wrap my head around this. The both of you can hear the voices of ghosts and other things?"

"I know it sounds hard to believe – but that is what happened to me and your nephew."

"So that's it," said Janie. "No wonder Samson barks for minutes on end. He can hear it, too."

"Why would a supernatural entity latch onto Jason?" suggested Dan.

"Why would it follow him? What does it want?" asked Justin.

"Whoa – parents, kids," said Roger, "that's the problem with this type of stuff. We have no idea, and it's hard to figure out these things – much like why people like pineapple on pizza. Like I said earlier, all this supernatural stuff is pure guesswork. One guess I have is that from what you all have been telling me is that it's using mirrors as its portal to go back and forth between our physical world and its metaphysical world. It's also using them to wear you out psychologically – mostly with Dan, Janie, and Justin staring at the mirror for minutes on end. As for me and your nephew, being blind, we might be immune to possession – if that's what this thing is doing."

"Why don't we smash the mirrors or at least throw them out so none of us can ever look at them again?" asked Justin.

"That doesn't solve the real problem," said Roger. "We need to destroy this entity – not trap it. Besides, there are so many things that create reflections: the screen on a TV, eyeglasses, and windows." Everyone got quiet for a moment. "Also, this is pure guesswork on my part. I could be totally wrong."

A stifled laugh partially escaped Dan's mouth. "I can't believe this. All my life I've been training a rational mind that uses logic and science – but here I am entertaining this idea. It's too …" He paused, apparently searching for the correct words. "Paradoxical. I want a straight answer instead of a theory. I … want to believe this. But it's hard. Very difficult. But I feel so goddamned scared I don't know what to do." Dan almost cried. "I want to protect my family – but I can't against this thing. I feel so helpless, overwhelmed and … **angry** … at this thing for killing my brother and sister-in-law and nephew." His whispers hit hard, as if trying to strike at the supernatural enemy. He inhaled deeply to prevent himself from crying.

Janie cried – almost sobbing. She wrapped her arms tightly around her husband. He pulled her tightly and kissed her on the forehead. He whispered. "I'm so sorry, baby. I don't know how to protect you and the boys."

"I think it's best," said Roger, "that you all at least get out of the house and do something normal – like go out to eat or see a movie or something like that. At least you'll get your mind off it while I contact my friends and do some digging so we can try some things."

"You said moving wouldn't help," added Janie.

"I didn't say to move, I suggested just getting out of the house for a while and try to do something else to get your mind off of it."

Dan sighed. "That's the best advice anyone has offered lately. Let's do it."

***

Jason and Robyn walked along the sidewalk. He noticed the scent of her perfume. It was sweet without being overwhelming. Mom complained that guys often wear too much after-shave, but Jason thought some girls wore too much perfume. He never realized how sensual a scent could be. All his life, he relied on his eyes to gauge a girl's beauty. He tried to imagine what she looked like.

"They're some outdoor tables and benches over here," she said while taking his empty hand and guiding him.

Her thumb quickly traced his palm. Unsure, but adventurous, his thumb traced her soft palm, and he slid his fingers between hers, interlocking them tightly. He smiled, wondering if she also grinned. Her fingers were thin, but warm – with just a little extra fingernail instead of the fake ones some girls liked to use. He followed her, listening to her voice, somehow weeding out all the noise of pedestrians, traffic, and various birds.

It was strange how they met just two days ago. It was strange that her dad was blind, too. Jason felt as if he could talk to her about anything. She listened to him intently but did not treat him any differently to any other guy – except that he was blind. He sensed that she found him attractive.

Uncle Dan, Aunt Janie, and Justin were eating at a burger joint, but Jason did not care for those. Toasted subs were his favorite – and he conned Robyn into going with him. That was the best part, he could be alone with her instead of having Justin act like a shithead around her.

After sitting at the table, he used his finger to locate the sandwich and unwrap it. He found his potato chips. His hands found the cold plastic bottle of Pepsi – at least he hoped it was. For some reason, Justin found it amusing to get a bottle of Dr. Pepper because Jason hated that taste. Justin sometimes treated everything like a joke too much. Of course, he could be the only one to get away with crap like that – or Jimmy could – if he was alive. However, he somehow knew Robyn would never do anything like that.

"You seemed to have adjusted to all this so well. Dad got therapy, and he also got involved with a group of people who went blind because of trauma. Do you do anything like that?"

"I started seeing a therapist – or rather he sees me. But it just got going a short time ago. I don't know how it's going to help me. A few of the kids at school went blind by disease or injury. But, at school we don't talk much about it."

"What about Justin? Do you talk to him? Or your aunt or uncle?"

"Yeah. I talk with Justin. Sometimes he listens well, but … too many things are a joke to him. I try to laugh, but … sometimes it makes me mad – and I just want to punch him." Jason grinned. "However, you know what Justin did a couple Saturdays ago? He went all day with a blindfold to try and get an idea of what life was like for me." A laugh emanated from his throat. "Sometimes he's really annoying and jokes too much – but I appreciated that. He fell a couple of times and hit the walls several times." This time, his laugh came through his mouth.

"Uncle Dan and Aunt Janie … well it seems like they don't know what to do or say. Know what I mean? It's like …" he searched for the right words to say. However, unsure of what to say, he hesitated. "It's like they're blind, too."

"They are," Robyn said quietly. "They don't know anything about taking care of a blind kid. Now you're different from them. Not a stranger, but just … different from them because you can't see. You also lost your family. They don't know that kind of pain – except, maybe, your uncle."

"I keep forgetting he lost his twin brother, too." Jason sighed. Pivoting his head towards Robyn's voice, he imagined being able to see her. "If I tell you something, can you promise to not say anything?"

"Sure."

He wasn't sure, hesitating before he answered. It longed to burst out and find ears that would listen to the confession he hid from Uncle Dan, Aunt Janie, and Justin. "Sometimes … I'll cry myself to sleep at night. A few times, by myself, I've gone to St. Thomas' Cathedral. It's where we got to Church. I go into the prayer room by myself and cry for an hour or so. Or I hide in the room down the hall from my room and cry." He wept a bit. "I can't stop. I want it to stop, but I miss them so much. And I miss being able to see. And it just hurts. I can't describe it, but it hurts." The last part of his words was lost in his sobs.

Her arms wrapped around him. The hug felt satisfying.

Do You Hear What I Hear?

Warm, it dispelled the cold that resonated in his chest over the last few months. He hugged her back, tight enough to show his vulnerability, but not too tight to hurt her. The emotions purged out again. He wondered if they would ever stop. Robyn's palms rubbed his back, and she whispered. "I'm so sorry. I don't know what to say. All I can do is listen."

The emotions waned, going back into hiding to gather strength. They rested just to rise again like the tide of the ocean. He wanted them to stay away. He didn't want to feel anything: no anger, regret, fear, or sadness. Jason wanted to go numb and avoid the pain at all costs.

"Tell me…" said Robyn, "what was Jimmy like?"

He smiled as his brother's image flashed through his mind. As usual, the image of Jimmy was a mischievous smirk. "Jimmy – he, uh … was a jokester like Justin. He once separated a few Oreo cookies, carefully scraped off the cream, and replaced it with mayonnaise and tricked me into eating it." He laughed. "I wanted to kill him. He was also the daring one – wanting to do crazy stunts off the trampoline or race a bike to jump a ditch. He got me in a lot of trouble. A few times, we would try to trick our teachers by going to each other's classes. Mom and Dad figured it out easily when we tried it on them. I really miss him more than anyone." He took a few bites of his sandwich.

"What was your dad like?"

He hesitated, finally letting some painful loss show. "Imagine Captain America from the Marvel Movies – and that's my dad. He was always trying to do the right thing and knew the right thing to do – like Cap. So, he was strong and could stand up to people like bullies or cheaters or jerks without being an asshole." He took a few bites of his sandwich and another sip of his drink. "And I know it sounds cheesy and corny, but that's the kind of guy I wanna be: tough and strong, knowing the right thing to do." He sighed, thinking about Dad's voice, what he looked like and his character. He smiled for a brief second, imagining Dad's face. At least the memories survived. They were still visual within his brain, but they had faded a bit. "I guess I never realized that – and how much I miss him – since the accident."

Robyn ate, too, and somehow let out another question. "What was your mom like?"

That answer came easily: "A worrier. She had to remind Jimmy and me about everything like 'wear your coat,' 'be careful,' or 'don't lie.' Like we needed that? She was also the one to embarrass us the most." His smile widened. "Just last year, Jimmy, Justin and I were playing basketball along with a couple of friends, and this girl named Sarah came by and started flirting with us. Mom saw us when she was bringing out lemonade. I don't think she liked the way Sarah was acting. Anyway, we decided to head over to Russo's to have some pizza and Mom quickly said, 'Now boys – be polite, be a gentleman – and **keep** your **dick** in your pants.'" Jason felt his skin blush. "Jimmy and I were so embarrassed – but our friends thought she was cool because she wasn't afraid to say 'dick' in front of us."

Robyn laughed hard for a minute. He liked hearing that laugh. It went on for a bit longer, exhausting her. Robyn sighed to catch her breath – as if the laughing was a physical workout.

She touched Jason's elbow and pulled him forward. "Last year, a boy named Ricky was taking me out to a dance. Aunt Natalie drove the car to get him, but Daddy rode with us. He made me sit in the front next to Aunt Nat, while he sat in the backseat with Ricky. Then, Daddy told him 'son, you better control your hormones while you're with my daughter'" she imitated her dad's voice, "'or I'll control them through surgery.'" She let loose some laughter before finishing. "Oh, how I wanted to kill him."

"Mom was also a Grammar Nazi," added Jason. "She was quick to correct our use of 'good' and 'well,' and the one thing she hated more than anything was when Jimmy or I ended a sentence with a preposition. Sometimes Jimmy and I would do it on purpose to piss her off." Jason remembered Robyn didn't have a mother, either. "What do you miss about your mom?"

Her abrupt silence and lack of emotion startled him. Was that too sensitive a question? He hoped she didn't hate him.

Robyn inhaled and hesitated. "She died so long ago . . . and I was so young ... sometimes I have trouble remembering her."

Guessing that her face looked down, he got quiet. He hoped to remember Mom and Dad well enough in the future. The thought of their images fading with time within his brain scared him enough. He felt it more with Jimmy.

Jason felt her move closer. Not just by the pumpkin-like perfume, but also by the warmth of her body. Instinctively reaching for her, his fingers brushed the top of her forearm. He took a gentle hold of it, followed it to her hands, then clutched her fingers. At least you're not ..."

"Don't say it." Her sharp words startled him – however he relaxed as Robyn sighed. "I may not be blind, nor know what it's like – but I've been taking care of Daddy for six years – and he's never been a victim. He didn't wallow in misery and depression. He didn't wait for someone to give his life back. He took it back." Her voice softened, giving him permission to move closer. "And you're going to do the same."

He sensed her smile – which softened the blow of her words. He appreciated her hand clutching his tightly. After being quiet for a moment, gathering his thoughts, Jason nodded. "Thanks. I ... don't think ... I've heard that from anyone else. I guess that's what ... I needed to hear."

"Trust me, hearing is what you do best. Daddy quotes this guy named Soren Kierkegaard a lot – and the one he uses quite a bit is 'the ear is the most spiritually attuned instrument.'"

Jason thought about it for a few seconds. Realizing his face contorted to a puzzled look, he verbalized his muddled thoughts. "What the hell does that mean?"

"I have to admit it," her laughter broke up her conversation, "but I'm not too sure, either."

After the short burst of laughter faded, Jason wanted to ask the one question burning in his mind the last couple of months. "Robyn ... am I ... ugly? I mean ... the scars ..."

"No! Not at all."

Hearing her soft answer immediately brought relief to his heart. Her voice sounded as if she smiled. Her hand spread over the left side of his face and gently took off his glasses. He cringed for a second, wanting to object. What was she up to? Breathing nervously, he hoped she didn't notice the bulge in his pants.

"Your face is so handsome." She traced his left ear and the left side of his nose. "The scars do not distract from your looks at all."

"Thanks." Hesitating, Jason did not know what to say.

Do You Hear What I Hear?

Often, thoughts poured into his head he needed to verbalize. Now, though, too many competed for his attention. Not knowing which emotion or thought to focus on, he merely smiled. "I wish I knew what you look like." He hoped she wouldn't get mad at him for that comment.

"I'll have you know I'm very beautiful and incredibly sexy."

He laughed. Robyn's voice was a lower pitch than most girls, and it had a slight rasp. Those features made her sexy to him. Their laughing mood died, not becoming awkward but rather quietly peaceful.

Something tickled his ears, calling out to him. Was it Uncle Dan, Aunt Janie, or Justin's voices finding their way through the traffic noise? His head turned right trying to pinpoint it, then turned left as if in search of a clearer channel.

"What is it?"

"I can hear the voices again."

He stood, turned, unfolded his cane, and waved it back and forth with Robyn next to him.

"What's going on?" she asked.

"Shh!" He had trouble hearing the whispers because of the traffic.

"Wait." Robyn pulled his arm to keep him from moving. "It's a crosswalk. Let me …"

Did she press the 'walk' button? Apparently so. Within a minute, not only did the traffic noise cease, but Jason also heard the "chirp" noise, indicating he could cross the street. After reaching the other side, he continued forward to the whispers that grew louder.

"Wait!" yelled Robyn.

Samson barked.

His body jolted to a stop as a cold hard bar – or rather two of them – hit him in the shoulder, arm, chest, and leg. Although shocked, the voices overwhelmed him. "Robyn, where am I?"

"You're in front of a graveyard."

Do You Hear What I Hear?

I See You

Jason absorbed the shower fully. It was therapeutic, allowing him to process the last few days. The returning memories, getting out of the house, and realizing he did hear voices of the dead. Yesterday, Robyn came over again and they went for a walk – purposely going by a funeral home ... and he heard voices again.

Jason smiled, thinking about Robyn. She was coming by today, and he had to get clean for her. He had spent almost an hour in the basement lifting weights with Justin. Sweat made him feel as if he was accomplishing something. Also, his muscles burned, and they felt sore – but in a good way. Unable to explain it, physical activity gave him a sense of accomplishment. Pushing himself beyond his capabilities made him feel stronger, better, and energized.

The drops of water not only carried away sweat and toxins, but also his fear, and frustration. He also found that the workout got his mind off everything: the noises at night, the whispers, the smells, the uneasy feelings. It helped him focus on his thoughts and work out his fears. Jason never noticed the mental health benefits of exercise.

The spray of water silenced as he turned the lever back to the left. Water dripped from the showerhead, splattered on the tile, then circled the drain, interrupting the quiet. Opening the door, he felt a presence displace the air. Catching a whiff of a familiar scent, his shoulders cringed, then his whole body curdled at the sound of a familiar feminine voice.

"I'm so sorry." Robyn's voice stammered. "I didn't mean to ..."

Jason immediately covered his private area with hands as he slammed his back and butt into the shower tile. Scared, embarrassed, his heart raced, yet his skin, his arms, legs, and whole body shrunk as he backed up. "Holy shit! What the fuck are you doing spying on me?" He felt just as embarrassed about his changing voice as it returned to a preadolescent pitch. "Seriously – the shower was running! Why'd you come in? What's wrong with you? Are you deaf?"

"I'm sorry, I was just ..."

"Will you get out of here? Now!"

"I'm sorry," her voice faded as she left the room.

Hearing the door close, he sighed, and his eyelids compressed as the wave of embarrassment returned. How could he face her ever again? He never realized how vulnerable he was until now. Still shaking, his head fell back, lightly hitting the cold, wet tile. He cringed, realizing she saw him fully naked. She'd have that image in her head forever. Every time she looked at him, that memory would return. How could he face her again? It added to the cold humiliation that swirled inside his chest. *Damnit, damnit, damnit, shit, shit, shit. Why'd she do that!*

Taking a huge breath, his racing heart slowed. Reaching out of the shower, he grabbed the towel angrily. Thank-God it was still there. It'd be worse if Robyn or Justin stole it. He fretted as the abasement returned. First Aunt Janie, now Robyn? What would she tell her friends? Would she laugh, thinking about the size of his ... "Fuck," he whispered. *She certainly heard the shower running and decided to peek. If I invaded her privacy like that, her dad would file charges against me!* His spirit froze like a statue. *Oh, no! What if she took a photo of me with her phone? Will she send it to her friends? Post it on the internet somewhere?* He shuddered at the thought of other girls gawking at his nudity and giggling. His throat collapsed on itself, almost strangling him. The blind boy naked for everyone to see. It would be passed around on the Internet for his entire life.

After his angry thoughts ran through, he wondered if he should tell Justin, or Uncle Dan or Aunt Janie? Or Natalie or Roger? No. He didn't want anyone to know. He'd been humiliated enough.

He finished drying himself and put on some clothes: boxers, jeans, socks, and a T-shirt. "Samson, come." Sensing the dog mostly by smell, Jason found Samson's leash and followed the dog downstairs.

However, reaching the bottom, he noticed the scent of Robyn's perfume and shampoo once again. Hearing her typing on her phone, he turned his head towards her. Humiliation returned. She was probably imagining him naked. "What the hell are you still doing here?" He made sure to let the anger hit his words hard, like a rock or a punch. "You better not have snapped a photo of me."

"No. I promise you that I didn't do that. Look. I'm really sorry. I didn't hear the shower running – really. Please, can you forgive me? I'm really very sorry."

Jason, knowing the living room well, and using her voice as a reference, sat on the couch across from Robyn. Keeping his distance, he still felt an awkward silence on her part. "Who let you in?" he asked sharply.

"Justin. He said you were up in your room and to go on in. So, it's his fault!"

"It sounds like an easy excuse for you. Sure, he'd

probably do that, but you heard the shower running and …"

"I had in my earbuds …"

"You still barged in," he said, not letting her finish. He scoffed. "I thought I could trust you."

"You can. I promise not to tell anyone. And you can have your aunt and uncle check my phone for pictures."

His eyelids shut tight – even though it did not help stop the embarrassment and shame he felt. He barely knew Robyn. They had only known each other for a few days. He had confided with her about things he didn't share with Uncle Dan, Aunt Janie, or Justin.

He felt her move closer. "Please forgive me," she said. "I promise you can trust me."

"I don't know," he said quietly. "It's just that you can see me, but … I can't see you at all. It's not fair."

After an awkward silence, he remembered his unanswered question from two days ago. "Robyn, what do you look like? He tried to think how to put his thoughts into words. "Well … I know how Justin looks, and my aunt and uncle look because I knew them before I went blind. But I don't know what you look like. What's the color of your eyes and hair? Can you describe yourself?"

Her voice softened. "I have a better idea." Her fingers took hold of his hand. At first, he was unsure what Robyn was doing. Strangely, her touch made him relax and feel excited at the same time. His fingers felt the back of her hand and her knuckles. They were soft and warm, helping him feel at ease. His fingertips glided over her fingernails. The wrist felt smaller, too – and it had a thin bracelet. He used his thumb to trace the circumference of her palm. Gently, her fingers clasped his hand gently. Slowly, his hand was guided higher. His fingers touched the outside corner of her left eye.

Do You Hear What I Hear?

His forefinger and middle finger spread as they traced the shape of her eye. It felt like the shape of a football, but sleeker, narrower, and more refined. His forefinger noticed the very thin eyebrow that acted like a cushion for his fingers to slide over. His fingers met on the inside corner, then they swept back along the underside of the eye. She blinked a couple of times. He felt the eyelashes tickling his fingers – reminding him of a butterfly he caught as a small child.

Concentrating, he gently pressed her skin while reaching towards her left ear. His forefinger and middle finger spread around the top of her ear and met at the narrow lobe. His nostrils caught the aroma of her shampoo and perfume. The two distinct scents mixed into a wonderful aroma that tickled the hairs in his nose.

His fingers dropped below her ear, and he traced her jaw. It was tight. It spread, indicating that she smiled. Reaching her chin, it narrowed into a vee shape, squared off at the end. His fingers dropped under her chin and down her neck. Robyn giggled, but only slightly. Her breath smelled fresh, as if she had some mint or perhaps some mouth spray. He traced the other side of her face, climbing towards her forehead.

Her hair draped over the back of his hand, tickling his skin. Turning his hand, her hair now became a blanket that warmed his palm and danced across his skin. He smiled while pushing her hair back behind her ear. His fingers now gently spread as he traced her hairline. Once his four fingers fanned out, he pulled them down on her forehead. The fingers met on the outside corner of her right eye. He outlined them, allowing his fingertips to meet on the other side. Finding the top, he gently sloped down her nose, feeling a slight bump. It was thin, even when the nares spread. As his fingers found her mouth, his forefinger and thumb spread to her mouth corners. They extended as he felt her smile again.

Pulling his fingers away from her face, he sensed her move closer. Was that his heartbeat he heard? Or was it hers? It wasn't racing, but felt calm, and at peace. Imagining her face from what he felt, he moved his head closer. Her face was closer as her breath bounced off his skin. It sounded like her breaths had quietened, as if she had found peace as well. Her breath smelled like peppermint candy. Slightly unsure of an urge, he decided to go ahead and follow it. Taking a breath, he moved forward, tilted his head, and hoped his lips would find hers.

As their lips met, he pressed a little more. As all uncertainty and fear vanished, he leaned forward and kissed her again. He hoped he was doing this right. She had not pushed him away, so she must have liked it. In fact, she kissed him, even tracing his lips with her tongue. He grunted. Her hand clasped the back of his neck and pulled him closer. Her fingers pushed through his hair. Her touch triggered so many reactions: a fast heartbeat, tingling skin, and a reaction he hoped she wouldn't notice.

He gently pushed his fingers through her hair. It felt so silky, so warm, and soft. Finding her ear, he gently traced it again with his fingers. He heard her gasp. He smelled the aroma of her hair, skin, and breath. None of them offended his senses. He wanted to dwell within them. He grunted as his right hand found the back of her neck. He gently stroked it. She grunted lightly – but as if she liked what he was doing. She rubbed the back of his neck. They pulled away from each other. Jason smiled and somehow knew she smiled back at him.

Do You Hear What I Hear?

Samson's bark startled him. Jason and Robyn both laughed as Samson kept barking. However, Jason's smile and exuberance faded as he sensed a chill in the dog's barking. It turned to a whimper. The familiar tension, paranoia, and dread nestled over them. The hair on the back of his neck straightened. His skin shrank from a ghastly cold. A giant thud echoed through the house as doors slammed shut. The temperature dropped suddenly, and a horrible stench fell – almost making him gag.

"Oh, my God." Robyn's whispers were laced in terror. Jason felt her hands shake as they clasped to his body and pulled him closer. He heard her breath range and felt the cold mist of her mouth hit his skin. He felt her trembling fingers and heard her shaky voice. "Jason, it's back. The lights … they're blinking. Can you hear anything it's saying?"

He kept saying "I don't know" as the haunting dread wrapped around him. He heard the whispers again, overlapping so much he could not understand them. The sounds tickled the hairs within his ears. A loud yell made the whispers go away. "Did you hear that?" he asked.

"I can't hear anything. Except the …"

Doors of cupboards, cabinets, and rooms opened and slammed numerous times. Robyn screamed as vibrant banging sounds echoed through the walls. He heard books, pictures, and objects fall from shelves. Other objects flew across the room, pelting him. The couch slightly jumped and moved.

Samson's whimper turned into a vicious growl. Three quick barks followed.

"Jason," Robyn's voice shrank to a whisper and shook. "It's above you."

A hot hand, or rather a talon, wrapped around his neck.

It pushed him onto the couch and growled. A horrific smell of excrement and death blasted across his face. Accompanying the odor, a disgusting drool sprayed. Unable to breathe, he grabbed the talon at its wrist and tried to pry it loose from his neck.

"Get away from …" It sounded like Robyn was slapped across the room. Chairs tumbled, and something like glass shattered.

A vicious barking moved towards him. Samson's yelp traveled across the room as if he was thrown by the demon.

A worse pain penetrated his neck, and his chest as Jason struggled for breath. The grip on his neck tightened. His skin burned, but he panicked more about not being able to breathe. His arms flailed as he desperately tried to find just a bit of air. His hands wrapped around the disgusting wrist that had cold, peeling, flaking skin. Jason tried to pull the strong claw off his neck, but the thing had immense strength.

Justin yelled something about Jesus. Or was he cursing?

A vicious low-pitched howl blasted across Jason's face, spraying the rank breath and more slobber on him. He could breathe! He coughed. A quiet enveloped the room. Still, Jason quivered. The tension, just under his skin, felt like a tiny surge of electricity. It shot through him like a dry heave. His explosive coughs expelled carbon dioxide to let his mouth pull in fresh air.

Someone took his hand. However, it wasn't Robyn's. The fingers were larger, as well as the hand itself. "Jason, Jason, it's me, Justin."

"Justin?" he said between coughs. "What happened?" More coughs. "Where's Robyn? Is she okay?"

She grunted and moaned.

"I don't know," said Justin, "I'll go check." He

stumbled through some fallen debris. "Robyn, are you okay?"

"Ow," she said several times. "My head."

"You gotta… a bad bruise."

Jason wept while shaking his head. His eyelids clamped shut in terror – or was it despair. "Why is this happening? Why? Why can't it just leave me alone? I just want it to stop. I wanna see again. I want Jimmy, Mom, and Dad. I didn't do anything to this thing."

Robyn pulled him upright and hugged him tightly. Her strong arms were warm and comforting. Her voice, though, did the most to calm him, possessing strength and solace. "You're right, it's not fair, but we're gonna figure this out. My daddy, your uncle, your aunt – all of us. We're gonna do something and … what is it?"

A lone tear streamed. "Mom?" he whispered. "Dad? Jimmy?"

Robyn eased him to sit on the couch. "You can hear them?"

"They need help. I can hear them asking me for my help. The creature … it has them … and many more as well." He turned to Robyn's presence. "What was-" he stuttered out his question, "it you saw? What did it look like?"

Dripping with terror, her whispers stuttered. "It was … too hard to … describe. Cold, dark …" her voice faded as she cried.

Samson came over, wobbling and whimpering – sounding as if he cried. He sniffed Jason and licked the boy's face. Jason kept petting Samson as the dog rested on his legs.

"Holy fucking shit!" Justin dropped his phone.

Startled by the outburst, Jason turned to the voice of his cousin. "What is it?"

"You're not going to believe what I recorded on my phone!"

***

Dan and Janie gathered around Justin's laptop. Looking back at Roger and Robyn, he quivered. He hugged Jason with one arm, and Justin+ with his other. Janie, standing behind him, cried as her strong hands clasped his shoulders. Dan flinched, worried about the video Justin downloaded to his computer. Anticipating the sight made him tense, but Dan had to see it for himself. It was not to admit to Jason and Justin they were right, but also to vindicate his own feelings and suppositions. They reached beyond science, logic, and reasoning.

"Okay," said Justin, "it's downloaded. Dad, Mom, you're not gonna believe this. I saw Jason and Robyn kissing on the couch, and …I thought it'd be cool to catch it on video for a joke … but I saw this." He hit the enter button.

There they were. Dan felt embarrassed seeing his nephew passionately kissing Robyn – and was grateful Roger could not see the images. Although he had no daughters, he knew how protective he would be with them – and he was sure Roger would feel the same way. Janie's eyes turned away, and Dan noticed Robyn blushing.

On the video, the lights went off and on while books, pictures and decorations flew off the shelves. Cabinets swung open and slammed shut. A shadow moved across the wall. A low, inhuman scream came from the laptop speakers, forcing Dan to cringe as if hearing high pitched squeaks. Loud bangs pounded reverberated, leaving behind a punch on Dan's chest. A strange voice, muffled and intermittent, was underneath the loud bangs. It sounded so despondent, desperate, and demonic. Between flickers, the shadow

Do You Hear What I Hear?

appeared again. Large, menacing, it moved with every flash of light. Cloaked, it glanced at Justin's camera and let out a guttural growl so loud the sound distorted. Even the recorded images – and more so the sound, left a lingering terror, indicating an unholy presence.

Dan saw a whitish face, no nose, pure black eyes, with peeling flesh mangled over its mouth – as if the lips had been stitched together. It changed color: black, red, yellow, black again. Justin cursed several times. Arms grew from the shadow with three long, narrow fingers that wrapped around Jason's neck. It lifted him off the ground, then slammed him hard into the couch.

"Get away from him!" Robyn screamed. The shadow slapped her with its free hand. Samson's barking reverberated louder and charged it, but the shadow slapped the dog back as well. Justin's phone fell and everything went dark. Facing up, the lights flickered and an image behind the shadow emerged. A human face flickered, returning between the flashes of light. Finally, Justin screamed, "In the name of Jesus – leave this place!" Everything went dark. Then the room lights came on. Dan rationality could not reconcile what he witnessed.

"Does anyone else hear that?" asked Jason.

"The footsteps? The scraping?" asked Roger.

"Yeah."

Samson growled.

Dan tried to listen, but the sounds eluded him. He looked at Janie, but she shook her head – as did Justin and Robyn. What did they hear?

Samson growled again. He let loose a few abrupt barks. Jason and Roger both looked at the room of Justin's wall. Dan followed their stares. Perplexed, he tried to listen to the footsteps and the scraping Roger and Jason mentioned. Suddenly, he heard the weight put on the wooden floor that moaned as if somebody or something walked through the hall. The creaks moved closer to the door.

A silhouette appeared as images emerged. An aging face with wrinkles faded in and out of existence. The military style suit held him at attention, as if an officer. The stature reminded Dan of that asshole sergeant from the Air Force. What was his name? Sergeant ... Simms. That was it. He was always yelling at the recruits, deriding their smile, or mocking how they talked, and questioned their sexuality. True, some military leaders were tough, pushing recruits beyond what they thought they could do. They forged a better man, a better soldier who had endurance against opposition and pain. The ones like Sergeant Simms, however, were simply bullies that bred resentment.

However, this figure in the hallway was not verbose. He was silent. The eyes had a subtle glow. A sense of dread invaded the room as if paving the way for the figure. Freezing air made Dan shiver. He felt a bit of nausea, as well as a headache. A ringing in his ears, although subtle, turned painful.

Do You Hear What I Hear?

As the fear spread under Dan's skin, he panted. The cold pricks on his hair felt like tiny stabs. His fingers shook. Goosebumps slithered across his skin. A depressing dread circled him like a predator. Turning, he kept looking for the being that surrounded him. Clutching the cross around his neck, he took a deep breath and closed his eyes. "Mother Mary, Christ the Son, God, the Father, spread your goodness and chase the evil away into the fiery pits of hell apart from your people who praise your name." It was a short prayer Father Simpkin taught them. Sure, it was often done during duress and fear, but this time Dan prayed as if his life depended on it.

He opened his eyes. The figure was gone. Letting out a sigh, he let go of the cross.

"Uncle Dan, do you hear what I hear?"

"Hear what?"

Roger interjected. "The heavy breathing? The bizarre words?"

"Yeah," said Jason.

Dan glanced at Justin's door mirror and saw it. The shadow changed size, shape, and height. The shoulders grew bigger. The arms stretched as three fingers appeared at the end of each hand. Pointed ears protruded from the head. Wings spread from its back and darkened the room. He clutched the cross again and repeated the prayer. He closed his eyes the second time, praying it over and over, hoping the prayer would make it go away.

The tension faded as the icy sensation disappeared. Warmth returned to his skin, and the dread abruptly vanished. Everyone seemed to share one collective sigh. Closing his eyes, Dan hoped he could open them without seeing some hideous thing hovering over him.

Stephen W. Scott

The doorbell rang.

Do You Hear What I Hear?

Old Man

The elderly man stood a bit over six feet tall. He was thin and had long arms and legs. His nose was a bit large, but only in length. On either side were two tired brown eyes. More skin wrinkled near the corners of his eyelids, the corners of his mouth, and his brow. Taking off his fedora hat revealed his white hair. It circled his head like a crown, leaving the top part of his head bald. Several misshapen spots had scattered on his scalp. They were not cancerous, but areas that received a lot of sun. He used a cane to help balance himself – although he seemed healthy for an elderly gentleman. He wore a gray, cotton overcoat. Dan guessed he was in his mid-to-late 80's.

The man seemed so out of place, even more so with the thick Eastern European accent – likely a Polish or Slovakian one. "My name is Nathan Oberst," he said quietly. "Rabbi Oberst."

Dan tilted his head. "Please, sit down." They all sat around the couch and chairs. "What is it that you want?"

"I am looking for …" his hand extended with Jimmy and Jason's school ID badges. His voice shuddered – looking at Jason. "Your son."

Nathan

Nathan wondered why everyone remained quiet. Looking around, a palpable tension seized the room – but it was far more than just meeting a stranger from a foreign land.

The man who opened the door, whom Nathan assumed

was the father, cleared his throat. "He's not my son, but my nephew. His father was my brother." said Dan. A pain stretched in his voice, trying to reign in the pain. "My twin-brother, and my sister-in-law and other nephew were killed." Nathan gasped. One set of twin boys – and a set of twin fathers! No wonder the Angel of Death latched onto them. "Which boy survived? James or Jason?"

"Me, sir. I'm Jason."

Nathan looked at the boy. Young, handsome, ruddy, thin, long sandy-brown hair that partially covered his eyes. He gazed at the scars on the left cheek that ran under his jaw. Part of his left lower lip was damaged, along with another short scar descending from the corner of his mouth. Nathan also saw part of the left ear lobe was missing. On the left hand and left forearm, he noticed more scarring – although one of them looked like a surgical cut. Perhaps an injury left him light sensitive as he wore sunglasses. A few tears, hidden by the glasses, streamed from the right eye, sliding underneath his jaw. Nathan sat to face him. "Child. You lost your twin-brother?" He pointed to Dan. "And you lost yours." His throat froze. Unable to talk, he stared in astonishment. The image of Noah raced through his mind, followed by his dying moans. They crossed the walls of time, making Nathan shudder in pain and weep.

"I, too, lost my brother," said Nathan. "My twin-brother, Noah. He died in the camps of Auschwitz when we were only ten." Sitting, Nathan sobbed more. "I saw the Angel of Death, slicing him open, taking his kidney, and then he ..." Nathan sobbed heavier. He had not talked with too many people about it. He did not tell much to his adoptive parents, although he did talk more to his wife, Rebecca. Nadia, his daughter, did not need to know much – except that her uncle died in the camp. He could not bring himself to tell her about the horrors in the barracks, and in Josef's so-called hospital. The only thing he told her was that he had seen the Angel of Death's Spirit, and that he had to stop it. She thought he was crazy. "We prayed to Yahweh every night. But he never came. We begged for the torture to stop. We prayed for warm beds, real food, compassion, and to be reunited with our father and sister. We prayed so much, but they fell back on us and crushed us like heavy weights."

Nathan found a handkerchief and wiped his eyes. "I'm sorry," he whispered. Putting his glasses back on, he surveyed the others around him. Dan, his wife, their nephew – and this other boy who looked sad. Who was this other fellow? The burly man with short, dark hair stood like a brick wall. He suddenly noticed the dilated eyes of the fellow who hugged a young girl. His daughter, perhaps? He guessed the burly fellow was blind. "You, sir – a friend of the family? Blind?"

"A recent friend, yes," he nodded. "I'm Roger Paden. I was a fireman but lost my sight in the line of duty. This is my daughter, Robyn."

Nathan briefly smiled, thinking of his daughter. "I, too, have a daughter, Nadia. She was named after my sister who disappeared in the camps." Nathan smiled wider. "She has three young ones. Grandchildren are such a delight." His smile faded thinking of all the years lost from his grandchildren – and the two great-grandchildren he met once five years ago. A direful regret lifted in his chest, triggering a sigh. Why didn't he spend more time with his grandchildren and great-grandchildren? Maybe he should have done that instead of tracking the demon and spirit over the last decade. Such a journey would have been more pleasant and fulfilling than his mission of madness.

A strong, determined sense of responsibility dug in, retrenching his stance. As far as he knew, he was the only one left from the camp who knew the truth and vowed to stop the entity from spreading more fear and hatred. The regret and doubt both vanished when a new breath filled his heart and lungs.

But now - what to say? The truth he knew – or should he make something up? He readied his cane, hand on top, prepared to stand and leave if they thought him crazy.

"Wait," said Dan, "what did you mean you were looking for my nephew?"

Nathan saw their confused and dejected stares changed to anxious hope. Their eyes begged for help – so much so that he found their anticipation intense.

First, Nathan explained how he found them. A Detective Agency helped, looking into the names, schools, obituaries, and articles that led him to the house of Derek and Susanne Collins. From there, the detective found the executor of the will, Derek's brother. Nathan, however, did not know they were twins.

Next, he told them the truth he hoped they would believe. "The demon twin is what it is." Unsure if he desired credibility or sympathy, he sighed before continuing. "According to his diary, Dr. Mengele met the demon twin while staring into the mirrors. It came to him because he was a twin. His twin died shortly after birth and was never mentioned to anyone outside of the household. In his diary, he bemoaned the loss of a brother he had but never knew."

"That's when Vodinion sought him out. You see, Vodinion, himself, was a twin. He too was once an Angel of Yahweh. When Lucifer rebelled, Vodinion sided with

Lucifer, but his twin, Dovinion, sided with Yahweh. Once they were separated and Vodinion was exiled, he dwelt on the Earth hating all the twins of the world. His one desire was to separate those twins. It is thought he was the one who cursed Esau and Jacob.

"Vodinion used the mirrors of this world. They were his portal. He would appear in the mirror of the twin it wished to torment. It assumes their identity. It uses memories, scars, and fears against them, and furnishes hatred for the other twin. In the end, he would prompt the possessed twin to kill the other ... and then turn on the family."

"Once he found the distraught Mengele, it seems it whispered his name at home, at school, in his sleep, and more-so when approached by the Nazis. Mengele wrote about this demon's manipulations on him in great detail throughout his diary. He kept this diary secret from Der Fuhrer.

"It was Vodinion I saw in the concentration camp from all those years ago. His diabolical vengeance lashed out not just on my twin, Noah, but all the others. It is why he took your brother," he said to Jason. Nathan then looked at Dan, "And that's why he took yours. He will not stop."

"Wait," said Roger, "I didn't think Judaism recognized demons and exorcisms."

Nathan smiled. "Some do. Originally, I didn't, but to stop this thing, I considered the doctrine of my brothers."

"Brothers?"

Nathan nodded. "Judaism is like the older brother to Catholicism or Christianity. You see, we have the same father, but father does not treat all his children exactly the same, does he? Here, my brothers are right."

After that, nobody said anything for a while. Nathan

thought it curious that none of them questioned his motives, his intent, and his sanity. The thick quiet had no tension, but rather a shared strength among this family … and the friend.

"But Uncle Dan's and my twin are dead," said the boy.

"He will seek to destroy your family next. Then, he will seek another twin to carry on this destructive cycle. He hasn't approached …" Nathan's thoughts shuddered to a halt as the boy, Jason, removed his glasses. Like the burly fireman, the boy's eyes were fixated and dilated. They had not responded, save for the occasional blink. "Child? Are you blind like this fireman? How did this happen?"

Jason nodded lightly, obviously reliving the sting of the trauma. He explained the hauntings, his twin's behavior, the voices, the smells, and the sights. As he finished the history of his twin's death, he cried again. "I miss him so much."

Nathan's own weeping compelled him to hug the boy tightly. "Child – I know the pain. It cuts deep – even after 70 years it hurts me like nothing else. I know what you are going through. I saw so many other twins in the camp suffer such anguish."

"I saw them," said Jason. "In some sort of vision – I saw the demon with Dad, Jimmy, and … dozens or maybe hundreds of people. It's like he's absorbing them."

Some illumination brightened Nathan's mind. Like the lighting of a candle, or the emergent flicker of a low wattage bulb, it was not too little to be of no use, nor was it too much to blind him. A tainted memory from the camp emerged. He remembered Michael and Micah who had their eyes removed. The recollection played like an old scratchy film.

***

(Auschwitz, 1945)

Nathan led Michael to the latrine. A depressing gray

color imbued itself into the camp. Hazy, the sun tried to burn through the clouds, but no shadows developed to follow the boys on the ground. Like their souls, the shadows had left.

"We're here," said Nathan.

Michael nodded. "I can tell by the stench."

To Nathan, the whole camp had one huge stink. However, over the months, the years, he acclimated to it. How could Michael possibly tell the difference in the odors of vomit in the barracks and mess hall as opposed to the stench of the latrines? To Nathan, the whole camp smelled the same: gross. Somehow, he got used to it but noticed it from time to time.

Michael carefully entered. He wobbled not only from the deteriorating balance, but also the heavy wheezing as his Asthma had grown worse. Nathan guided him to the door, not wanting his friend to fall. Was it the weakness and hunger that made his legs shake? Or was it difficult breathing?

"Nathan …"

The sole shadow of the camp enveloped him. Josef stood a couple of feet taller, somehow making the gray haze darker. Although the man smiled, Nathan refused to trust it. Josef leaned over to face him. "How is one of my favorite children today?"

After a … was it two or three years? He had lost track of time. Still, Nathan stopped believing in Josef's kindness and compassion a long time ago. Sure, he took chocolate when it was offered – but only in a vain attempt to appease his stomach's ravenous hunger. The hand that cradled Nathan's chin felt cold, scaly, and sinister. Josef's face changed too as his eyes sank into the pitch-black sockets. The skin reddened and wrinkled as the head morphed into a long, tired face. While the nose faded, Josef's teeth grew, and the horrible thing snapped at him – emitting a horrible growl. The smell of the breath, although unique, could not compete with the stench of the camp.

"Nathan?"

Yanked from Josef's cold shadow – Nathan saw Michael emerge from the latrine. He took Michael's hand to guide him.

"Ah, Michael," said Josef, "How are you this beautiful morning?"

Michael spoke through his wheezes. "How would I know if it's beautiful?" he whispered. "You do not fool me," his words gained strength, moving from a weak whisper to a strong assertion. "I know what you are. I hear your real voice. It sounds like rocks in your throat. It's deeper and says frightening things like 'hurt them,' or 'I want more.' I can hear the voice of Micah. He wants to leave the camp but can't. Savan and Stanley said the same. They are still crying, you know. I hear them mostly at night. I no longer can smell your cologne. It is lost to the stench of your breath and rotting flesh. It's strange, sir, but since I cannot see, I know your true form. I cannot see myself in the mirror – so I cannot see the thing that comes after me anymore. I'm blind, but at least I am free from you."

Josef withdrew the candy. Nathan led Michael away from the latrines – and back to the barracks.

***

Nathan finished his account of the camp at Auschwitz. Tears flowed heavily revisiting those memories. Nathan took a sip of the tea and set it on the table. They had stopped eating and remained quiet – not knowing what to say to him. He noticed the wife of the gentleman was crying – along with the daughter of the fireman. Even that burly, strong man cried, too – along with the blind boy. Nathan recalled Michael crying many nights in the barracks after he was rendered blind.

The embarrassing silence lasted a second. "I never could have imagined that," said the blind boy, Jason. "I thought losing my brother and parents and my sight were the worst things in the world. I'm really, really sorry you had to go through all that, sir."

The man's wife hugged her nephew. The fireman did the same to his daughter. "Jason, you, and the fireman have a great advantage over this Angel of Death. Not being able to see him, or the mirrors, helps you."

Jason snapped. "How can you say that? It tried to strangle me!"

"The demon cannot take you. It cannot dwell inside as it did your brother." Nathan looked at the uncle, trying to remember his name. "You, sir," he said pointing to Dan, "and myself are in the greatest danger. Being the twin who can see and stare into the mirrors. I must act quickly with the ritual. I may ask for the boy and the fireman…"

"My name is Roger," he said curtly.

"Forgive, please. When you are 87 many things go fast: memory, balance, strength, bladder, and bowels, too."

Everyone chuckled. It lasted not even a second as their faces turned white and frozen.

Nathan continued. "If I can enlist Roger and Jason to assist, it would be helpful."

Uncle Dan's voice ended with the eerie silence. "How soon can we do this? What do we need to do?"

Nathan shook his head. "I have never performed this ritual of casting out a spirit. And there is no guarantee it will work."

"Couldn't a Catholic Priest help you?" Roger asked. "I'm Catholic, and I think Dan mentioned he is. That way we could have the world's first inter-faith exorcism." Nobody followed Roger's chuckle.

"Possibly – but they do not actually perform the exorcisms. That is done by a Jesuit Priest, and they may take weeks or even months to determine if an exorcism could or should be performed. The Vatican wants to be very sure before indulging in such things. Moreover, the Jesuits need time for preparation. Even I must prepare. I cannot just rush in. I need at least three days of fasting, prayer, and study. I must go now."

Everyone spoke at once. "Wait. What is your number?"

"How can we reach you?"

"Where are you going?"

Using his hands, Nathan quieted everyone. "I am at this place called Holiday Inn. I will need your number – because I am not smart enough for a smartphone."

Some of them chuckled for a split second.

Nathan smiled and nodded. He put on his hat and turned. His breath stilled as his heart shuddered to a halt. He felt cold as an old, familiar dread awakened within him. The hairs on his arms and legs stiffened, and his fingers trembled.

In the mirror, he saw it again for the first time in 75 years: the hideous face, wrinkled, scaly and flaking skin, and fang-like teeth. It scowled and huffed – a cold breath forming on the inside of the hall mirror. It said something to him. Although whispered, he could make it out. The voice, all too familiar, echoed as if the sound emanated from a deep cave. Nathan said a quiet prayer to Yahweh, then turned to the images. "Hello, Josef."

Do You Hear What I Hear?

"*It is good to see you, Nathan.*" The voice whispered.

"I wish I could say the same to you, Josef."

"*They're mine. They're his. We will stop you as we should have all those years ago.*"

Nathan shook his head. "I am the last one. Stanley, Savan, Micah, Michael, Omri, David, Erik, and Noah and I all made a promise. I am the last one – and I will fulfill it – but Yahweh will do the fighting."

The creature tried to leap from the mirror, but it was stopped. It pressed hard from within. It growled hideously.

Nathan walked by the mirror. The rage exploded within him. Lifting the cane, he smashed the mirror. The breakage spread out like a spider-web, reflecting many parts of the room and the people in it multiple times. Nathan turned to the desperate families. "Cover all the mirrors. Do not look at them. Do not trust any image you see. Do not talk to it. Talk to God. Pray. Prepare. Fast."

"But …" Dan stammered, "we're not Jewish. We're Catholic."

Nathan pointed to the mirror. "Nor is the Angel of Death. It is simply evil."

Stephen W. Scott

The Conflict

Nathan

Nathan turned to the burly fellow. "Roger – be ready." He now turned to the boy. "Jason, be ready. Remember, you two, I think, are immune from possession. It might still strike at you – especially you, child. You are a twin – one he cannot penetrate. So, he will strike at you with physical force." He turned to Dan. "You are the one most vulnerable. You can see. You are a twin. He will try to get you. Do not argue with it. Do not talk to it when it whispers. And do not look at any reflection."

Nathan put the kippah on his head. A tallit draped over each shoulder. The Star of David rested at each end of the tallit prayer shawl. Gently falling to his knees, he kissed the Torah.

Only focusing on Yahweh, he repeated his prayer for deliverance. He kept thinking of the plagues beset on Egypt by Yahweh – ending with the deaths of the firstborn Egyptians. His mind focused on the people of Israel caught between the armies of Egypt and the churning waters of the Red Sea. If God had helped them with such miracles – surely, he would help this family. Nathan prayed for them, and against Vodinion.

Jason

Justin poked Jason. "What's he saying?" he whispered.

Jason poked him back, whispering a "shhhh," to get his cousin to be quiet. "How should I know?" he murmured, "I don't know Hebrew."

Do You Hear What I Hear?

Jason took a deep breath as a strange cold circled down and surrounded him. A serious dread followed, stilling the air. An electrical current danced on the hairs of his skin. His breaths shortened – and he felt mist drip from his mouth. As the air became stagnant, a quiet, nefarious fear seized him. The feeling thrust itself on him, digging deep into his belly where it curled up into a tight, cold ball of ice. Jason felt the urge to cry as all his emotions swelled: fear, anger, despondence. They weakened as he felt Robyn's hand gently clasp his. Some warmth returned to his skin, as well as the blood speeding through his veins. His heart slowed, syncing with his calmer breaths. He tried praying, but felt as if a strong, scaley hand hovered around his neck. Was it going to squeeze his throat again?

Jason's mind kept racing, thinking about everything that happened. Was this his life running through his mind? So fast, it became a blur, making it impossible to discern which events occurred, when they occurred, and with whom. Strangely, it was only the times when he was frightened – if not terrified. He saw the shark in the Sao Paulo Bay, the pictures of the children tortured by Nazis, the car wreck, the time when the family hid from a tornado, and the pain of being blinded.

Jason's head exploded as a demonic wailing burst through. High-pitched, it resembled a woman's scream. So annoying and painful, Jason covered his ears and recoiled. It made no difference as the scream felt like an icepick jabbing in his ears. Dropping to his knees, he sobbed as his fears descended again, crushing the tiniest bit of hope.

"Jason, what's wrong?" Was that Robyn? He barely heard her. Could she not hear it? Images flashed in his mind of a … hideous, deformed creature covering its ears and trying to drown out the prayers.

Roger

Roger heard an agonizing scream. Covering his ears, he fell to his knees, praying fervently to God. The sounds pierced through his hands, muscles, and bone. Much of the high-pitched sound resembled metal scraping on a steel floor. His skin, hands, legs, and even his spirit shook uncontrollably.

Roger heard his wife screaming at him.

"It hurts it hurts so much. Why'd you let me die? You did this to me!"

He felt scratches from dead souls, trying to cling to him for life. The scars felt deep and bloodied. He felt the warm blood ooze onto his skin and cake.

Suddenly remembering one of the three Latin prayers taught to him by Father Nelson, he spoke it softly. It was supposed to be a special prayer against demonic forces. He knew it in English, too – but for some reason, used the Latin.

Roger had investigated about 30 hauntings – most were not valid. Of the real ones, this one eclipsed all of them. The terror pierced his chest, vibrating like the bass from a huge concert speaker. He called out to Robyn. She quickly responded, hugging him on one side. He pulled her tight – then realizing Jason was on her other side. He wondered if the boy heard the same screams he heard.

Nathan

A loud pounding reverberated throughout the house. Cabinet doors and drawers opened violently, then closed with the same force. Objects like pictures, decorations, and books flew across the room at random. Everyone backed away, trying to find cover from the flying objects.

The air turned still and cold, outlining everyone's misty

breath. Some lights went out, while others burst as if a firecracker was inside. The sounds stopped, along with the opening and closing of doors, drawers, and flying objects. The air stilled, however, the rancid stench of excrement and spoiled meat tried to trigger Nathan's gag reflex.

The few lights remaining outlined the grainy image of a man. It became a heavy, weighted shadow as the head and arms moved. Nathan prayed to Yahweh while gently talking to the man who stood a few feet away from him. It whispered back, but Nathan heard it clearly. "No," said Nathan. "You must go."

An indiscernible whisper.

"No. Yahweh will send you to the pit. Sheol is the place fitting for you."

The whisper returned – only louder.

"Yes, I hate you – but I do forgive you. But that does not let you off the hook. You hid behind this thing. You listened to it. You carried out what it wanted, so there must be consequences. When you face Yahweh, there must be justice."

The whisper yelled back, but it drowned quickly as a blinding flash of light wrapped around it. The image vanished, although Nathan felt a horrid, cold dread barely escape. The horrible, freezing sensation barely touched his spirit, indicating this darkness was the one he and every remaining soul wanted to avoid in the afterlife.

Dan

Dan shined a light from his smart phone as the shadowy presence near Nathan disappeared. Still, he felt a heavy insidious existence wrap around him like strong, frightening hands. His light swiveled, trying to find the unsettling presence that surrounded him. It watched him – although he could not see it. His eyes scanned the dark as his heart frantically raced. He wanted to see it, but also didn't want to see it. Why? Maybe he hoped it was not real. Perhaps he might find a logical, rational explanation. The dreadful terror would not let him find such answers as the darkest imaginations pumped cold blood through his body. He relaxed as Janie put her arm around his side.

A huge bang brought it all back: the smell, the cold, the dread. The cabinet moved towards them. Another bang seemed to make it lurch another foot or so. The cabinet lurched forward again. Dan's eyes widened as he backed up a few steps, then stumbled to the floor.

The mirror's periphery iced. Cracks spread from the corners and base to the inside. The demon's large head appeared – revealing a sunken, morose face. It had no nose but rather slits where nostrils might be – resembling a snake. One set of fangs jutted down. Its arms, long and sinuous, had a dry, flaking skin – along with the head and torso. It howled at them, pounding from the inside of the mirror again. Its hands pushed. The mirror cracked, spidering from within. The head lurched in, breaking through. The low, thunderous howl sprayed drool on everyone.

Dan fell back and stared at the mirror, locking eyes with the being that rested inside the mirror world. Almost hypnotic, Dan heard nothing but a low-pitched hum. His breaths formed a perfect four-beat rhythm as his consciousness faded. Dan wondered where he was … and who he was. In a daze, it seemed like a tunnel of mist swirled on itself. Hideous roars, screams and moans resounded as if they came from a cave.

The creature howled again, pushing itself through the mirror which had cracked in several places. It lurched more, breaking free, flapping its wings. The wind pushed their hair back. Its vile smell – beyond description – made everyone vomit.

The demon's obsidian eyes locked with Dan's. Somehow this reality only contained Dan and the demon. It glared at him, putting him into a trance. It moved closer, slowly, forcing its will onto Dan. His identity faded as memories were cast out of his mind, taking away his identity and agency. Who was he? He fought, using his will to cling to his personhood, agency, and soul. He cried at the last thought of Derek, Janie, Justin, and Jason. He had a brother. What was his name? His sister-in-law – what was her name? Where are they? Who were his parents? Were they still alive? What did he do for a living – and what had he done before?

Janie

Janie cringed. She knew her husband no longer existed under those eyes. They turned upward. They glossed over with an albino-like whiteness and then faded to black. Now normal, Dan's eyes only contained an icy stare. Blank, void of any character, soul, or personhood, Dan's face whitened. She screamed his name, hoping to pull him from the demon's grip.

Stephen W. Scott

The Last Twin

Nathan moved closer to Dan and prayed. The Yiddish prayer, repeated over and over, had no effect. Still an icy-cold stare radiated from Dan's eyes, glaring a subtle red glow at Nathan.

The lights blinked off and on. Every time the lights dimmed, so did the room's temperature fell. Nathan fought the chills in his spine and focused on Yahweh. The fireman repeated his Latin prayer. As the lights flashed on, Nathan saw Dan standing there. The darkness made him vanish. The lights came on, this time revealing the hideous demon bellowing a loud, inhuman scream. The lights faded then lit up again, revealing Dan's sinister smile. The lights gave way to darkness, lasting longer as if something waited to pounce on him. As the lights returned, the ugly thing flailed its claws at Roger and Jason – knocking them both backwards into some bookcases. Robyn screamed and ran to comfort her father.

Nathan's fears thudded as each thump of his heartbeat faster. The pulse in his chest thundered, resounding louder and louder. Feeling the terror morph into anger, he sought the peace Yahweh promised. Closing his eyes, Nathan concentrated on his prayers, and the presence of the Almighty.

A brilliant flash lit up the room as something else appeared in glorious light, displaying magnificent and beautiful wings that spread in authority. In it was a resounding power – but there was no fear, nor cold, nor dread. Full of hope and light, it resonated with everyone. Nathan, glaring at the new thing, noticed more prominent things: the face glowed, the arms were not sinuous but proportional. It sounded as if it was singing a mighty chorus instead of the dissonant clicks and growls. Although he did not know for sure, Nathan sensed it was the angelic Dovinion. It would be the one to drag Vodinion into the pit.

Dovinion grabbed its twin by the neck, squeezing tightly with one hand while bludgeoning Vodinion with its free hand. Every blow flashed an eerie light – alternating with the beast's faded image with Dan's real image. Also, a vicious sound exploded with every hit. The thunderous sound resonated out, pushing through his skin, muscle, bone, and his soul. Everyone covered their ears.

The demon howled, but the servant of Yahweh – would not stop. He kept pounding at the demonic entity, landing more blows that sent out a deep, bass sound that vibrated through Nathan's chest. Three more blows from the angelic being knocked the demon out of Dan. He slumped to the floor. The two entities clashed. More hitting, more strangling. At one point they wrestled, turning over a few times and slamming into a wall, knocking over and breaking furniture. The demon swiveled and finally delivered its own blows and caught the angel in a vice-like grip. It glanced at the mirror. Was it seeking escape?

Nathan took a heavy book and slammed it into the mirror – shattering it. The ugly, angry cracks divided into shards that dislodged. The demon howled at him, almost knocking him down. Nathan screamed. "Break the mirrors! It's trying to escape!"

Justin

Justin led Jason towards the other mirrors – starting in Mom and Dad's bedroom. Justin first shattered the closet door mirror with a broom. He rushed to the bathroom mirror, turned on the light. The sight horrified him. It was his own image looking at him, with a scowl, glowing eyes, and a sinister smirk. Horrid, disfigured creatures surrounded his image and pressed forward. Hands emerged from the mirror – breaking through like fingers pressing out of the water. They grabbed Justin's wrists and tried to pull him in. The grip was tight, strong, and incredibly cold. Justin tried to brace himself, but found his body pinned against the bathroom counter. He tried to push with his legs but found no gain, but they were too strong. These ... things had the advantage. Justin screamed. "Help! Help! Mom! Dad! Help me!"

"Justin," yelled Jason, "what's happening?"

Justin knew his skin turned white. Sweat poured viciously while his heart chilled. Would he freeze to death or succumb to terror? Panicked, unable to think, he begged for help. "It's pulling me in. Help!"

Jason tried to pull Justin back. He grunted. "What is it?"

"Just break the fucking mirror! It's in front of you!"

Jason let go, flailed his arms, somehow grabbed something, and threw it at the mirror. Bits of glass ricocheted back while most of the shards sent a high-pitched squeal as it fell to the ground. Justin huffed when he fell to the floor – feeling a sharp cut on his right palm. "Shit! Shit! Shit!"

"What is it?"

He panicked seeing the blood gush from the cut – then grunted as his nerves fired from the wound. "A shard of glass cut on my hand. Ow! Never mind me, break the other mirrors."

"I can't see them!"

"I'll show you!" he said while wrapping a towel around his hand. Justin stood and grabbed his cousin's wrist and yanked him through the house. "It's in front of you! Holy shit! Just smash it before those things …"

Jason, using his cane, smacked the mirror three times – then it finally collapsed into another rain of crushed glass. It was almost as deafening at the thunderous hits going on in the living room between the demon and angel.

Robyn

Robyn's eyes blinked hard. Overwhelmed by the lights flickering, she had to use her hands to guide her up the winding staircase. Her feet climbed the steps, leaving behind a hollow thud that echoed. The sounds surrounded her while dread and fear closed in. Her breaths, visible in the flickering lights, dispersed as they fell. Stopping, her lower jaw quivered. Part of it was the freezing cold that seized her skin. Her hair stood on end while an electrical, yet icy, sensation wrapped around her body. Panting hard, her chest almost hurt. *Remember what Daddy told you!* She stopped, closed her eyes, and took a deep breath.

Inhaling, feeling a bit calmer, she lifted her eyelids. The vanishing fear exploded when she saw hideous creatures surrounding her. Barely in view were misshapen, bald heads and black eyes that refused to blink. They possessed malnutrition as the joints were much larger than the limbs they supported. Their rank breaths nauseated her, and almost caused her to vomit. The voices were garbled and stifled, sounding as if they tried to inhale and talk at the same time. It actually sounded like an unholy chorus or a moaning full of despair. Their bony arms and fingers reached for her. "Get away from me!" she screamed.

Reaching the top of the stairs, she turned first to Jason's room. Glancing around, it was hard to tell what was there. The flashing lights continued to leave glows around her vision. They were reddish – and some took the form of the hairless, hapless creatures that were just there. Barely seeing a baseball bat, she grabbed it and rushed into the bathroom.

The lights, fully on, showed a young, malnourished boy. Naked from the waist-up, it had pale skin and black, sunken eyes seemed dead. The mouth opened, revealing a darkened hole and crooked, blackened teeth. Robyn smashed the glass with the baseball bat – leaving the glass splintered into dozens, perhaps hundreds of pieces.

She rushed to the hallway and down towards Justin's room. Mirrors? Where are they? The lights flickered fast, causing shadows and light to dance around her, making everything resemble a stop-motion camera. She started with the bathroom door mirror. There was Justin, naked, pressing his fingers from the inside, sending a frozen, spider-like kaleidoscope outward. At first, she thought he pleaded for help, but realized it was a trick when his eyes turned red, and the rest of his body became a hideous beast. She smashed the mirror, turning the single image into multiple ones within the shards of glass.

"Robyn, where are you?"

"I'm in here." Emerging from Justin's room, she saw Daddy feeling along the walls as a guide. "Daddy ..." Her voice trailed at the sight of thin arms, large heads with glowing eyes in the long, horizontal mirror. The still air emitted an awful smell, forcing her eyes to water. The lights faded for good, only leaving the glowing eyes from the reflective glass. The hallway spun slightly to the left and grew longer. Or did it? She almost lost her footing but kept her balance while Daddy fell.

Hands lurched out the mirror, desperately reaching for anything. Somehow, several got ahold of her hair and pulled. One seized her by the neck and another by her right arm. She screamed and tried to resist, but her strength was too weak. Unable to pull free or back away, her feet slowly gave way to the dark forces, and she dropped the bat. "Daddy, help me!" she screamed several times while trying to get the cold, strong grips off her body. "Smash the mirror." She glanced down at him trying to stand. "The bat's next to your hand. No! The other one."

He recited a Latin prayer he often used as a horrific, dissonant, low chorus built. No distinct melody, the music bellowed like the ominous sound of an organ. Each note cut through Robyn like a shard of glass. As Daddy prayed, the unholy forces weakened, and she broke free from the icy grip - falling backwards against the opposite wall.

The creatures seemed to hold their ears as the red glow in their eyes faded. As she got a look at their eyes, her mind cleared. As her thoughts, memories, and agency faded, something cold and insidious entered her mind. It looked everywhere, like a hacker looking through a computer's hard drive. It examined her thoughts, feelings, memories, and fears.

The creature vanished and Robyn broke free of her trance as Daddy smashed the mirror with the baseball bat. She covered her ears as the sound of splintered glass pinched her mind and made Robyn cringe. Once the sound dissipated – she felt a warm, familiar hand grasping her shoulder. Instead of pulling away from Dad, she rushed closer to hide in his arms. After a few seconds, she led her father downstairs.

She halted at the sight. The hideous demon had grabbed the angelic creature and slammed it into the wall. The house shook – almost knocking everyone over. The white creature flipped and held the demon at bay, then delivered hit after hit. The blows reverberated through the house, through their chests, ribcage, and heart – then bounced back like painful sonar. It chilled the awe-struck humans.

Nathan

Vodinion broke free and pulsed violently into Nathan. He instantly heard screams erupting in his mind as unfamiliar memories race through his head. They swirled, taking Nathan back to the dawn of time: the rebellion, the creation, the fall, histories of nations as the demon hid from the brothers and spread misery to all of those made in the image of God. No! After all these years, his quest halted in the midst of a worn, sad heart. The horrors he witnessed had already worn his spirit. He had lost.

Shocked, Nathan felt the pain explode in his chest, left arm, and his head. Falling to his knees, he tried to clutch his heart and put it back into rhythm. It bounced like an old record player needle that kept hitting a scratch. It was like a marching band that was both out of step, out of tune, and not in sync with percussion. The pressure on his chest tried to crush him. His life's memories darted through his mind. Nadia, Father, Mother, Grandma, and Noah.

A single laugh escaped. He knew if he died, the demon no longer had a place to hide. The breath exited his body, but the pain prevented Nathan from pulling in fresh air. Able to get a huge breath, he stood again, fighting the unbearable pain in his chest, arm, and back. It felt as if all his veins constricted to the max – as if they were about to break. His head pounded with every erratic heartbeat.

The angel, Dovinion, stood before him. His radiant cloak, powerful wings, and piercing eyes displayed the majesty of Yahweh. A trumpet blared loudly, along with the Yiddish words, "Be not afraid." Dovinion reached inside Nathan, seized Vodinion and yanked him out. The bellowing scream drew a dark, black hole that surrounded both angel and demon. A brilliant light flashed, accompanied by a loud bellow and a hideous scream. In an instant, both creatures vanished as the air became quiet and still. The presence was stronger than contentment and peace, but rather a powerfully majestic holiness.

After feeling the full presence of Yahweh, Nathan experienced joy in his demise. Falling on his side, the coarse pain rippled through his limbs, head, and torso. He cried as the room quieted. Everyone turned on the lights – or at least the ones that worked.

The only sound remaining was Nathan's gasps and grunts. The blood pressed in his vessels, trying to break free. The pain spread to his shoulder and his neck. Rolling on his back, he somehow found a prayer and thanked Yahweh for getting him through the depressing time in the concentration camps, his nightmarish memories in recovery, and his painstaking journey to this moment. The presence calmed him, and he found regular rhythmic breath for one last beat. His final breath exited … and he heard something: Noah calling his name.

Robyn

"Daddy – help him! Please. He's dying."

Robyn rushed to Nathan's side as his eyes glazed, and his final breath faded. Jason, Justin, Janie, and Dan gathered around as Roger squatted on the floor. Robyn guided her dad's hands to Nathan's neck, to search for a pulse. She cried while pumping his lifeless chest. "Daddy, you do it. You can save him. Please, right there," she said while guiding his hands to Nathan's sternum. Daddy used his own short, quick breaths to provide the rhythm for compressions. Robyn checked for a pulse but found nothing. Tears not only flooded her eyes but also dampened her hair. "Do something," she begged while looking at the family.

Justin activated his phone and within a few seconds, he bellowed, "Our friend is having a heart attack. Please help him ... our other friend is doing CPR ... our address ..." His one-sided conversation faded as everyone focused on Nathan.

On the verge of tears, Jason knelt next to Robyn. "He's not gonna die, is he? Please don't let him die." They all heard a crack, followed by another snapped rib. "Don't! Stop it," blurted Jason. "You're hurting him. You're hurting him." His pleas turned to sobs.

Dan and Janie dropped to the floor to hug Jason. "It's okay. It's okay," Dan and Janie told Jason. "Roger's helping as best as he can. Chest compressions often break ribs. It's quite common. Shhh. It's okay."

Nathan

Nathan uttered a breath that sent immense waves of pain through his rib cage. He coughed, making the pain worse. His eyes looked around at the family above him. He silently prayed as his heartbeat strengthened just enough – yet he knew the actions of the fireman only bought him a few minutes – perhaps seconds. His spirit started sinking again. Blackness surrounded his vision and slowly encroached. With the little strength he had, he reached up and grabbed

Do You Hear What I Hear?

Dan's arm, as well as Jason's. He had to tell them the voice that surged in his ears. "Twins," he whispered. "Don't worry. I can hear my brother calling my name." He cried – although he felt happy. "I can be with Noah once again – along with Nadia and Father." He smiled as his last breath left his body, and his spirit followed.

Jason

"I'll miss you, bro. I love you."

"We're proud of you, son."

"Thank you. We love you."

Jason smiled and wept as he heard the whispers from Jimmy, Mom, and Dad.

Stephen W. Scott

Great News

Justin trotted up the sidewalk, finding a starker chill in the shade of the old towering Oak and Elm Trees. Not only did the shadows chill the already cold air, but they also prevented the sun from melting stubborn snow and ice. Fortunately, Albany had its usual spring struggle: cold nights, mild days, with chances of light rain or snow. Fortunately, the area of upstate New York was almost out of the crushing and depressive winter melancholy.

The stately urban homes along the street were old, but strong. Made of solid wood and brick, they shielded families from the harsh elements, and the cruelties of the world. His exuberance faded as he thought of Nathan's death. Somehow, it felt like losing an old friend.

The whole ordeal happened three months ago, although it seemed like only a few days later. Of course, it took forever to clean up the mess and get repairs done to the house – and it was expensive. *"Apparently our insurance doesn't cover acts of God – so I'm reporting the incident as an act of Satan."* Justin smiled, thinking about Mom's joke.

During the last few months, he and the rest of the family had no feelings of being watched, no noises, no dread, no foul smells, and no fear. Justin suddenly appreciated the repetitious rut of everyday life, realizing how he took boredom for granted. He had been able to sleep so much better.

Now, though, he may not be able to sleep because of the exciting news he had for his cousin. Justin burst through the door and yelled. "Jason? Are you home?"

"Up here, shithead."

Justin sprinted up the stairs, excited to share the news with his cousin – or perhaps his brother. They did grow up together. However, the struggle sealed the whole family tighter.

Jason was reading a book through the braille scanner. Although he could not see, his head swiveled towards Justin. "What's up?"

"I got something so cool for you. You're gonna love it."

"Something cool? What is it? An air conditioner?"

"No, shithead. I got an email at school, and I forwarded it to you. You gotta read it now."

Jason sighed. "Okay." His fingertips worked intently to align themselves on the special keyboard so he could type.

The program opened. A small feminine voice said, "Two new messages."

"Wait," said Justin as he clicked on the correct message,

"let me do it." The computer audio read it to them:

Do You Hear What I Hear?

Dear Justin, thank you for reaching out to me about your cousin. Jason, you're going to have the longest and hardest struggle ahead – not just in losing your sight, but your family as well. My father was killed by a black-market cartel when I was 15 – and they burned our house to keep us from talking to the government of my country. Then, after moving to Brazil, I used surfing to get my mind off that tragedy. I was good, winning many competitions. Mama and my sister, Sierra, cheered me every time I won. I was the Brazilian Champion two years in a row when I was only 18 and 19. But then my eyesight was destroyed by a virus. I woke up blind in one eye one day, then the next day my other eye was blind. It took a lot of tears, adjustment, and so much work. It was then I wished my father was around. But it made me stronger and resilient. At first, I thought my whole life was gone, especially since I could not do the one thing I loved the most: surfing. But after two years, I was able to overcome that and continue to surf. I started winning competitions again. So, you can still surf even though you're blind. The lack of sight allows your mind to focus more on balance, and what you feel and hear. However, in your blindness, you must rely on those around you: your aunt, uncle, and cousin. You must also rely on your faith. I attend Mass weekly and work close with my Catholic Priest,

Father Diego. As long as you believe in God, you will know he can inspire you to do great things. Finally, this August is my second surfing camp for the blind. You are cordially invited. Fill out the attached form and email it back to me. Thanks to donations and charity, your flight, boarding, and equipment are all taken care of. That does include either your aunt or uncle. If both want to come, along with your cousin, they will have to come up with their own travel fare and lodging. I look forward to meeting you. Stay strong. Your friend,

Pablo de la Hoya Cardinal

The computer voice faded, leaving behind a comforting silence. Jason cried, but he refused to wipe the tears. At that moment, he felt something in his life return. The sting of losing Jimmy, Mom, and Dad subsided, and suddenly faded into oblivion. "Justin," his voice quivered, "I can't thank-you enough for this. You're the best cousin a guy could have. I love you."

Do You Hear What I Hear?

In the Water

"That is so wonderful!" said Robyn as Jason told her the story of the email. "I can't explain how glad I am for you." She kissed him on the cheek.

Smiling, he took her hand and squeezed tightly. Feeling at ease, he walked with her along the shore path around the small man-made lake. He wished he could see it, but Robyn explained it well. "The sunset is beautiful. The sky is orange, leaving purplish colors underneath the spreading clouds. Kids are playing in the playgrounds. People are walking their dogs, feeding the ducks with pieces of bread. The water's almost still, reflecting all the people, the trees, the clouds, and the sky. It's beautiful."

Jason whispered. "I feel like I have a brother again. And that, I have parents, too." Thinking of Nathan, Jason sighed. He wished that he could have seen the old man's face. Robyn told him what he looked like – but it wasn't the same. He remembered the night three months ago. He had no way to thank the old Rabbi for saving him and his family from the demonic creature and vengeful ghost. Again, just like earlier this afternoon, the tears felt as if they contained some sort of healing property. Nathan saved them from the demon. Aunt Janie, Uncle Dan, and Justin saved him from the loss of his family.

"For some reason, I feel like we're going to be alright. I haven't felt this peaceful since ..." He imagined surf water splashing over him as he guided a surfboard into the tube underneath the waves. Smiling, he finally found the words to finish his thought. "Since I was surfing."

"And you'll get to do it again."

Somehow, he heard her smile. "Surfing's a source," said Jason, "it'll change your life … swear to God."

"What?"

Jason had to get Robyn to share his favorite movie, Point Break. "I'll explain later." Somehow, he sensed Justin's presence had disappeared. "Robyn, where's my shithead cousin?"

"Justin!" yelled Robyn. "Come on."

Justin had lost himself in thought. Or was he thinking? He had been staring into the water at his reflection. At first, he admired how the sky above him reflected perfectly. A quiet ringing lulled him into a trance. Faint whispers barely entered his ears. Was that something behind him?

Do You Hear What I Hear?

Scotland

Nadia clutched her husband's hand. As their fingers interlocked, Ian gently squeezed. She stared at the tombstone over the freshly dug grave. The dirt had piled a few inches above the greening grass of Scotland. It was near the borough of Glenfinnan, an outlying Edenborough town. This was the place where her father's adoptive parents lived. She still thought of them as Grandma and Grandpa.

Still cold, Nadia moved closer to Ian, hoping his broad shoulders would give her shielding from the winds. Her long, dark hair flapped across her eyes, almost slapping her skin. She recited the prayer for the dead her father taught her.

"Foolish old man," she whispered. A faint smile stretched for a second. She had not seen him in almost six years. He had become obsessed with such outlandish ideas: demons, ghosts, the Angel of Death. She had no hatred – only sadness, and pity for her lost father. She could not imagine the horrific trauma and fear he and the others suffered.

Choking back her tears, Nadia read the grave: "Nathan Oberst – the foolish old man I love." It was in the place where he wanted his body buried. The tombstone to the left of her father's grave was for her mother, Rebecca.

On the right of her father's grave was the uncle she never met. She read her uncle's tombstone. "In loving memory of my brother, Noah." She found it strange that she knew what Uncle Noah looked like, but never knew the man, himself. Somehow, though, hearing Father's stories of Uncle

Noah gave her some understanding of his personality, demeanor, and sense of humor.

Aunt Nadia, whom she was named for, had a grave, too. She wished to know her lost aunt as well, but her short life did not have the numerous vibrant stories Uncle Noah had. However, Uncle Noah's and Aunt Nadia's lives were taken by the tangible evil of a despotic ruler who existed in the real world – not by the mythological and supernatural forces her father spoke of.

Nadia turned to her grandchildren, Phoebe and Lydia. Phoebe looked at the grave while Lydia looked into the pond. She coaxed Lydia to see the grave. Sure, they were a bit too young to understand the finality of death. However, Nadia knew they had to be introduced to it sooner or later. "This is your great grandfather's grave. Do you remember him?"

Both shook their heads quietly as if they were ashamed.

"I wish I remembered him," said Lydia.

"When was the last time we saw him?" asked Phoebe.

Nadia stooped and wrapped her arms around both girls. "It was five years ago when both of you were celebrating your second birthday."

The four of them turned from the graves. Nadia turned her head and saw Lydia looking at the pond again. Nadia picked her up.

Lydia waved at the pond. "Bye, bye."

Do You Hear What I Hear?

About the Author

Stephen W. Scott was born in Tulsa, OK. He attended the University of Oklahoma and graduated with a degree in Journalism – Professional Writing. He has worked for a few newspapers, then moved to Wilmore, KY in 1991 to attend Asbury Theological Seminary where he received his Master of Divinity in 1995. After returning to Oklahoma, he served as a pastor and chaplain in the United Methodist Conference. He has been working in education since 2001 and resides in Tulsa, OK. He enjoys bicycling, weightlifting, photography, reading, playing guitar and writing.

Other Books by Stephen W. Scott

The Blind Faith Series:
Do You Hear What I Hear?
The Demon Inside Me
My Best Friend is a Demon

Other Books:
Wonderful & Terrifying Nightmares
Abandoned

Visit him at
www.swscott-author.com

www.ingramcontent.com/pod-product-compliance
Lightning Source LLC
LaVergne TN
LVHW021805060526
838201LV00058B/3239